CHAINS

Night Rebels Motorcycle Club

CHIAH WILDER

Copyright © 2020 by Chiah Wilder
Print Edition

Editing by Lisa Cullinan
Cover design by Cheeky Covers

All rights reserved. This book or any portion thereof may not be reproduced or used in any manner whatsoever without the express written permission of the author except for the use of brief quotations in a book review. Please purchase only authorized additions, and do not participate in or encourage piracy of copyrighted materials.

Your support of the author's rights is appreciated.

Disclaimer: This is a work of fiction. Names, characters, businesses, places, events and incidents are either the products of the author's imagination or used in a fictitious manner. Any resemblance to actual persons, living or dead, or actual events is purely coincidental.

I love hearing from my readers. You can email me at chiahwilder@gmail.com.

Make sure you sign up for my newsletter so you can keep up with my new releases, special sales, free short stories, and other treats only available to newsletter readers. When you sign up, you will receive a FREE hot and steamy novella. Sign up at: http://eepurl.com/bACCL1.

Visit me on facebook at facebook.com/AuthorChiahWilder
Visit me on twitter at twitter.com/chiah_wilder
Visit me in Instagram at instagram.com/chiah803

Insurgent MC Series:

Hawk's Property
Jax's Dilemma
Chas's Fervor
Axe's Fall
Banger's Ride
Jerry's Passion
Throttle's Seduction
Rock's Redemption
An Insurgent's Wedding
Outlaw Xmas
Wheelie's Challenge
Christmas Wish
Animal's Reformation
Shadow's Surrender
Insurgents MC Romance Series: Insurgents Motorcycle Club Box Set (Books 1 – 4)
Insurgents MC Romance Series: Insurgents Motorcycle Club Box Set (Books 5 – 8)

Night Rebels MC Series:

STEEL
MUERTO
DIABLO
GOLDIE
PACO
SANGRE
ARMY
Night Rebels MC Romance Series: Night Rebels Motorcycle Club Box Set (Book 1 – 4)

Nomad Biker Romance Series:

Forgiveness
Retribution

Steamy Contemporary Romance:

My Sexy Boss

Chapter One

THE SCENT OF jasmine and the high-pitched chattering in the room were nauseating. Through the slats of the shutters, Autumn saw two children playing with an orange frisbee beyond the sprawling maple tree in the front yard. Her tongue felt thick and her head pounded like someone had come up from behind and sunk a meat cleaver into it.

"At least *try* and look like you're having a good time," Sadie whispered while nudging her best friend.

"Why didn't I listen to you last night? And why the hell did I ever think that martinis were the way to go? I don't even *like* them." Autumn lightly rubbed her aching temples.

"That's what Alicia, Rachel, and I were trying to figure out." Sadie giggled.

"Open my gift next," Barbara Davis said, a smug smile creeping over her doughy face as she handed a brightly wrapped box to Autumn.

"I can't believe I let Bret talk me into having his ex-girlfriend's mother at *my* bridal shower," Autumn said through clenched teeth as she took the gift from Barbara.

"Me neither," her best friend agreed. "But then Bret's not exactly Mr. Sensitive, is he?"

Autumn clutched the box, irritation pricking along the back of her neck. *What does Sadie know about Bret? Sure, he can be selfish and self-absorbed, but he's always there for me when I need him.* The memory of Bret canceling their meeting with the caterer floated through her mind. *I didn't need him for the tasting anyway.*

"Autumn, are you going to open the present or just hold it?" Rachel asked.

She glanced at her friend, then chuckled. "I guess I'm a little out of sorts."

"I bet you are." Rachel's blue eyes twinkled. Alicia and Sadie chortled softly.

"I think there's an inside joke going on between the three of you," Bret's mother, Regina, said. "I'm still so sorry your mother couldn't make it in from Denver to come to your shower." Her future mother-in-law leaned over and plucked another mini quiche from the tray on the table.

"She'll be here for the next one," Autumn answered while ripping off the yellow paper dotted with colorful umbrellas. The truth was that she'd hadn't told her mother about the shower until it was too late for her to make the long drive to Alina. Her mother had always been afraid of small airports, so landing at the one in Durango some sixty miles away would not have been an option.

For the past couple of weeks, Autumn had started having doubts about marrying Bret, but she didn't tell anyone. She chalked it up to having cold feet, which she'd read was perfectly normal.

Pushing aside the glittery tissue paper, Autumn stared at a single saucer and tea cup. A narrow gold band encircled the rim of the cup and china plate, and there was something engraved on the side of the saucer: *Barbara and Teresa Singer*. Staring at it, she couldn't quite process that the names on the gift were Bret's ex-girlfriend and her mother. *What the hell?* She glanced up and met the determined eyes of Barbara.

"Don't you love it?" the woman gushed.

"I … uh … am speechless." Autumn closed the lid to the box.

"I know Bret will love it. Yellow is one of his favorite colors." Barbara sank back into the couch and patted Regina's knee. "Remember all the summer picnics we used to have when Teresa and Bret were dating? He always insisted on her wearing that cute yellow top he'd bought her during one of their many trips to Mexico."

Regina cleared her throat and slightly pivoted her body away from Barbara's touch. "Autumn and Bret are planning a beautiful honeymoon in Italy, and it was all his idea." She bent down and picked up a large box. "Here, dear, this one is from Stanley and me."

The awkward moment passed, and Autumn plastered on one of her biggest, most sincere-looking smiles and took the box from Bret's mother.

"It's so heavy," she said.

"Only two more to go. Hang in there," Sadie whispered as she helped Autumn unwrap the gift. A picture of a shiny black KitchenAid mixer on the box had several of Regina's friends and family cooing.

"I don't even bake," she said under her breath before pushing the gift aside. "I love it. Thank you, Regina."

"You're welcome. I know how much Bret loves my brownies, so I'll give you the recipe." Regina smiled.

Bret's mother put Suzy Homemaker to shame, to say the least. Not only did she make everything by scratch, including mayonnaise, ketchup, and mustard, she made and sold beautiful and delicious cakes for weddings, birthdays, quinceañeras, anniversaries, and many other events. She also kept an immaculate house and sewed like a professional. Oh … and she spoiled the hell out of Bret. Autumn had lost count of how many times he'd compared her ineptness to his mother's superhuman domestic skills. Not that Autumn resented Regina. She wished she could be more like her future mother-in-law, but Autumn just hadn't inherited the domestic gene. Her mother wasn't that handy in the kitchen, but she at least could make bacon without burning the hell out of it.

Unlike Bret's childhood of homemade sloppy Joe's, chewy chocolate chip cookies, and freshly squeezed lemonade, Autumn grew up on takeout cartons, cookies out of a tube—her mother thought by baking them, it had meant she'd "made" them—and pitchers of Kool-Aid. Autumn was totally content with it, but sometimes when Bret made snide remarks about her domestic abilities, it made her want to enroll in a cooking class or take up crocheting. Unfortunately, with the hours she spent at the veterinary clinic, Autumn barely had time to go to the grocery store to pick up fixings for a salad. One thing she *could* make were super salads.

The afternoon seemed like it would never end, and finally, Sadie—her best friend since she'd had moved to Alina a few years before—stood up.

"I have somewhere to be. Are you ready, Autumn?" she asked, gathering up some of the gifts.

Autumn nearly stumbled over her own feet as she jumped up from the chair. "I am." She gripped two large shopping bags Regina had given her and began to pile the presents in them.

"Let me help you," Alicia said, crossing the room.

"I feel terrible leaving you with such a mess. Please let me help you at least put the food away," Autumn said.

Regina shook her head, her hands on her hips. "I wouldn't hear of it. Besides, my sisters are putting things away already."

"I had a wonderful time. Thank you for throwing such a nice shower. I now have so many things to stock my kitchen."

"You'll have to get used to saying *our* instead of *my*." Regina smiled.

"That's true." Autumn's head still ached and she longed to just get home, throw off her heels and clothes, and veg in front of the television with a cool rag across her forehead for a couple of hours. Later that night, she and Bret had dinner reservations at one of the new restaurants in town—Spice Room. It had taken her a lot of persuading and doing favors for Bret to finally convince him to try one of her favorite cuisines—Indian.

"Don't mean to rush you, but I really have to go." Sadie walked over to the door and held it open.

Regina nodded. "Have a good time tonight. Bret told me you talked him into going to that new place from India. I don't think he'll like it, but it's good to try something at least once."

"I agree. Indian food is so varied that I'm sure he'll find a dish he'll like. Thanks again." Autumn scooped up the bags and walked toward the door with Regina following behind her.

"Bret wants me to teach you how to make homemade tortillas. Give me a call next week and we can set something up." Regina stood in the doorway as Autumn stepped onto the porch.

"Okay, but I'm very busy at the clinic. I worked way less hours when I had a boss." She tipped her head toward Bret's mother, then quickly thanked everyone again and waved goodbye as she scurried down the walkway.

"I thought we'd never get out of there." Sadie switched on the ignition. "It was nice but too long. How many more do you have to go to?"

Autumn groaned. "Too many. One shower, maybe two, but not a slew of them. I wanted a simple wedding, and my mom and dad were on board with that too, so why is Bret insisting on all this fanfare? My parents and I are the ones paying for the wedding, so I should be getting some of what *I* want."

"I can't believe Bret's this involved in the whole process. I guess that's kind of cool, but then again, it could be a pain in the ass."

She leaned back against the passenger seat. "It's a total pain in the ass because he's really not being all that helpful. Whenever we make plans to meet with various people, like the florist or the caterer, he cancels at the last minute by text. It's so damn annoying. It seems like he enjoys the *idea* of being involved but that's where it ends."

"He does like getting the attention," Sadie said.

"Yeah, and at six feet, piercing blue eyes, and sandy brown hair, he gets it … especially from women. It seems like every time we go somewhere in Alina, some woman he used to date or knew comes out of the woodwork."

"Alina is a small town, and I can see how that would be real infuriating, but I guess it depends on how he handles the situations with these women."

Autumn stared out the window at the passing trees and houses. "He absolutely loves it. It doesn't make me jealous or anything, but Bret keeps talking about it afterwards. It's almost like he *wants* me to be jealous."

"I can see that though. I'd be pissed if it didn't bother Mitch that men kept flirting with me. And I wouldn't be too happy if women kept coming over to him when we're out together."

Autumn shrugged slightly. "I'm just not that way." She gripped the door handle.

"Not even when you found your ex-fiancé with your friend? What was his name?" Sadie asked.

"Dylan, and not even then. I was devastated and hurt, but not jealous. Maybe something's wrong with me." She opened the door.

"Or maybe you've never been in love."

Autumn turned toward her friend. "I loved Dylan at that time in my life, and I love Bret."

"Loving and being in love are totally different," Sadie said, her gazed fixed on Autumn.

"I hear that all the time, but I don't agree with it. Are you going to help me with these gifts that'll just collect dust on my granite counter?"

Sadie laughed. "I can't believe Regina gave *you*—of all people—a *kitchen* shower. Doesn't she know that you don't cook?"

"Apparently not. Bret keeps trying to turn me into the happy homemaker as far as his stomach is concerned." Autumn caught Sadie's eyes, then the two women busted out laughing. "Yeah … *that's* not gonna happen."

Sadie slid out of the car and filled her arms with several boxes. "Where do you want me to put these?" she asked as she walked toward Autumn's house.

"I guess in the kitchen. I'll just put them in the cupboards and figure out what I'll do with all these gadgets and machines at some point." Autumn pushed open her front door and held it open with her foot while Sadie passed through.

"How's your hangover?" her friend asked.

"Better, but a nap on the couch with a cool washcloth across my forehead is my plan for the next two hours." She hoisted up the bags in her hands to the counter. "I'll deal with all this later. Do you and Mitch have plans for tonight?"

"We're going to Vesta Grill with Alicia and Juan. Remember we asked you guys to join us?"

"That's right, but we already had plans. Maybe next time." Autumn walked her friend to the front door.

"It seems like we never go out as couples. That's kind of strange, don't you think?" Sadie stepped out onto the porch.

Autumn raked her slender fingers through her auburn hair. "Bret and I are both so busy in our careers that when we have time to go out, he prefers to just be with me." As Sadie stared at her, Autumn cut her gaze to the swaying branches of the tree in the front yard. "That was one of the reasons why I bought this house. I love weeping willows—they stand so firm, yet their branches are flexible and strong, bending without breaking."

Sadie glanced over at the weeping willow then stepped off the porch. "This has to be one of your better ways of changing the subject when it comes to Bret."

Autumn lifted up one shoulder and smiled weakly. "Have fun tonight. Let's get together for dinner one night next week."

"Sounds good. Let me know how you like the new restaurant."

Autumn watched as her friend drove away, then she closed her door and climbed the stairs to her bedroom to change clothes. Sadie was right about one thing: whenever she started to probe into Autumn and Bret's relationship, Autumn steered the conversation away from it. And there was no way Sadie didn't suspect that Bret was the reason they weren't joining her friends for dinner. The truth was that Bret didn't like her friends and didn't want to hang out with them. They'd gotten into several fights about it, and the few times he'd acquiesced and gone out with her group, he acted like a pouting, spoiled child, so she'd just stopped asking him. Once they got married and were bonded as a couple, she was sure things would fall into place. Sometimes, Bret could be so self-centered and selfish, but other times, he could be so loving and attentive by sending her a bouquet of flowers for no reason or whisking her away to Aspen for an unexpected romantic weekend. It was true that the impromptu acts of love had dwindled in the last several months, especially after they'd become engaged, but Bret had it in him, and when this whole wedding fanfare was over, they'd settle down into their new life and everything would be wonderful.

I hope. Of course it will be. Look at Mom and Dad and how happy they've been for the past thirty-five years. Everything's going to be just fine. It seemed that had become her mantra for the past few months, and she recited it more often whenever doubts niggled at the back of her mind.

Squeezing out the excess water from a washcloth, Autumn decided to forgo the couch in favor of lying on the bed. She pushed aside the many decorative pillows and eased down on the mattress. After several minutes her phone beeped, and she groaned as she reached for it on the nightstand.

Bret: *My mom said the shower was great. U'll have to have her come over & show u how to use all the things u got.*

She rolled her eyes and sighed loudly.

Autumn: *It was good. Just resting b4 tonight.*

Bret: *Yeah … well, I can't make it tonight. Sorry.*

She sat upright, ignoring the dull pain of blood rushing to her aching temples. "What the hell?" she muttered under her breath.

Bret: *U still with me? My boss wants me to entertain a client who got in this morning. It can't be helped.*

Autumn: *Really?*

Bret: *I resent the implication from that comment.*

Autumn: *Whatever.*

Bret: *I'll come over afterwards. We can have some fun together.*

Autumn: *No, don't. I won't be in the mood.*

Bret: *Why r u being so difficult? Do u want me to say no and risk* *my job?*

Autumn: *I'm not saying that. I'm just disappointed, that's all.*

Bret: *Me too. I'll make it up to you next Saturday. Flanigan's, okay?*

Autumn: *I don't want to go to a steakhouse. I want to try the Indian restaurant.*

Bret: *We can do that another time. A five-star steakhouse is what my sweet fiancée deserves.*

"Such an asshole. It's what *you* want," she muttered under her breath.

Autumn: *We'll see. I may be on call next Saturday. I have to go. Bye.*

Bret: *I can't believe ur pissed at me about something I can't help. How selfish.*

Autumn: *I'm not pissed. I have a headache. It's been a very long day. Bye.*

Bret: *I'll call u later tonight. Love u.*

She swiped out of the screen, then turned her phone off. Another last minute cancelation. Bret's excuse didn't ring true, and she was pretty sure that he'd made plans to go out with his friends to the sports bar. Bret loved hanging out with his buddies, and he acted like he was still in a fraternity. *So damn immature.*

Autumn leaned back and rested against the headboard. "I'm not going to freak out. I really don't feel like dressing up anyway. I'll do a takeout order from the Spice Room, watch a thriller and then a few reruns of *Seinfeld*."

She swallowed past the lump in her throat and pulled her knees up to her chest and wrapped her arms around them. Autumn looked out the window and watched the tree branches swaying in the wind.

Chapter Two

"Do you want me to hang around for another go, baby?" Ruby pressed her soft breasts against Chains's back, draping her arms around him.

Sitting on the edge of the bed, he shook his head. "As tempting as that is, I'm gonna pass."

"I'll make it worth your while," Ruby whispered into his ear.

Chains reached behind him and patted her leg. "You always do. I'm going to Chaco Canyon for a bit."

"Need a companion?"

He untangled her hands and stood up. Pointing at the Siberian husky sprawled across the floor under the window, he smiled. "I already got one."

"There's no way I can compete with him." Ruby pouted and scooted back against the headboard.

Chains laughed and pulled on his boxers. "No one can compete with Thor." As if on cue, the dog sat up and barked, his tail wagging and his blue eyes sparkling. Chains bent down and petted Thor's thick white fur. "We're going for a hike, buddy," he said, which made the dog's tail thump energetically against the hardwood floor.

Ruby ran her hands over her full breasts, lifting and cupping them while she stared at him. "Are you sure you don't have time for a quickie, baby?"

He winked at her. "Another time," he said before walking into the bathroom.

When Chains came back into the bedroom, Ruby was gone. He glanced at his neatly made bed and smiled. Of all the club girls, Ruby was the one who never left a club member's bed unmade. For the last few months, Ruby had been his go-to girl, but he'd been feeling a bit restless the past few weeks, so he figured he'd try out Lila for a while. Unlike many of the other members, Chains preferred to stick with just one club girl at a time for a while before he rotated to another one. Lila was one of the newer girls, becoming involved with the club just eight months before. As was the norm, the men were crazy about her because she was new and different, but now she was part of the club fabric so her popularity had waned a bit.

A rap on the door pulled Chains out of his thoughts, and he quickly fastened the belt on his jeans and crossed the room.

"Hey, dude. You wanna join us on a ride?" Crow said when Chains opened the door.

"Now?"

"Yeah. Aztec, Eagle, Metal, Rooster, Army, and Goldie are going. Army mentioned that you said you were wanting to go to Chaco Canyon. That's where we're heading." Crow walked into the room.

Chains leaned against the door frame and watched his friend squat down and pet Thor.

"I'm not riding there because I'm taking Thor with me."

Crow looked over his shoulder at him. "It fuckin' sucks that you gotta go in a cage on such a perfect riding day."

"Yeah ... well, that's the way it is."

"Why don't you take Thor for a walk on our property, then join us for the ride?"

The Night Rebels' large three-story clubhouse was set well back from the road and sat on several acres that mostly consisted of grass, wild brush, and standing trees. A ten-foot-tall concrete wall topped with two feet of barbed-wire surrounded the motorcycle club's property, and access was through a steel gate as tall as the wall. Security cameras lined the perimeter of the property, and the gate's control and intercom system allowed the club members to screen out undesirables. A sign attached to the gate read in bold white lettering: Trespassers Will be

Shot.

"I want to take him somewhere different. The run up some of the trails will be good for him."

Crow straightened up and jammed his hands in the pockets of his jeans. "Are you still thick with Ruby?"

Chains shrugged and shifted from foot to foot. "I was just thinking about that when you knocked on the door. I'm thinking to move on to Lila. Why?"

"Just wondering. I met this cute citizen the other night at Cuervos and she called me today. Said she wanted to get together over the weekend but her cousin was visiting, so she asked if I had a buddy. I could hook you up with her. Are you interested?"

He scrunched his face, deepening the lines on his forehead as he shook his head. "I don't go for citizen chicks, you know that."

"Yeah, but this cousin doesn't live in Alina, so I figure she's a good bet. You won't have to worry about her getting too clingy or shit like that. It's a change from the club girls."

"Yeah, but I'll pass. Ask Aztec or Eagle. They're always looking to get laid without any attachments."

Crow laughed as he walked toward the door. "Aren't we all?"

Chains nodded, a smile spreading across his face. "Good point. Have a good ride."

Crow lifted his chin. "Okay, dude. See you later," he said as he shut the door.

Chains pulled on his boots, then tucked his wallet in the back pocket of his jeans. "You ready to go?"

Thor barked and ran to the door, then looked over at Chains expectantly as he waited for his owner. Once Chains opened the door, Thor bolted out and charged down the stairs and into the big room.

"Hey there, boy." Aztec's loud voice wrapped around Chains before he entered the main room. He laughed when he saw Thor leaning toward Aztec—his tail held out behind him in a wide, sweeping wag as the club member stroked the dog under his chin.

"You're spoiling the shit outta him," Chains said as he strode over to the bar.

"And you don't?" Aztec replied, a smile in his voice.

Chains picked up his shot of tequila and threw it back, then asked the prospect to bring him six bottles of water.

"Crow said you and Thor are headed to Chaco Canyon," Aztec said.

"Yep. Maybe we'll bump into each other." He pushed away from the bar.

"Only if you're going to Glacier Lake. We're gonna have a few beers and smoke some weed, then we're heading to Stella's. I got my eye on one of the waitresses," Eagle said as he walked over.

"Which one?" Aztec said.

"Do you have to ask?" Chains replied. "It's the redhead with the big tits and shapely legs."

Eagle slapped his hand against Chains's shoulder. "You know me too well, bro. She's been giving me the eye for the last month or so."

"Is that why we keep going to Stella's when we're riding?" Metal asked before bumping fists with Chains.

"Fuck yeah. Once I get her to spread those pretty legs for me, I'll be a regular at the roadhouse." Eagle held up his hand and Ink rushed over with a bottle of Corona, then scurried back behind the bar.

"You're already a fuckin' regular," Army said as he strode over to the group. "Are we ready to roll? I gotta be back before the gym closes, so I'll probably opt out on going to Stella's. Diablo, Paco, and I are going to move the new equipment into another room. Mia's reminded me a million times not to be late."

"And she can literally kick your ass if you are," Crow said.

Chains and the others laughed while Army nodded. "Yeah … she's got some wicked moves. In a few weeks, she's competing in Denver at the MMA Mania. Any of you guys wanna come and cheer her on?"

"Count me and Hailey in on that," Goldie said.

"I'll go. I like watching chicks fight," Crow added.

"Me too," Metal said.

Army took out his keys. "Let me know—Mia can get a good rate at the hotel. So, are we riding?"

"Let's roll," Goldie said, then looked over at Chains. "You coming?"

"Not this time." He snapped his fingers and Thor came running, and the two of them walked out into the late afternoon sun as the group of riders followed behind. The spicy fragrance of chrysanthemums mingled with the autumnal smell of leaves, and the gravel crunched under the bikers' boots as they walked over to their motorcycles.

Chains opened the driver's door of his black Tahoe. Thor jumped inside and settled on the passenger seat, his cold nose pressed against the window. Chains slipped inside and turned on the ignition and then rolled down the windows; Thor stuck his head out and lifted his nose up in the air.

In less than thirty minutes, Chains was at Chaco Canyon. The second he opened the passenger side door, Thor bolted out and ran ahead a few yards, barking and then sniffing the plants and bushes. Chains followed behind and soon was hiking on a trail that led steeply up the side of a hill overlooking the canyon. Once they reached the top, Thor rushed off to the left into a thicket of trees, and Chains sat down on the ground. He swept his glance over a seemingly infinite expanse of mountain ranges that melted into each other as mist swirled around the jagged peaks.

"As long as I live, I'll never get tired of this view," he said under his breath, loving the peace and stillness he always felt whenever he was there.

Several minutes later, Chains put two fingers in his mouth and whistled for Thor, but he didn't come.

"Thor! Come here!" His voice echoed off the rocky cliffs.

He expected to see the Siberian run out from the brush, but the dog was nowhere to be seen. Chains pushed up to his feet and trekked through the thicket, whistling and calling Thor's name. Then he heard a ringing bark in the distance, and he picked up his pace until he found Thor nestled between trees and surrounded by overgrown mountain laurel and thick vegetation. The dog's ears pricked up while he chewed something in his mouth as his blue eyes fixed on Chains.

"What the fuck are you eating?" Chains's gaze darted to several clusters of orange-yellow berries that covered a vine climbing up the trunk of the trees. "What the hell are those?" He stooped down and plucked a few berries and brought them to his nose. A rank, bitter odor invaded his nostrils, making his nose run and his eyes water. "Fuck, that's nasty. Did you eat these?"

Thor barked then slowly trudged through the undergrowth.

"I don't know what this shit is, but you gotta be careful what you eat, buddy." Chains slipped the orange-yellow fruit into his pocket and made his way back to the car.

On the ride back, Chains kept looking over at Thor to make sure he was doing okay; the fact that the husky had probably eaten the berries concerned Chains.

His phone went off just as he pulled into the dirt lot in front of the clubhouse. When he saw his mother's name on the screen, he gritted his teeth and swiped to answer.

"What's up, Mom?"

"Nothing. I just haven't heard from you in a long time. I was getting worried. Bret said he saw you and those guys you live with at Leroy's a few days ago. How you can eat at that place is beyond me. When you were young, we never ate at diners. I always cooked good homemade meals and …"

Chains tuned his mother out and buried his hand in Thor's fur, smiling when the dog looked over at him. He leaned over and opened the car door, and the husky bounded out and ran toward the club, barking excitedly.

"Are you listening to me?" Irritation laced his mother's voice.

"Yeah. Did you call to chew me out about eating at the diner?" Chains slid out of the SUV.

"No, and I'm not *chewing* you out. I think you need to find a nice girl to settle down with, get a house and stop living like you're in a fraternity. Don't you want to get married?"

"Been there—done that."

"I told you Krystal wasn't the right girl for you, but you didn't listen. The minute I saw her with that low-cut top and heavy eye makeup, I knew she wouldn't be faithful."

"Let's not get into all that. I've been divorced for six years—end of story." Chains kicked at a stone as he walked toward the club. The last thing he wanted to talk about was that bitch and her cheating ways.

"If it's the end of the story, then why aren't you with a nice girl? You haven't brought a woman home for Christmas since the divorce."

"I'm not interested in going down that road again. Once was enough. Leave it alone, Mom." He leaned against the stucco wall and took out a joint and lit it.

"Just because one of the apples was rotten in the basket doesn't mean they all are. You have to move on."

"I have. I'm kinda busy right now, so why did you call?"

"All right … go ahead—keep your head in the sand. It's your life, but you'll be sorry when you're old and all alone."

Chains inhaled deeply, then slowly blew out the smoke and watched it dance in the air before dissipating.

"You can be so stubborn. That's always been your problem. I remember—"

"I gotta go," he said.

"Wait. I wanted to let you know that I'm hosting a brunch for Bret and his fiancée." A small pause. "You know, she's got the oddest name. I mean who names their daughter—"

"Mom," he prodded. "When's the damn brunch?"

"There's no reason to curse. Your brother really wants you to be there."

Chains dropped the spent joint on the ground and stubbed it out with the tip of his boot. "I doubt that. *You* want me to be there."

"That's not true."

"Mom, I'm hanging up, so just tell me the date and I'll let you know in a couple of days if I can go."

"It's two weeks from this Sunday. It's going to be real nice. Maybe you'll like one of the bridesmaids. A few of them are very pretty and smart."

"Gotta go. I'll let you know. Bye."

He ended the call and rested his head back against the wall and watched the falling leaves swirl in the light breeze. The early evening sunlight bathed the mountain peaks in a golden glow, and Chains breathed deeply several times to calm his rising anger.

The relationship with his family was like oil and water; it had been that way as far back as he could remember. His dad had been riding his ass since the age of six, and his mother always sided with his father.

Chains had a brother, Bret, who was two years younger than he, and two sisters who used to drive him up a fucking wall with their constant chattering. Amelia and Emily were real close to their mother, and Bret was close to their dad, so that left Chains as the odd man out. And that was exactly how he'd always felt—like a fish out of water—when it came to his family.

"Hey, bro," Jigger said as he walked out of the club. "How was your hike?"

"Good. Thor ate some shit from a vine and I'm not sure what it is." Chains took the berries out of his pocket and opened the palm of his hand. "Do you recognize these?"

Jigger dipped his head down and picked up one and examined it. "Sorry, bro. I don't know shit about plants. Did he eat a lot of them?"

"I don't know. He was chomping on something when I found him in the woods." He ran his hand through his brown hair. "Fuck, I'm probably worrying for nothing. How's your kid?"

"He's great. I'm going to Durango at the end of the week to spend a few days with him. This shit of not having him full-time is wearing thin, and the thing that really pisses me off is that damn ex-bitch of mine is fucking a new guy who doesn't like kids."

"Damn, that's tough. Is that why she's letting you see more of Abe this last month?"

"Yeah." Jigger pulled out a cigarette and dangled it between his lips. "I just want him to live with me. Morgan's just being a bitch about it because she wants to get back at me for leaving her *and* she doesn't wanna give up the child support. What a damn mess." He clicked a lighter then inhaled the cigarette.

"Yeah, citizen women are the fuckin' worst. You need to get a lawyer. Get the name of that attorney who defended Army. Maybe he knows someone who can help with a child custody case. I'm glad I didn't have any kids with Krystal."

"Why are women such bitches?"

"The club girls are cool. It's the citizens you gotta stay away from."

At that moment, Lila opened the door and looked at him, concern etching her face. "You better come inside. Something's wrong with Thor."

"Fuck," Chains said as he dashed past her. "Where is he?"

"Over there," Lila said, pointing to the northwest corner of the room. "I think he's throwing up."

He saw Thor's head dipped down real low and could hear the sounds of gagging coming from him. He rushed over and dropped down on one knee.

"What's wrong, buddy?" Chains put his hand on the husky's back.

Thor whined then stepped back, his body swaying as if he was dizzy. Chains looked down at the vomit on the floor and stiffened: there was a fair amount of blood in it.

"Fuck," he whispered. He cut his gaze over to Thor who lay on his side, his bright eyes dull and glassy.

"How is he?" Lila asked as she bent down and stroked the dog's fur.

"Not good. Stay with him—I'll be right back." Chains ran from the room and sprinted up the steps two at a time. He rifled through a drawer in the nightstand until he pulled out the card his retired veterinarian had given him four months before. He quickly tapped in the number as he walked down the stairs. By the time he was back at his pet's side, Chains had secured an appointment with the animal clinic right away.

"Come on, buddy," he said as he gingerly picked up the big dog and walked to his car.

Lila, Ruby, Jigger, Razor, and the two prospects—Ink and Vegas—followed behind. Jigger and Razor pushed down the back seat, then Ruby and Lila spread a blanket over it. Ink and Vegas helped Chains lay Thor on top of it.

"You want me to go with you to help out?" Jigger asked.

"Yeah," Chains said. His mouth was dry like sand, and sweat formed along his hairline.

They drove in silence as Chains maneuvered the SUV through traffic. He kept glancing behind his shoulder to make sure Thor was okay, but the dog's breathing was labored and his eyes were shut.

I just gotta get him to the clinic in time. Chains pushed the thought that Thor could die out of his head. Thor had been a puppy when Chains found him shivering in a window well one cold January night seven years before. He had been at one of his lowest points after having caught his fellow brother and best friend, Crossbones, fucking Krystal. After that, everything was a blur: beating the shit out of Crossbones, kicking his cheating wife out on her ass, the club's decision to throw Crossbones out of the Night Rebels, and his family's smug faces when he'd told them he and Krystal had split.

And then a ball of fur had come into his life, and the only thing that mattered was saving the little guy. From that moment on they'd become fast friends, and Thor was always by his side.

He glanced back at the dog and clenched his jaw—the taste of blood pungent. Thor wheezed as he struggled to breathe.

"He's gonna make it, bro. I know it," Jigger said.

Chains nodded.

He just fuckin' has to.

Chapter Three

"They're here, Dr. Stanford," Christina said, standing in the doorway.

Autumn looked away from the computer screen and smiled at the veterinarian tech. "Have the owner bring his dog to Room Three. I'll be there in a fast minute."

"Will do." The tech turned around and her ginger-brown hair swung around her shoulders before she disappeared down the hall.

Autumn rolled her shoulders back and stood up from the chair. She raised her arms above her head and stretched, then slipped on her white lab coat and headed out of the office.

When she entered the examining room, she saw a large Siberian lying on a multi-colored blanket on top of the steel table. Beside the dog was a tall man with tattoos running up and down well-defined arms. He wore a white T-shirt and black jeans, both of which fit him like a second skin.

Then he turned around and her pulse raced. A close-cropped beard accentuated his firm jaw. Her gaze quickly ran over his muscular chest, tapered waist, and narrow hips. But it was his eyes that held her—the kind that could easily distract a woman. They were the brown shades of acorns, just bright enough to shine in the shadows. When she looked into them, a shiver of golden light raced down her spine.

"Are you the doc?" His voice was husky baritone—sensuous and commanding.

Dragging her gaze from his, Autumn looked at the Siberian. "Yes. How long has he been this listless?" she asked, walking over to the table.

"Since he ate some of these on our hike in Chaco Canyon a couple of hours ago." He pulled something out of his pocket and opened his hand.

The slight distraction from before evaporated immediately when she saw several orange-yellow berries lining his palm.

"Those are American climbing bittersweet. Did you actually see him eat them?"

"No, but he was chewing something when I found him. There were a bunch of these on vines around the trees, so I'm pretty sure they're what he was eatin'."

"Did he vomit?"

"About forty-five minutes later and there was blood in it. What the fuck's going on with him?"

She glanced up and saw the worry etched all over his face, and she offered him a small smile. "The fruit from this plant makes humans have a stomach ache and diarrhea, but for dogs it's poisonous. It's good that you brought him in right away. What's your dog's name?"

"Thor. I'm Chains."

"And I'm Dr. Stanford. I guess we started backward." Another smile. His gaze bored into hers and she looked away. "Thor's suffering from hematemesis or, simply put, vomiting blood. I'm glad you thought to bring in the berries since it helps me isolate the cause of his hematemesis."

"Can you help him?" Chains stroked his pet repeatedly as he spoke.

"I'll do my best. The first thing I need to do is give him an activated charcoal. That'll help to prevent further absorption of the poison into his body. Do you know how many berries he ate?"

"No idea. Fuck, I shouldn't have let him wander off, but we go there a lot and it's never been a problem."

Autumn opened one of the cupboards and took out what she needed, then pulled on a pair of gloves. "Don't blame yourself—dogs are notorious for ingesting a lot of things."

"He's never done this before. I should've given him a damn treat before we went."

Autumn smiled. "Again, don't beat yourself up over this. Did you want to stay while I begin treatment?"

"Yeah, of course. I'm here for the whole fuckin' nine yards."

A soft knock on the door made Autumn look up. "Come in."

Mary entered and quickly came over to the table. The nurse had a silver tray filled with syringes, tubes, gauze, and surgical tape. Autumn told her what needed to be done at that moment, then Mary put the tray down on the counter, walked around the table, and stood beside Chains.

"If you could help us hold him down while I administer the charcoal, that would be great," Autumn said to him. He tilted his head and placed both hands on top of Thor's body.

"After we wait for a bit, I'm going to do a *gastric lavage,* which is basically an internal washing."

"What's that for?" The fine lines in his tanned forehead deepened.

"To directly wash any residual poison from Thor's stomach. It's a highly effective way to remove a toxin from the stomach before the body ingests the element."

"What do you have to do for that?" he asked.

"I'll put a tube filled with water into Thor's stomach to flush his system. Diuretic drugs will enhance the secretion of the substance through the urinary tract."

"That doesn't sound too comfortable."

"I'll have to administer an anesthetic, but before I do that, I'm going to run blood work and some other diagnostic tests. Once we begin the procedure, you'll have to wait in the lobby. It won't take more than thirty minutes, and I'll come out and get you once it's done."

"All this shit from eating just a few berries?" Chains ran his fingers through his hair.

"A few *poisonous* berries." She stroked the dog's soft fur. "Thor has a very good chance of recovery. I just need you to let me do my job, okay? Time is really of the essence."

"Yeah, okay … sure."

"Great. While Mary draws blood, let's go to my office and we'll go over the paperwork."

An hour later, Autumn called Chains into the recovery room, then rushed out to examine another patient.

The clinic had three veterinarians on staff, two nurses, four techs, and two receptionists. Ever since Autumn had graduated from veterinary school, it had been her dream to own a clinic, and when the opportunity to buy a retiring vet's practice arose, she jumped at it and moved from Denver to Alina.

"Chains is asking for you," Mary said as Autumn finished up with an ailing Persian cat. "I still can't get him to tell me his last name. He's a bit odd, don't you think?"

Autumn chuckled. "I suppose we're all odd in some way. I think it's sweet that this tough-looking guy adores his dog—you can see it in his eyes."

"I wasn't paying *that* close attention to him." The older nurse moved away from the doorway. "I'm just wondering why he doesn't want us to know his real name. I highly doubt any mother would name her son *Chains*."

"I don't know … some parents give their kids some pretty crazy names. Frank Zappa named his daughter *Moon Unit* and the name *Semaj* cracked the top 1000 names for boys in 1999—it's *James* spelled backward."

Mary clucked her tongue. "Well, I think he's hiding something, but you seem to be taken with him."

Autumn's jaw muscle tightened and irritation pricked the back of her neck. "Please ask Dr. Jenkins to take my walk-in appointment in Room Four." Shoving her hands in the pockets of her lab coat, she strode over to the recovery room.

I'm certainly not taken with him. That's just nonsense … Mary's full of it.

When she opened the door, Chains was leaning over Thor, whispering into the dog's ear while he stroked his side over and over. For some reason, the sight of this very masculine man soothing his dog struck her as incredibly sexy. As if sensing her presence, Chains looked over his shoulder and his gaze locked on hers for a half second, then slowly moved down her body.

Autumn cleared her throat and walked over. "How're you holding up?" she asked.

His eyes lingered on her breasts and then her lips before meeting her gaze again. "Okay. Is Thor good now?"

Feeling uncomfortable with his undisguised scrutiny of her, Autumn took a pen from her pocket and fiddled with it while walking to the other side of the table. "He's doing better than when he came in. I'm pretty sure he's out of the danger zone." She ran her hand over the waking dog and looked at Chains, faking nonchalance. "But I'd like to keep him here for a day or two to monitor his condition. I'll hook up an IV for fluid therapy to make sure he's well hydrated and that the electrolyte levels are where they should be."

"Yeah … do what you think is best."

"You can come and visit him while he's here if you'd like to."

Chains nodded, his gaze fixed on her face. "So, you're the one who bought Doc Nelson's practice."

"Yes. I'm assuming he was Thor's vet."

"Yeah, he was until he retired, then I went to Doc Eisenberg. He's the one who gave me your card when he retired about four months ago. I didn't figure a chick owned the clinic."

A small smile danced across her lips. "Believe it or not, us *chicks* comprise more than fifty percent of the student body in veterinary schools."

Chains's eyes didn't waver from her face. Autumn's breath *whooshed* out of her lungs as she felt her heart rate increase under his intense gaze.

"Don't take offense—I didn't mean anything by it."

"None taken," she said, trying to keep her voice casual as she turned away from his stare. "If you don't have any questions, I have other patients I need to check on. One of the techs—Christina—will be in shortly. Thor's vitals look strong, but he'll be a little woozy until the anesthetic completely wears off." Autumn's lips turned up.

"You got a damn pretty smile, Doc." His voice had lowered, giving his words an intimacy that made her insides tingle.

She let out a small, nervous laugh. "Thank you. Let Christina know if you have questions." Autumn rushed across the room, stumbling over her feet as she grabbed for the doorknob. Behind her, Chains chuckled, a deep vibration that echoed in her ear.

She leaned against the wall in the hallway, trying to steady her breathing while chastising herself on acting so ridiculously. Yes, Chains was a ruggedly handsome man, but she'd seen other good-looking men before. The image of Travis Krichmar came to mind. The thirty-two-year-old single dad made her female staff swoon every time he brought his golden retriever, Casey, into the clinic. Autumn thought he was an attractive, physically fit man who could easily be a model. *But I've never acted like this around him ... or any guy for that matter.* She grimaced. *Especially a client.* She shook her head slightly. *It must be the upcoming wedding. I'm just nervous. Yeah, that's it. I know it.*

"Are you all right?" Mark Jenkins asked.

Autumn nodded. "Yes. I was just feeling a little warm, that's all. I'll have to check the thermostat. How did you fare with the cat in Room Four?"

"Fine. The little guy had a thorn in one of his paws. It's all good now."

"Thanks for handling that for me."

Mark smiled. "No problem."

Autumn pushed away from the wall, then slowly walked back to her office.

An hour later she was sitting behind her desk, reviewing the lab results for a Jack Russell terrier when Christina poked her head inside the door.

"Thor's resting real well. I just changed his IV bag. Did you need me to stay the night to monitor him?"

"No, I'll stay for a while. Rodney has the nightshift, so he'll be at the clinic tonight. Lauren will be here as well."

Christina wrinkled her nose. "I hope you don't take this the wrong way, but Lauren's just plain weird. I don't really trust her."

Concern washed over Autumn. "Why do you say that? Have you seen her mistreat the animals?"

Christina shook her head. "No, not at all. I actually think she relates way better to them than to people. I just meant that she always wears black and never talks or tries to mingle with any of us. I'm always suspicious of people who aren't social. I don't know… she's just strange."

"She is a bit of a loner, but so was I when I was growing up. She's only twenty and probably still trying to figure out her place in life." Autumn laughed. "At thirty-one, *I'm* still trying to figure out certain things about me. What's important here is that she's great with the animals."

"I know. I wish she were more like Rodney. He's super friendly. He definitely makes us laugh."

"He's pretty social." *To the point of being annoying.* Autumn glanced back at the computer screen. "Did Chains leave?"

"Who?" Christina said.

She looked up. "Thor's owner—did he leave?"

"Is that his name? He never answered me when I'd asked him earlier. Yeah, he left with another guy about twenty minutes ago."

A thread of disappointment wove through her, which irritated the hell out of her.

"He's pretty cute." Christina giggled. "I like bad boys, but I'd be too afraid to go out with one."

Autumn nodded then turned back to the computer screen. "Can you please bring me the X-rays for Daisy—the Siamese?"

"Uh … sure," Christina said before walking away.

Autumn stared at the monitor for a long while, then pinched the bridge of her nose and returned to her work.

By the time she had seen her last patient and turned the lock on the front door, smoky purple clouds had absorbed the last of the sun's rays. She strolled down the hallway to the back room and walked inside to check on Thor, and Oscar—a pit bull who was also recuperating in the clinic after minor surgery.

"How're they doing?" she asked Rodney.

The vet tech stood up from a chair that he'd placed between the two beds. "Good. Mrs. Shively's been calling every half hour to check up on Oscar. I told her she could come in and spend the night if she wanted to."

"Is she going to?" Autumn asked as she skimmed over the charts for both dogs.

"No, she said she'll just keep calling throughout the night." He chuckled.

She slipped on a pair of gloves, then walked over to the dogs and checked their IV bags. Thor cracked his eyes open a bit, then licked her hand when she reached over to check one of the monitors hooked up to him.

"You're a beautiful dog," she said under her breath before turning her attention to the pit bull. "And you're a real cutie." She swiped her hand over the black dog's side.

"You look beat," Rodney said.

"I am. It's been a long day." Autumn smiled.

"And night. You were here until the early hours of the morning with Oscar. You should go home and get some rest. Dr. Jenkins is on call, so if something comes up, I'll give him a buzz."

Autumn nodded in agreement as she pulled off the gloves and discarded them in the trash can; then, she turned away from the table and walked to the door. Hesitating, she looked over her shoulder at Rodney. "If something changes with Thor, give me a call in addition to Dr. Jenkins, okay?"

The vet tech's eyes widened slightly. "Uh … yeah … sure."

"Thanks. I'll see you later." Autumn strode out into the hallway and went to her office. She swapped out the white lab coat for a black wool peacoat, then slung the strap of her purse over her shoulder and walked out of the clinic.

It was a lovely fall night: cool, crisp, and clear. She tilted her head back and stared at the twinkling stars in the dark sky, mentally connecting them together like she used to do when she was a young girl. One of her favorite childhood games besides word searches had been connecting the dots, and on warm summer nights, she and her friends would lie on a blanket in her parents' front yard and try to make shapes out of the stars by connecting them.

"I haven't thought about that in years," she muttered under her breath as she tore her gaze away from the inky canvas and fished out the ringing phone from her handbag.

"Hi, Bret." Autumn unlocked the driver's door and slipped into the car.

"Hey. Whatcha doing?"

"Just leaving the office so I'm running about thirty minutes late."

"Yeah, about that …"

Disappointment sank to the pit of her stomach.

"Are you still with me?" Bret asked.

"Uh-huh."

"Something's come up at work. I hate like hell doing this, but I can't go out to dinner tonight."

"And you just found this out *now*?"

"Yeah, it fucking sucks. I told Travis that too."

"Don't you *claim* to tell him that every time this happens?"

"What do you mean by that? You act like I'm lying or something. Why wouldn't I want us to go out to dinner?" Irritation crackled through the phone.

"It's just been happening a lot lately. It seems like the closer we get to the wedding date, the more you push me away," she said softly.

"What the hell? That's a load of bullshit. I thought you, of all people, would understand about working late. How many times have I waited around for you because you were preoccupied with some damn dog or hamster? Fuck, Autumn, I don't need this. I'm stressed over finishing this software project that I've got to present to the parent company in San Francisco in a few weeks. I thought I could count on your support."

A thread of guilt wove through her. "I'm sorry. Of course you can count on me. I've had a really long day, and I'm operating on just a few hours of sleep. I didn't mean to upset you, but I was really looking forward to the two of us having dinner together. It seems like we've hardly seen each in the past few weeks."

"I was looking forward to it too, but what can I do? We can go to Aspen for a romantic weekend once I get back from San Francisco, okay?"

"Okay," she whispered.

"I can come by after I get done at work."

"What time will that be?"

"Not sure—maybe midnight or a little later. I miss getting it on with you. You know how good we are together." A low chuckle.

A dull throb pulsed in the back of Autumn's neck. She massaged it, hoping to stave off a headache. At that moment, all she wanted was to change into her fleece pajamas and curl up in bed with the covers tucked snugly under her chin.

"So I'll see you later, right?" he asked.

"I'm too beat tonight. I don't think I'll be able to stay awake past ten o'clock."

"I can wake you up, sweetie." Another low chuckle—they were really starting to get on her nerves.

"Another time. I'm just too tired." She switched on the ignition.

"You're telling me *not* to come over?" Anger laced his voice.

"I guess I am. Don't work too hard. Let's touch base tomorrow when we're both refreshed."

Bret didn't answer, and she could hear his short puffs of breaths. The windows in the car rattled as a truck passed by.

"I'll talk to you later." Her voice sounded weary and somewhat strange, echoing through the car. She cleared her throat. "I'm sorry, but I really am tired."

When he finally spoke, his words dripped ice. "No, you're not. You're punishing me because I have to work late. You're playing a dangerous game, Autumn."

A small sigh escaped through her lips. "I'm not a game-player. You should know that. I'm sorry you're upset."

Then he hung up. At first, she thought the phone had disconnected, but when Bret didn't call back, she realized he'd hung up on her. A wave of anger washed over Autumn, and the urge to destroy something reverberated in her so deeply that she pushed her purse off the passenger seat as the contents inside scattered across the floor.

"I'm so sick of this!" She slammed her hand on the steering wheel. "Why do I always feel like I've done something wrong when he's the one being a jerk? I'm tired and he should damn well get *that*."

She stared at the phone for several minutes hoping he'd call back, but he didn't. Determined not to be the one who'd apologize *again*, Autumn threw the phone on the floor. The dull throb at the base of her neck had now blossomed into a raging migraine.

Blinking back tears, she turned out of the lot and headed home.

Chapter Four

JIGGER BURST OUT laughing as he tipped the chair back against the wall in the main room. "The look on your face is classic." He slapped his knee and gestured to Kelly to bring him another beer.

Chains laid his phone on the table and looked over at Crow, who wore a big shit-eating grin on his face as he watched Eagle study the balls on the pool table.

"I'm guessing you bet on Crow to win this round," Chains said.

Jigger glanced over at the two men in the corner of the room. "I'm not involved in that."

"Then, what the fuck were you laughing at?" Chains patted Kelly on the ass when she placed another shot of whiskey in front of him. "Thanks." He winked at her.

"Any time, sugar." She squeezed his bicep. "Ohh … I like this."

Chains chuckled and picked up his glass.

"You looking to have some fun later on?" Kelly ran her fingernails down the length of his arm.

"Probably not, but if I change my mind, you'll know." Another wink then he turned his attention away from her as she sauntered away.

"How can you turn down Kelly? She's one of the hottest fucks in here," Jigger said as he brought the beer bottle to his lips.

Chains shrugged, then glanced over to the pool table. "Crow's got this game."

"Maybe you're turning her down 'cause you got that doctor chick on your mind," Jigger said.

Chains jerked his head back. "What the fuck are you talking about, dude?"

"I saw the way your face fell only a few minutes ago when the doc wasn't there. You had to talk to some dude. It was classic. I should've taken a picture of it." Jigger laughed again. "Just fuckin' classic."

Irritation pricked at Chains's nerves as he watched his friend turn red from laughter. "What the fuck's the matter with you? You look like a crazed hyena or something. I'm just worried about Thor, that's all."

Jigger calmed down a bit. "How's he doing?"

"The tech said he's resting and all his vitals are good."

"That's cool. The chick knows her stuff."

"Yeah." Chains threw back the rest of his shot.

"She's hot too."

He shrugged, then turned his chair away from Jigger and faced it toward the pool game. Eagle was sweating bullets, and several of the members had walked over to watch the match.

"There's no fuckin' way you don't think that doc chick is a sweet piece."

"She's attractive," Chains said without looking at Jigger.

"You're not fooling me, bro." His chair slammed back down on the floor, then Chains heard it scrape against the linoleum. "I'm gonna see if Kelly's still in the mood. Catch you later."

Chains grunted his reply, his gaze never moving from the corner of the room. Instead of seeing Crow swagger to the table for his turn after Eagle missed a prime shot, he devoured the image of the pretty veterinarian's curves in his mind, admiring every inch of it. At that moment, all he wanted was to explore her naked body as she gasped and pleaded for his dick. He could see her almond-shaped eyes dazed, hear her soft moans, and feel her full lips wrapped around his cock, sucking the hell out of it.

A streak of lust seared through him. "Fuck," he muttered as the crotch of his pants grew tight. Glancing around the room, he scooted closer to the table then leaned back. With one foot propped up on the chair across from him, Chains crossed his arms over his chest and glared at the wall behind the pool table. The fact that he was attracted to her rankled him. It'd been a long time since a citizen had piqued his interest.

"I'm grateful that she saved Thor's life—that's all," he muttered. It had nothing to do with her warm smile, her lush auburn hair shining under the fluorescent lights, her button nose, full lips, or her perfectly rounded tits that turned up slightly as if begging for his mouth. "Fuck," he growled, shifting in the chair. Yeah … it had nothing to do with any of *that*.

"You look like you need a friend, baby," Lila said. She glided her fingers over his back and massaged his neck and shoulders.

Chains let his head fall back slightly.

"You're so tense, baby. What're you thinking about?" The scent of her floral perfume made his nose twitch.

"Nothing much." Doc Stanford's deep brown eyes flashed through his mind. *Damn, if they aren't beautiful.* They were the color of the soil after a rainstorm with flecks of gold sunlight.

"See, you're getting all tense again, baby." Lila's soft voice blurred out the image of the sexy vet. "Are you worried about Thor?"

Nodding, Chains straightened up in the chair. "Yeah, that's it."

"Do you wanna take this to your room? I can give you a real good body massage." Her breath was warm next to his ear.

"Thanks, but I'm gonna step out and give the clinic another call."

"I'll still be here when you get back, baby."

Chains grasped her hands and squeezed them. "Don't waste tonight waiting for me. Another time, okay?"

Lila pulled her hands away. "You still with Ruby?"

He rose to his feet. "I'm not with anyone." He pursed his lips, then strode across the room to the front door.

Once outside, Chains pulled out his phone and tapped the clinic's number. He looked at the black sky filled with sparkling stars and wished that Thor were standing next to him.

"Highlands Animal Care Center," a male voice said.

"I'm calling to see how Thor's doing," Chains replied.

"And who are you?"

Anger bristled along his spine. "The fuckin' owner."

"Uh … sorry, but I need a name," the man said.

"Is Doc Stanford there?" Chains gritted.

"No, but she'll be in tomorrow morning. I can help you if you just give me your name."

"Chains."

"Hang on."

Chains heard the clack of fingers on a keyboard over the phone.

"Okay. Thor's doing fine. He's resting and all his vitals look good."

"What time do you open in the morning?"

"Seven thirty."

"Thanks." Chains ended the call and slipped his phone into the pocket of his leather jacket. The pulsating strains of hard rock filtered through the windows, and he looked at a group of scantily-clad women in high heels ambling toward the clubhouse. These women were the *hang-arounds* who lined up outside the concrete walls four nights a week, hoping to be one of the lucky ones chosen to have a good time with the members. The parties, booze, weed, and lifestyle were a draw for many women who wanted a walk on the wild side.

Not in the mood for a club party, Chains strode over to his Harley and threw his leg over the leather seat. He switched on the ignition, then roared past the huddle of women waving at him. Chains turned left onto the old highway and increased the speed as he headed toward the small roads crisscrossing the desert. The cool wind brushing through his face, the spicy aroma of sagebrush washing over him, and the sound of the motor filling his ears embraced his senses and acted as oxygen to his soul. And it was exactly what he needed. Riding his bike always rebooted his system, bringing a sense of calm and ease to his mind and body. For Chains, it was the best and only therapy he knew that made him forget everything for a while.

An hour later, he pulled into the parking lot of Leroy's—one of his and the club's favorite diners in town. Feeling energized and refreshed, Chains hopped off the bike and sauntered into the eatery.

"Hey, good-looking," Loretta said as the corners of her mouth turned up.

"Hey." He pulled off his leather gloves and stuffed them in the pockets of his jacket.

"You got others comin'?" The curly-haired cashier asked.

"Nope—just me."

She pulled out a laminated menu and came out from behind the counter. "Same booth?"

"Yeah," he replied, following close behind her.

A table of three women in their early twenties smiled and whispered among themselves as he passed their table. When he winked at them, they tittered, and one of them threw back her shoulders and thrust out her breasts.

"Is your motorcycle a Harley?" she asked in a breathy voice.

"Yeah," he said without stopping.

"I bet you get that a lot," the cashier said, looking over her shoulder at him.

Chains shrugged. "Chicks dig bikes."

Loretta put the menu down on the table. "And the men who ride them."

"I guess." He slid into the booth facing the front door, then shrugged off his leather jacket. Like most outlaws, Chains always sat where he could see who was coming in and out of a place. In his world, a split second of unawareness could change everything in a bad way.

"Water and coffee?"

He looked up at the dark-haired hostess. "Yeah, thanks. Is Tammy working tonight?"

"She is. I'll send her over in a few. Be right back with your drinks, handsome."

He watched Loretta walk away, positive that the exaggerated sway of her hips was for his benefit.

When she disappeared into the kitchen, Chains settled back into the booth and looked at the clock on the wall above the food window: 8:50

p.m. He rummage through the pocket of his jacket and took out the phone.

"Highlands Animal Care Center." It was the same man Chains had spoken to earlier.

"Chains here. How's Thor doing?"

"Good. He's resting peacefully. Dr. Stanford just left. She came by to check on him and another patient."

At the mention of the veterinarian's name, the image of her in the white lab coat and nothing else streaked through his mind. "Thanks," he mumbled, then ended the call.

"Hiya, sugar. You solo tonight?" Tammy asked as she approached the booth. She was one of the club's favorite waitresses at Leroy's, and Chains and the other members admired her tenacity in providing a good home for her kids after her asshole husband ditched her for another woman. Chains could definitely relate to the sense of betrayal and anger that consumed the spouse of a cheater. When he'd found out Krystal had fucked Crossbones, rage had been his constant companion for a long time.

"Yeah, I just came back from a ride. How's life treating you?"

"I can't complain. In a couple of hours my shift will be over, then I can go home and soak in a hot tub." She laughed. "Believe me, that's the only thing keeping me going tonight."

"One of those days?"

"Busy as all hell. How've you been?"

"Good."

"Did Loretta tell you about the specials?"

"Nah. Whatcha got?"

"Chicken fried steak, meatloaf, and pot roast."

"What do you recommend?"

"They're all good, but the pot roast is awesome—even better than mine." Tammy glanced over at the kitchen, then lowered her voice. "Don't go tellin' Chubby that. His ego's big enough without any more help from me."

Chains chuckled. "I'll go with the pot roast."

"It comes with a salad. Ranch, right?"

"Yeah." He handed her his menu.

"I'll go see what's taking Loretta so long with your drinks." She hurried away.

Soon, Tammy was back with his coffee, water, and dinner. Chains poured the dressing over the salad and began to eat. A steady stream of customers continued to file into the diner, and the three young women who'd flirted with him earlier kept staring over at his table, but he ignored them and looked down at his food.

Unlike some of the brothers at the club, Chains preferred women closer to his thirty-two years, and these chicks looked like they were barely twenty-one. He also wasn't in the mood for any company.

A pang of loneliness shot through him. He missed Thor. Even though Chains knew he was safe and doing well at the clinic, it didn't mean that he couldn't pine for his furry buddy like hell.

He pushed the empty plate away and placed his crumpled up napkin on top of it. A bell above the door sounded, and Chains looked up and saw the sexy veterinarian, who'd been on his mind too damn much that night, enter the diner. As if guided by radar, her captivating eyes turned to his table, then her mouth opened and color rushed to her cheeks. She held his gaze a fraction too long before blinking and then focusing her attention on the cashier.

Chains watched as she leaned against the counter, looking at everything but him. Loretta rang something up on the register before walking over to one of the wired shelves and took down what looked like a cream pie. As the cashier cut a slice, Chains gazed back at the veterinarian and caught her staring at him. An embarrassed expression covered her reddened face and she looked away. He kept his eyes fixed on her, wondering why the hell he was letting this woman get to him. She took the bag from Loretta, and the way the vet tossed her head made his fingers itch to grab all that long, wavy hair and yank it hard, making her cry out before crushing against him. *Fuck!*

With the paper bag in hand, Dr. Stanford locked her gaze on his before she began walking toward his booth.

"Hi." She approached his table and gave him a quick once-over.

"Hey," he replied.

She pulled up the bag. "My chocolate cream pie run." A small laugh burst through glossy peach lips. "I stopped by to check up on Thor—he's doing great." She switched the paper bag from her right to her left hand.

"Yeah, that's what the guy told me when I called. Can he come home tomorrow?"

"Maybe. Let's see how he does through the day. He was a pretty sick fella." Tiny fine lines around her eyes crinkled when she smiled.

"Thanks for helping him out."

"You're welcome. Thor's a beautiful Siberian."

"Yeah. So, do you got a first name?"

There was a slight pause, then a soft chuckle. "Autumn."

"That's a pretty name." His gaze dropped from her eyes to her shoulders and then to her breasts. "It suits you."

Autumn cleared her throat. "Uh … thank you." She quickly looked away.

"Why don't you have a seat? I can get you a cup of coffee."

She fidgeted with the bag in her hand for the umpteenth time, then glanced at the wall clock. "Thanks, but I have to get going. I still have some work I need to do before I call it a night."

Shrugging, he leaned back into the cushion and propped his leg on the seat across from him. "Okay." He locked gazes with her, enjoying the way it made her fluster.

"Okay then." Autumn pointed to the door. "All right—I'll be going now."

"I'll come by in the morning to see Thor."

A big smile plastered across her face while her head moved up and down like one of those bobble-head dolls on the dashboard of cages.

She's so fuckin' nervous. Yeah … she's interested.

"Thor will love seeing you." After a pause, she turned away mumbling, "Goodbye" as she rushed to the front of the diner. Without a backward glance, Autumn pushed open the glass door and hurried toward a dark-green two-door Audi.

Chains chuckled when the cage sped out of the parking lot.

"I'm guessing you liked the pot roast," Tammy said as she leaned over and picked up his empty plate.

"It was good."

"You want any dessert?"

One corner of his mouth hitched up in a smirk. "Yeah ... I'll take a piece of chocolate cream pie."

Chapter Five

AUTUMN TOSSED ANOTHER blouse on top of the growing pile on the floor as she tried to decide what to wear to work that morning. She didn't want to admit she was nervous about seeing Chains, especially since running into him the night before at Leroy's. She didn't like the way he looked at her, the way he'd made her feel nervous and all mushy inside.

The previous night, Autumn had planned to go to bed earlier, but the more she'd thought about Bret hanging up on her, the madder she became, and the more intense the craving grew for a piece of Leroy's famous chocolate cream pie. Bret usually disapproved when she'd order anything sweet, so her trip to the diner was a small act of rebellion and defiance. The last person she ever thought she'd run into was Chains.

Autumn sighed as she shook her head. *Damn, that man.* There was something dark and dangerous about him. Just by looking at him, any woman would know she'd be taking a risk in getting involved with him. There was no doubt that the sex would be awesome, but the chance of him stealing then breaking a woman's heart would be pretty damn high.

"Grr … just stop it," she said aloud. Cinder, her bluish-gray cat, meowed and rubbed against her legs. Autumn looked down and into the cat's bright copper eyes. "I'm acting like an ass, you know," she said, bending down to rub Cinder under the chin. "I should be thinking about Bret instead of a patient's owner. I'm being shameful."

Cinder purred and nuzzled the side of her face against Autumn.

The truth was that Autumn was *very* attracted to Chains, and she was pretty sure a lot of women would be. Just because she was engaged didn't mean she'd never find another man besides Bret attractive. There had been numerous times when Bret had done a double-take when a pretty or curvy woman passed by them on the street or in a restaurant. "That's just normal human behavior. I'm making too much out of all this." Without another glance in the mirror, Autumn fastened her blouse and tucked it into her pencil skirt, then slipped on her heels and walked out of the bedroom with Cinder following close behind.

On the way to the clinic, Autumn kept glancing at the phone laying on the passenger seat of the car, hoping Bret would man up and give her a call. When the phone finally rang, she was so startled by it that she jumped a bit in her seat. Glancing over, her heart sank when she saw it wasn't Bret calling.

"Hello?"

"May I speak with Autumn Stanford?" a woman asked.

"Speaking." Autumn turned into the parking lot, found a spot and then shut the ignition.

"This is Jenny from Gateaux Bakery. I'm just confirming your 4:30 p.m. appointment today."

"Oh, right." Autumn slid out of the car.

"Is the time still good for you?" Jenny asked.

"Yes." She slammed the car door. "I actually forgot about it, so I'm glad you called. I'll be there. Thanks."

"Is your fiancé coming as well?"

"He said he wanted to, but I'll be there for sure. Thank you."

Autumn slipped the phone into her leather tote bag and walked across the lot. A black and gray Harley-Davidson with a ton of chrome gleamed under the morning sun. She paused to admire the beautiful motorcycle and wondered what it would feel like to ride on it. When she was in college, a friend of hers had a scooter and would take her on rides around the city and countryside. She'd loved the way she was immersed in the world around her and connected to it. It was unlike anything she'd experienced from inside a car.

Autumn ran her hand over the soft leather seat and massive handlebars. "This beauty is a million times more powerful than Declan's scooter. I bet it would be thrilling to be on the back of this one."

"Hi, Dr. Stanford," a woman's voice rang out behind Autumn.

Looking over her shoulder, she smiled when her gaze met Silvia Sanchez's. "Hi. Is Poppy not feeling well?"

The middle-aged woman held a small Pekingese in her arms as she ambled over to Autumn. "She hasn't eaten in two days. I made her lamb stew and rice yesterday, and she just turned away. Her back leg seems to be giving her trouble too. I think she may have a splinter or something."

Autumn ran her hand over the fawn-colored dog. "Did you step on something, Poppy?" She smiled. "I'll take a look at her as soon as I check on a couple of patients." She held the door open for Silvia, then followed her into the reception area. "I'll see you soon," she said before disappearing behind one of the doors.

After putting away her coat and tote bag, Autumn slipped on her lab coat and rushed down the hall toward the recovery room that housed Oscar and Thor. She had planned to be at the clinic thirty minutes sooner, but trying on a multitude of blouses had made her late. Again, she cursed her foolishness and made a vow that it would never happen again.

When Autumn entered the room, she saw Chains standing by the cage that held Thor. She stayed rooted to the spot as her eyes roamed over him. His navy blue T-shirt fit nicely, showcasing his firm chest. Toned shoulders and firm biceps bulged under the fabric, and Autumn had the unfamiliar impulse to simply run her hand over the sculpted flesh in admiration. Tearing her gaze away, she inhaled deeply and then walked slowly toward him.

Chains turned and gave her a nod, took her in with one of those bright, disarming glances, then fixed his brown eyes on her.

"You must've come in early," she said, stopping in front of Thor's cage. Chains was so close that she could smell his spicy cologne along with the scent of leather and sun-warmed skin. She gripped the clipboard hanging on a hook and perused the chart.

"How'd you like your pie last night?" he whispered, except his mouth was close, *too close* to her ear. His warm breath sent an unwanted tingle of desire to every nerve ending in her body.

Flustered and angry, Autumn moved away to put some distance between them.

"Good. Thor's doing very well," she said.

"He's still pretty groggy."

"That's because he's on an IV. I'd like to keep him overnight again, and if everything is looking as good as it is now, you can bring him home tomorrow." Suddenly feeling awkward and exposed, she pressed the clipboard against her chest.

The corner of his mouth tugged upward as his gaze rested on the form holder for a second then slowly traveled up to her lips.

"That's great news, Doc."

She cleared her throat. "I'm sure you're both anxious to get back to your routine." Scribbling notes in the chart, she feigned indifference even though she was acutely aware of his presence.

"Do I make you nervous?" His voice was like a low roll of thunder.

Glancing up, she shook her head. "Not at all." Inside, her nerves were snapping, but a cool smile spread across her face.

He took two steps toward her, making her stomach twist into a knot.

"Are you sure about that?" he whispered.

Not knowing what to say, she just stood there grinning like a damn fool.

"Dr. Stanford, we have an emergency. Dr. Jenkins needs you to take his appointment in Room Six."

"I'm coming," Autumn said as she placed the clipboard on the hook. She quickly walked over to Oscar's cage and read the charts before rushing out of the room.

For the next forty-five minutes she hurried from room to room, tending to her patients as well as Mark Jenkins'. After administering a shot to a large tabby, a deafening roar rattled the windows of the examination room.

"What's that?" the tabby's owner asked.

"I have no idea," she replied as she walked over to the window. Autumn sucked in a small gasp as she watched Chains turn around the black motorcycle she'd admired earlier that morning. *I should've figured the Harley belonged to him.* She watched him until she couldn't see the bike anymore.

"They should make it against the law for people to have such loud motorcycles," Patty Timbers said as she picked up her cat.

"I'm pretty sure there's a law against it," Autumn said, turning away from the window. *But he wouldn't care about that.* A small laugh escaped through her lips.

"The police are never around when you need them." Patty placed a kiss on top of her cat's head.

"I'll see you in six months for Othello's next shot." Autumn pulled off a pair of nitrile gloves, then tossed them in a bin next to the sink before walking out of the room.

The rest of the day was so busy that Autumn and the rest of the vets didn't have time to take more than a ten-minute break. Mercifully, she'd didn't have any extra time to think about the unnerving encounter she'd had that morning with Chains. There was this vibe in the air between them she couldn't quite put into words. It felt like high school all over again, and it angered and confused her. Autumn had never felt this drawn or attracted to a man she didn't know, and the fact that she and Bret were getting married in less than three months made the guilt factor overwhelming.

Tomorrow Thor's going home, so that will be it. I need to concentrate on the wedding. Autumn looked at the clock, then rushed over to the closet. "Dammit! I've got to be at the bakery." She hurried out of the room, telling Mary that she had an appointment and to call her if anything came up before she came back to the animal clinic.

Her day had been so full that Autumn had forgotten to call Bret to see if he still planned on meeting her to discuss the design of the wedding cake. She rummaged through her tote when she got into the car and dug out her phone, quickly tapping in his number.

"What's up?" he said on the second ring.

"I forgot to remind you that we have an appointment at Gateaux for the cake. Are you still planning to go?"

"Of course. I told you I'd be there. I don't need you to remind me."

She bit the inside of her cheek.

"Are you on your way?" he asked.

"Yes. I'm running a bit behind because it was crazy at the clinic today."

"I'm just pulling in front of the place."

"How was your day? Did you finish your work last night?"

"Still working on it. My day was good. I'm going in now."

"See you in a few," she said before hanging up.

Autumn spotted Bret's yellow Mustang convertible in front of the bakery and parked behind it. Three- and four-tiered wedding cakes with columns, cascading flowers—real and sugar—and dozens of miniature pastries filled the two display windows of the brick storefront. Interspersed between the goodies were pumpkins, acorns, berries, greens, and sateen leaves in fall colors.

"Sorry, I'm late," Autumn said when she walked through the glass doors.

A woman around Autumn's age nodded while pulling out a wooden chair beside her. "No worries. I'm Jenny. Catherine had something come up with one of her children, so she had to leave. I've been working in cake design for the last twelve years. I studied and worked in Paris for four years." Jenny smiled widely. "I just wanted you to know that I have a lot of experience in everything sweet, and my specialty is in designing unique wedding cakes."

"I'm not worried. Catherine sings your accolades all the time to me." Autumn sat down then leaned over and kissed Bret on the cheek. "Hey," she whispered.

"You're looking good, sweetheart." He squeezed her hand, then looked down at his phone.

As she and Jenny discussed various designs, Bret focused his attention on the phone, making no effort to be part of the decision process. The incessant beeps drove Autumn crazy, and she seriously thought about flinging the damn phone against the wall, then laughing maniacally as the broken pieces flew around the room.

"Do you want the sugar flowers or something a bit more modern?" There was an edge in her voice.

Bret shrugged. "Whatever you want. You're the one paying, right?"

Jenny shifted in her chair while clearing her throat.

"I thought you wanted to help out with the design," Autumn said.

He looked up. "I'm here, aren't I?"

"Not really," she mumbled.

An hour later, Autumn walked out into the cool air and headed to her car. She'd just plunked down another five hundred bucks for the cake, making the entire price a little over a grand. At the end, she decided on the sugar flowers tumbling down the side of the four-tiered cake with simulated lace and pearl accents around the borders.

"Do you want to go out for a beer?" Bret asked as he slipped his arm around her waist.

"I was hoping we could go to the Spice Room."

He scrunched his face. "I'm not feeling *that* tonight. Anyway, I told Liam, Colin, and Oliver that I'd hang out with them tonight. We're going to the Beer Shack. You love their burgers."

"Why didn't you tell me you already had plans?" Autumn pressed the remote and the Audi's headlights turned on.

Bret pulled his arm away from her waist. "I want you to be there with me tonight. I thought you'd want to spend some time together."

"I would, but I don't feel like competing with your friends. Anyway, I'm on call tonight. I'm going back to the clinic to check on two of my patients and one of Mark's."

"Okay. I'm not going to jump down your throat because you have to work late. I understand, which is more than I can say about you and my work. Last night, you really pissed me off."

"I already told you I was sorry about that." She leaned against the car. "Are you sure you want to get married?"

Bret jerked his head back and a frown burrowed between his brows. "What the fuck kind of question is that?"

"It's a fair one. It just seems like instead of this wedding bringing us closer together, it's pushing us farther apart."

"I don't know what the hell you're talking about."

"Like this whole cake designing thing. I bet you don't even know what I decided on for *our* cake. I'm just wondering why you even bothered to come. You were glued to your damn phone the whole time."

"I came because I knew you wanted me there for you. You're just never satisfied, are you?"

"Forget it." She pushed away from the car and opened the door.

Bret slammed it close. "Don't be this way, Autumn. The last few months you've become a real pain in the ass. I try and do all this stuff for you, and you don't even care."

"What are you doing for me? Canceling engagements at the last minute? Wanting to come over at one or two in the morning to have sex? Not giving a damn about the wedding plans? Tell me all the things you've been doing for me."

Bret shook his head, then pounded his fist on the top of the car. "I can't talk to you when you're like this. I love you and I want to marry you—it's that simple. Now, I have to go. I'll call you later." He gave her a quick peck on the lips, then went over to the Mustang and slid inside.

She watched in disbelief as he merged into traffic before she opened the car door and slipped inside. Something wasn't right between them. *Is it me?* Autumn didn't think so because Bret had definitely been pulling away from her in subtle ways for the past two to three months, but she couldn't figure out why. It appeared as though their lives were the same in regard to hours and intensity, so what was the problem, and why didn't he want to talk about it?

Sighing, Autumn drove the car away from the curb and headed in the direction of the clinic. For a split second, she wondered what Chains was doing at that moment, but she quickly banished all thoughts of the ruggedly handsome man who rode a Harley.

Tomorrow, I'll pick up a couple of steak dinners and have Bret come over. We just need to make time for us.

Happy with her plan, she decided to send Bret a text once she got back to her office. Every couple had their rough patches, and planning a wedding when they were both so busy was just plain stressful. Bret was the man she loved and wanted to marry. There was no confusion; he was her happily ever after.

Autumn kept telling herself that, hoping to snuff out the doubt niggling at the back of her mind.

Chapter Six

"WE MISSED YOU at Cuervos last night," Eagle said as he slipped into the chair beside Chains.

"I had a website I had to finish," Chains replied. For the past seven years, he'd been running his website design company, and it had proven to be quite lucrative.

"The chicks were outta control." Eagle chuckled. "This busty brunette wanted it so bad that she practically begged for my cock in her mouth. Damn … could she give head."

Chains laughed. "So you've lost interest in the redhead at Stella's?"

"No. I'm still priming her, but this sweet piece from last night is worth another round or two." Eagle tilted his chair back. "Jigger had a sexy blonde throwing herself at him all night. Crow didn't do too bad either. You missed a good time, bro."

"I'm sure the next time I go to Cuervos there'll be chicks wanting to have biker cock. It never fails." Chains picked up a bottle of water and took a deep drink.

"You sound like that's a fuckin' bore."

"Most chicks are too eager, and sometimes I like the chase."

"This is coming from a guy who'll only fuck club girls?" Eagle laughed.

Chains shrugged. "Whatever."

"What's gotten into you lately?"

A vivid image of Autumn in her pencil skirt flashed through his mind. "Nothing," he muttered.

"It's Thor," Jigger said as he plopped down next to Eagle. "When's he coming home?"

"This afternoon," Chains replied.

"I'll go with you to help out. I'd love to get another glimpse of that sexy vet." Jigger waggled his brows then leaned his elbows on the wood table.

Chains shook his head. "Thanks, but I'm good."

"Sexy vet? What the fuck, dude? You've been holding out on us." Eagle pounded his fist on the table and several members looked over. "Thor's vet is sexy as fuck according to Jigger."

Chains clenched his jaw.

"That's why you've been spending a shit load of time over there," Crow said. Aztec, Skull, and Brutus guffawed.

"When were you gonna tell us about this?" Rooster asked.

"Never—he wants to keep her to himself," Cueball said.

Chains narrowed his eyes. "Just shut the fuck up about it. My ass was at the clinic because of Thor, and you all know it."

"Is she sexy, bro?" Rooster asked.

Chains just glared.

"Fuck, dude. Deny it or embrace it, but don't just sit there lookin' pissed 'cause that tells us you got a hard-on for this sweet piece," Eagle said as the members burst out in laughter.

"I don't have a fuckin' hard-on for anyone," Chains replied.

"Then, why're you getting so damn mad?" Goldie chuckled.

"Because you're all such fuckin' morons." Chains guzzled the rest of the water and glanced at the door. Relief washed over him when he saw Steel and Paco walk in. He didn't want to *think* let alone *talk* about Autumn, especially to his brothers. The fact that he was bothered by their ribbing spoke volumes.

After Chains had left the clinic the day before, he'd gone back to the clubhouse and holed up in his room, burying himself in work; he needed something to take his mind off of *her*. By the time he'd packed it in at four in the morning, he was so damn tired that he fell asleep the minute he hit the bed. But the morning brought thoughts of Autumn, and as hard as he tried, he just couldn't get her out of his mind. Her smile, her sexy-as-hell curves, and those captivating eyes all overwhelmed his conscious thoughts.

The gavel pounded, and Chains jerked his head up and looked at the club president who stood at the head of the table. The noise in the room came to an immediate stop as Steel called church to order.

"The first thing we have to discuss is whether or not we want to sell weed to this group in Kansas. Chains ran a background on these guys, and I've checked them out with some of our other contacts as well. So far it looks okay," Steel said.

"Would this be an ongoing business?" Army asked.

Steel shook his head. "Nah. We don't need the fuckin' ATF in our business, but we need the cash to buy more weapons. We stand to make a shitload from this sale." He glanced over at Chains. "Give us the lowdown on these buyers."

He lifted his chin as he rose to his feet. "The buyers are a father-and-son team. They work outta Wichita and have thirty people on their payroll. The dad, Gary, runs one of the most prestigious real estate companies in Wichita, and I bet none of his employees suspects he's the head of a drug-smuggling ring," Chains said with a laugh. "He and his son have a bogus company from where they launder the money. They sell natural stuff like soaps, lotions, and other shit."

A low murmur of laughter filled the room.

"Love those states that haven't legalized weed—gives us a good revenue," Muerto said.

"Yep. These dudes distribute weed to about ten of them," Chains replied. "The kick in the ass is that this dude's wife's all over the society pages in the newspapers. I bet the people they hobnob with at the country club don't have a fuckin' clue where the money comes from. Posers to the max."

"I hate posers," Diablo said.

"I second that," Sangre added.

Suddenly Goldie shot to his feet. "Who wants to beat the shit outta posers?"

And then the room exploded with strings of expletives as some of the members pounded their fists on the tables while others jumped to their feet. Chains laughed, then plopped down on the chair, waiting for Steel to hit the gavel and bring church back to order.

Paco pushed away from the wall and put two fingers in his mouth, then whistled so loudly that Chains thought his eardrums would burst.

"Fuck, dude," he said.

"You're better than the damn gavel." Steel laughed, then looked over at Chains. "Are we ready to roll on this deal?"

Chains nodded. "Pretty much. I just wanna check a few more references who've done business with these buyers. If it all checks out, we're good to go."

"Okay. Let me know and I'll set it up," Paco said. "To change the subject, we got the Steamboat Springs rally coming up soon. Hawk and Banger told Steel and me that they expect some trouble from that fucking MC one of their ex-members joined." He snapped his fingers several times. "I can't remember the name of the damn club. It's on the tip of my fucking tongue."

"Are you getting old or is Chelsea keeping you up all night?" Rooster joked.

"Rising Order," Paco blurted out. "That's it"—he glanced over at Rooster—"and fuck you."

Rooster guffawed and flipped the vice president his middle finger.

Steel leaned forward. "I told the Insurgents we'll help if those assholes start up any shit."

"Damn straight," Chains said.

"Hawk knows he can count on us," Eagle added.

"It's been a while since we've had a good fight." Brutus tipped back on his chair.

"Fallen Slayers said they'd join in too," Skull said.

"I didn't think they were gonna come. They seemed lukewarm about it last week when I went to their club party," Eagle said.

"They got a couple of new members, and to hear Roughneck say it, the two dudes are crazier than shit." Steel chuckled.

Roughneck was the president of the Fallen Slayers MC, which was located in Silverado—an hour's drive from Alina. The two MCs were friendly and often partied or helped each other out when rival clubs tried to mess with either of them.

"If there's nothing else, get the hell outta here and go find a drink and a good lay." Steel tapped the gavel on the table.

A mild commotion rippled through the room: metal chairs scraped against the concrete floor as members stood up, voices echoed and reverberated, and heavy boots left the room.

"Are you sure you don't want me to go with you to pick up Thor?" Jigger asked.

"Yeah," Chains replied as he headed to the bar.

"It wouldn't be any trouble." Jigger followed behind him.

"I'm good, so leave it alone." Chains held up two fingers to the prospect manning the bar.

"What's the name of this clinic Thor's in?" Eagle asked as he sidled up beside Chains.

The prospect placed two shots of tequila, some lime wedges, and a salt shaker in front of Chains, then scurried away. He licked the back of his hand, sprinkled a pinch of salt on it, then licked it again before he threw back the tequila in one gulp. Heat slid down his throat to his chest, and he finished it off by biting into a lime slice.

"Do you know the name, Jigger?" Eagle said.

Ignoring the impulse to smash Eagle in the face, Chains picked up the salt shaker for his second shot.

"Are any of you guys going to take me and Angel to the drugstore? We need to get a few things," Lila said.

The cloying scent of perfume overwhelmed him, and he pushed away from the counter.

"I'd help you ladies out, but I've got to pick up Thor."

A wide smile lit up her pretty face. "I'm so happy that he's all better. I've missed him."

Chains squeezed her shoulder. "Me too." He glanced over at Eagle. "You're not doing shit, so why don't you take the women to town? You got too damn much time on your hands."

Eagle slowly brought the beer bottle to his mouth. After a long pull, he set it down on the bar. "I'm gonna find out the name of the clinic, bro." He then turned to the Lila and said, "I can only spare an hour for your shopping trip."

Lila squealed and rushed away.

"You're a softie," Jigger said as he stared at the club girl's ass.

"Don't give me that bullshit—you were one second away from offering to take them," Eagle replied.

Chains pulled out the keys to his SUV and chuckled. "Have fun with the girls."

"Fuck you," Eagle muttered.

He turned away and walked out of the club. In less than thirty minutes he was pulling into the clinic's crowded parking lot. When he entered the building, several people with dogs, cats, and a couple of guinea pigs littered the reception area. Chains walked up to the counter and rang the chrome call bell. A woman who looked vaguely familiar came up to the front.

"May I help you?" the short-haired brunette asked.

"I'm here to pick up my dog—Thor." He wanted to ask if Autumn was around, but he didn't. The doctor was just Thor's vet, and after today he wouldn't see her again unless Thor needed some medical attention. Asking about her would be lame as hell, and besides, interest in a citizen wasn't his thing.

"Okay." The receptionist looked at a computer screen. "Dr. Sanford wants to talk to you."

An annoying streak of excitement surged through him. *Fuckin' pussy.* "Okay."

The woman leaned back in her chair and stared at him. "I think I know you." She squinted her eyes, then they widened as a pink flush spread over her face. "Chet Graver, right?" A smile spread across her face.

"Yeah—but the name's Chains now."

"Chains?"

"Yeah. You look familiar." He tried to remember if she was one of the many girls he'd hooked up with before he got hitched to Krystal, but he was drawing a damn blank.

"Shelia Bixby. Alina High—class of 1987. Remember?"

A memory of them climbing into the back seat of his used Camaro flashed through his mind. "Oh yeah. How've you been?" They'd hooked up after a football game, and for him, it had been a one-time deal, but Sheila had interpreted it as the beginning of a relationship. For the rest of their senior year, she'd chased the hell out of him.

"Real good. I have a couple of kids—a son and a daughter. What about you?"

"No kids."

"What about a wife?" Sheila leaned forward slightly.

"Nope."

"I'm divorced."

Chains nodded.

"I just moved back from Carbondale a year ago. I wondered if you still lived here."

"Well ... now you know. So how long do I gotta wait before I can get my dog?"

She shrugged. "I'm not sure. What do you do?"

"Web development." He glanced over his shoulder and spotted an empty seat.

The door opened and one of the techs walked into the reception area. She glanced over at him and smiled.

"Hi. I bet you're here to pick up Thor." He didn't miss the way she checked him out. He looked at her nametag. *That's right—the chick's name is Christina.*

"Yeah. I was just wondering when I can get him."

"Soon. Dr. Stanford should be finishing up with her patient. Thor's been such a good boy."

"Didn't you come out here to bring a patient back to one of the rooms?" Sheila asked, irritation punctuating her words.

Christina gave her a sidelong glance, then cleared her throat. "Minnie Cuellers," she said.

A woman jumped up from her seat, and a white bichon frise barked.

"Hi, Minnie." Christina crouched down and rubbed the dog under its chin. "How are you doing?"

"She has a bad case of the runs," her owner said.

Christina stood up and held the door open.

"That doesn't sound too comfortable." The tech glanced over at Chains. "Nice seeing you again."

He lifted his chin and began to walk toward a vacant chair.

"So maybe we can go out for a coffee to catch up," Sheila said.

Chains looked over at her. "My schedule's pretty full." The last thing he wanted to do was encourage her. She'd been a major pain in the ass, and he didn't want to invite her into his life.

"I'm sure you have a free hour—everyone does." She licked her lips and held his gaze.

"Chains," a soft voice said.

He glanced over at the door and saw Autumn: hair pulled up in a messy bun with tendrils hanging down around her slender neck, high-heeled ankle boots that made him think lecherous thoughts, and a sheen of gold shimmer over her full lips. He sucked in a breath. *Damn.*

"I'd like to speak with you before I release Thor." She held the door wide open.

"Sure." Chains shoved his hand into his front jeans pocket and swaggered over. As he walked past her, the scent of her perfume enticed him: vanilla with hints of cinnamon and musk. It was sweet and spicy and sexy as hell, and it was the first time he'd smelled it on her. Something told him that she wore it for him, and if she was trying to beguile him, it was working.

He stood aside then followed her down the hallway, admiring the way her hips swayed and her ass wiggled; once again, nasty thoughts filled his mind.

"Here we are." Autumn looked over her shoulder at him and color rushed to her cheeks. She quickly turned away and scurried to her desk.

Chains sank down on a black leather chair and locked his gaze on hers. For a second everything in the room stood still, then she shifted her eyes away and pushed papers around on her desk. He settled back in the chair, smug that he seemed to have an effect on her. The doc was acting damn cute, pretending that he didn't make her nervous as hell.

"So," Autumn said while glancing at the computer screen. "Thor's doing great. He's a little weak from everything he'd gone through, but he should be back to normal in a few days."

"That's good."

"For the next few days, feed him a bland diet. Some suggestions are plain, unseasoned boiled chicken or turkey breast, the skin off and shredded, with some rice. You can substitute a yam for the rice." Her gaze was still fixed on the screen.

"Got it."

"None of his usual treats or dog food. After a few days, you can gradually introduce his dry and wet food and see how he tolerates it."

"Okay. Are you gonna keep talking to that damn screen, or are you gonna look at me?" His question made her visibly stiffen, then she swiveled around slowly.

"I was making sure I didn't miss anything important to tell you."

"Yeah ... right." A smirk tugged at his lips.

"If Thor's not feeling well, or if you notice anything unusual, call me." She stared at him as if to show him that she could do it without any qualms, but her tight facial muscles and that adorable pink sheen coloring her cheeks gave her away.

"Sure. So, do you want to get a slice of chocolate cream pie at Leroy's after work?"

Her eyes sparkled for a split second, then she looked back at the computer. "I'm sorry but I'm not able to." Her shoulders sagged a bit.

"I'm engaged."

Surprised, Chains glanced at her hand. "I don't see a ring."

"I don't wear any jewelry at work"—Autumn looked over at him—"but I'm flattered."

"Don't be. I was just asking because you saved Thor's life. I used to grab a cup of coffee with Thor's old vet all the time." Chains jumped up. "I gotta get going."

Autumn stood up. "Of course."

"Just tell me where he is—you don't have to tag along."

Her face fell. "I'm sorry that I upset you."

"You didn't do shit. I know you got a full house, so there's no need to take up any more time with me. Christina can help me out with Thor. Is she engaged?"

Autumn's mouth opened slightly as she shook her head.

"Good to know."

The vet picked up the phone and pushed a button. "Have Amanda go to Recovery. Thor's owner is ready to take his dog home." A pause. "Thanks." She placed the phone back on the cradle. "Christina is assisting Dr. Jenkins."

"Whatever. I know where the room is," he said as he walked out of the office. While Chains ambled to the recovery room, he was madder than hell at himself for succumbing to such juvenile and cheap antics back in Autumn's office. He grimaced when he replayed the comment he said about Christina. What the fuck had possessed him to act like such a pussy? Playing games and trying to make a chick jealous wasn't his style. And why in the hell was he so damn bothered by the fact that she was engaged. *I don't even know her. So she's got a sexy bod—Lila, Ruby, Alma, and Kelly have great asses and tits too. And she sure didn't act like she was engaged. I wonder what her fiancé would say about that. I didn't figure her for a cheating bitch, but most women are. She's just like Krystal, only classier. Fuck them all.*

By the time Chains arrived at Recovery, anger was pumping through his veins, but one look at Thor, whose tail was thumping against the floor, and the fury evaporated.

"Come here, buddy." He crouched down on his haunches and grinned. Thor ran over, barking excitedly, and Chains put his arms around the dog's neck and hugged him gently. "You ready to go home, buddy?" He ran his fingers through Thor's fur. Another excited bark had Chains standing up, and he noticed the tech had Thor's leash.

"He's certainly happy to be going home." The young woman extended her hand. "I'm Amanda. Christina told me about you ... and Thor."

He studied the cute blonde, who seemed to be about twenty-four or so. "I'm Chains. Can I have his leash?"

She giggled. "Oh, of course. I'm sorry."

Chains took it from her hands, then attached it to Thor's collar.

"If you need anything, you can call me." Amanda slipped her hand into the front pocket of her turquoise smock, pulled out a card, and handed it to him.

"I already have a couple of business cards."

"This is my direct number so you don't have to bother with the answering service during after-hours."

He took the card and the large smile plastered across her face told him she'd be an easy lay. Chains shoved it in the pocket of his cut.

"Let me walk out with you," she offered.

"I'm good." He threw her a stern look—the one that stopped citizens in their tracks—then left the room with Thor bounding in front of him.

Once Thor was settled in the car, Chains pulled out of the lot. The dog hung his head out the window, and Chains decided that it was time he found another clinic for Thor. He had no interest in seeing Autumn again. For a small slice of time, he'd lost his head and let a pretty woman get into his system, but not anymore. He never had to see her again. Afterall, she was nothing more than a mere blip on the timeline of his life.

Chains rolled down the rest of the windows in the SUV, letting the fresh, crisp air rush over him as he and Thor headed back home.

Chapter Seven

"I HOPE YOUR parents are coming to my Mom's brunch in a couple of weeks. She's starting to think they don't give a damn about the wedding," Bret said before popping an olive into his mouth.

"They are, and I'm the one who told my mom to not worry about coming to every shower. Denver's a good eight-hour drive to Alina, and my mom's afraid to fly," Autumn replied.

"It's just that my mom thinks your parents should be more involved."

"I actually wish that *we* were the ones involved. It seems like I'm doing a lot of the planning without you, and whatever I do, you or your mother veto it. What happened to the small wedding we wanted?"

"*You* wanted it, remember?"

"You told me you did too."

"I was just trying to keep the peace." Bret motioned the waiter over. "Another martini." He looked at Autumn. "Did you want another drink?"

"I'll have a glass of merlot this time," she said to the waiter. Autumn waited for him to leave, then shook her head. "I thought we were in this *together*. And what does 'keeping the peace' mean?"

Bret reached out and grasped her hand. "With my mother—not you. She's going nuts because I'm the first one of my siblings to get married."

Autumn sighed. *He has an answer for everything.* "I'm surprised Emily and Will haven't tied the knot yet."

"Me too. My parents are mad as hell at her for shacking up so long with him. I can't blame them. He should either marry her or move on. Emily wants to get married in the worst way." He laughed. "It feels sort of good one-upping the golden child."

"I can't relate to the dynamics you have with your siblings since I never had any."

"Count yourself lucky. Sometimes they can be too much."

The waiter placed the wineglass in front of her.

"Thank you," she said before taking a sip out of it. "I've met everyone in your family but your brother. Will he be coming to the brunch?" A knot of muscles at the side of Bret's jaw pulsed, and she knew she'd hit a nerve.

"Who knows or cares?"

She lifted one shoulder slightly. "I was just wondering. I know the two of you aren't that close, but you *are* brothers."

"Unfortunately." Bret took a big gulp of his drink.

"What's the cause of the bad blood between you two?" Since she and Bret had been together, he rarely spoke of his brother.

"Chet's a fucking loser. He's always thought he didn't have to follow the rules, and he gave our parents a real hard time, especially our dad, when he was in high school. The guy's bad news, and if I never see him again, I wouldn't give a damn." He drained the rest of his martini, then gestured the waiter to bring another.

"What does he do?"

"How the hell should I know? He's in that criminal gang—the Night Rebels." Bret glanced at his phone.

"The motorcycle club?"

"Yes. It figures he'd get mixed up with them. It's an embarrassment to our family." Bret tapped something into his phone. "Why the hell are we talking about that *him* anyway?"

"I was just wondering if he'd be at the brunch. There was this client at the clinic who had the most beautiful Siberian husky. He rode the coolest-looking motorcycle I'd ever seen." Autumn took another sip of wine.

"Anyone who rides a motorcycle is either a thug or doesn't give a damn about his life. There's no way I'd get on one of those death-traps."

Bret's phone beeped again.

"They can be freeing," she whispered under her breath. "The guy had an air of defiance … rebelliousness about him," she said wistfully.

"Who're you talking about?"

With a slight shake of her head, she answered, "No one."

"Oh." He glanced at his phone again. "I wonder what's taking so long for us to get our dinner."

"Why? Do you have somewhere to go?" Tension crept into her voice.

"It's because I'm fucking starved," he said a bit too loud.

Several diners around them looked over, then spoke in hushed voices.

"Keep your voice down. Maybe you shouldn't have any more to drink," Autumn said.

"Don't tell me what to do—you're not my damn mother. And besides … I'm fine." He craned his neck. "Where the hell's the waiter?"

The phone beeped *again*.

"Can you cut off the texting conversation you've got going there?" she asked, pointing to the cell. "I'd hoped for a dinner with just the two of us, not you, me, and your phone."

Bret scrunched up his face. "Aren't you the funny one. I've got some business going here."

"Can't it wait until after we're done eating?"

"No."

Before Autumn could answer, the waiter arrived with a large tray filled with food; he placed the rare T-bone in front of Bret and the medium-well filet mignon in front of her. Baked potatoes, sautéed mushrooms, and lightly steamed asparagus rounded out the meal. Bret ordered two more martinis, and Autumn's stomach twisted: her fiancé wasn't a jovial drunk. Whenever he was plastered, he became loud, obnoxious, belligerent, and rude—nothing she was looking forward to.

"I need to ask a favor of you," Bret said before cutting into the steak.

"What is it?" She popped a morsel into her mouth and chewed.

"I need to borrow some money from you. I hate asking, but I'm running a little short and I have some bills to pay. I've never asked you before."

Autumn set down her fork and knife, and caught his gaze. "How much do you need?"

Bret glanced down at his plate and cut into the meat. "Ten grand."

He said the amount so offhandedly that, at first, she didn't think she'd heard right. She watched him slather butter on a slice of bread and then her gaze went back to him.

"Did you say *ten thousand dollars*?"

He stuffed a big piece of bread in his mouth and nodded while chewing.

"You need that much to pay a few bills?" Autumn was confused because Bret had constantly bragged to her about how much he'd made at work and how many company bonuses he'd received. "It's not that much. You probably make that in a couple of weeks or less." He picked up his drink and gulped it down.

"I wish. I don't have ten thousand to loan you. I have a lot of expenses and even more now with the wedding and all."

Bret's fork stopped in mid-air. "I can't believe you're using the wedding as a reason not to help me out." He fixed her with a steely look.

"I'm not using anything as an excuse. I don't have that kind of cash to give you." All of a sudden she'd lost her appetite. "What do you *really* need the money for?"

"A business venture I want to get off the ground. You can be part of it if you want. I just need some capital to invest."

"What kind of business?"

"Why all the fucking questions? I thought you wanted to support me." Anger oozed from him.

"Calm down—I'm just asking. It's a legitimate question."

The phone beeped several times. Now when Bret looked at it, worry etched his face.

"So do you want to help or not?"

"I can loan you three thousand," Autumn answered.

"That's it?" He quirked his lips.

"That's all I have. I'm sorry," she said.

"Then I guess it'll have to do. See if you can get another grand or so, okay? It's for our future—remember that. I'll need it by tomorrow though, can you swing it?"

"Yeah, I'll take it from one of my bank accounts."

"Cool, but try and scrounge up another thousand." He winked. "Love you."

For the next hour, Bret had gotten so drunk and loud that by the time they'd finished dinner and exited the restaurant, he was in one of the foulest liquor-induced moods she'd ever seen. When she suggested they call a Lyft, he disagreed with her very loudly. The valet stood sentry as if waiting to see who would win the argument.

In the end, Autumn wound up taking a Lyft by herself, while Bret stubbornly insisted he could drive and refused to go with her. By the time she arrived home, her stomach was in knots, and she worried endlessly about Bret making it home safely. She repeatedly called his number until he finally picked up and told her to "leave him the fuck alone." Autumn had, at least, managed to get him to tell her he was at his apartment, which eased her mind.

"How did such a perfect night end so shitty?" she asked aloud.

Cinder curled up against Autumn on the couch after she had changed her clothes, washed her face, and poured herself a glass of red wine. As she sipped it, Chains flitted through her mind as he'd been doing since she'd first met him. When Autumn had told him she was engaged, she could've sworn she saw an angry, betrayed look flash in his eyes. And then he asked if Christina was engaged. That question had played through her head for the rest of the day.

To Autumn's surprise, she felt an unexpected twinge of jealousy as she wondered whether Chains had asked Christina out on a date. The reaction surprised and frightened her. It wasn't any of her business if he made plans with the tech, and Autumn certainly shouldn't be feeling jealous, especially since she was engaged and planning a wedding.

"Why am I feeling so restless?" she asked her cat, who just stared and then nuzzled against her. After the night she'd had with Bret, she wondered if she even wanted to get married. "Maybe we need to get away like he said. He wants us to go to Aspen," she said to Cinder.

The phone buzzed and Autumn picked it up.

"Hi, Mark. What's up?" she asked the veterinarian.

"Not much. I was just wondering if you wanted me to do follow-up calls for your patients."

Hesitating, she reined in her professionalism. "No, I'll do it, but thanks for offering. You must be beat after last night's emergency surgeries."

"I am. I'm spending tomorrow on the golf course."

"Good for you—you deserve a break."

"So do you."

"I'll be taking a long one for my honeymoon," she replied.

"That's not for a while. Just take a day or two off—we all need it."

"I know. Have fun tomorrow."

Autumn made all the calls except for one: Chains. Chiding herself for acting like a schoolgirl instead of a professional, she tapped in his number quickly.

"Yeah?" His voice rumbled with a low, sexy timbre.

"Hello, Chains. This is Dr. Stanford and I'm calling to see—"

"We're back to Dr. Stanford?"

Autumn poured more wine into her glass and took a quick sip. Ignoring his question, she said, "I'm calling to see how Thor's doing."

"He's doing great."

"Did he eat well?"

"Yeah. One of the club girls made him chicken and rice like you said. He seemed to love it."

Club girls? "So he tolerated it?" *Don't ask any personal questions. This is a business call.*

"Yeah. Whatcha got going on?"

"I just got home from dinner. I'm sorry I'm calling so late."

"It's not even ten. Damn, you need to really get out." A small pause. "Anyway, it's all cool. I'll let you get back to your *fiancé*." Chains sounded casual and jovial, and it bugged the hell out of her.

"He's not with me. I mean we don't live together." *Why the hell did I say that?*

"Okay. Are you trying to tell me something?"

"I don't know why I told you that." She took a gulp of wine.

"I do … and so do you, but we'll play like we don't." His low chuckle rattled her nerves and sent shivers up her spine.

"I have to go. I'm glad Thor's doing well. Call the clinic if things change. Bye." Without waiting for his response, Autumn clicked off. *What the hell's wrong with me? Ugh!*

Picking up the phone, she stared at the screen then called Sadie.

"It's about time you returned my call," her best friend said.

"I'm sorry," Autumn groaned. "We've been swamped at the clinic for the past two days. How're you doing? How's it going with Mitch?"

"Doing great, and Mitch and I are still dating, so that's a good thing. What's going on with you?"

"Bret got stinking drunk at dinner tonight. We ate at Flanigan's, and he insisted on driving home."

"Tell me you didn't go with him."

"I didn't. I called a Lyft but he refused to go with me. I was scared the whole time until he finally got home. I don't understand him sometimes."

"Drinking too much is one thing—we've all done that more times than we'd like to confess, but driving home drunk is stupid and selfish. What about the innocent people on the road?"

"I know … I agree with you, but Bret can be so fucking stubborn."

The conversation turned to planning a shopping weekend in Denver at the end of the month. While they talked, Autumn wrestled with telling Sadie about Chains, but in the end, she decided not to say anything. What was there to say? That she was attracted to a hot-looking guy? That was really the extent of it, wasn't it? Anyway, Thor was back home and doing fine. When a patient returned home, her protocol was to call the day of to make sure all was going well, then to close out the case.

Well, Autumn had made the obligatory call and it was time to move on. She walked into the kitchen, washed the wineglass, then ascended the stairs.

She probably wouldn't see Chains or his dog again for at least six months when Thor was due for his shots, and by then she'd be blissfully married to Bret. Happy that the rugged biker would be nothing but a memory, Autumn slipped on a nightgown and slid under the sheets. In a matter of minutes, she was out like a light.

Chapter Eight

Two weeks later

ON HIS WAY to town, Chains drove by the clinic and looked over at the parking lot, his jaw clenching when he saw Autumn's car in the space at the far end of the building. That seemed to be her usual spot since her vehicle had been parked there each time Chains had passed by, which had been more times than he'd ever admit.

A picture of Autumn petting Thor while warmly smiling at Chains had taken up residence in his mind, and he couldn't shake the image no matter how hard he'd tried. No amount of tequila or weed could rub it out. And various images of Autumn in her lab coat—on and off—factored into some pretty graphic fantasies while he was in the shower or lying in bed in the late hours of the night.

If any of the brothers got a whiff of his little detours each time Chains rode into town, they'd *never* let him forget that he was acting like a fucking grade-A pansy-ass. In anger, he revved the engine at the stoplight, then sped off the minute the light turned green. A few cars honked at him, so he stretched his hand out the window, lifted it in the air, and prominently displayed his middle finger.

Ever since the night Autumn called him when Thor had come home from the clinic, Chains had debated about giving her a jingle. The fact that she'd stated she didn't live with her fiancé told Chains that she wanted to have some fun on the side before donning the ball and chain. Autumn was looking to cheat and would make a shitty partner like his ex-wife had, but if the woman wanted to spread her legs and have some fun, he was down for it. There was no way he'd get emotionally involved with her, but Chains couldn't deny the attraction they had for each other. But in the end, he hadn't called her. His pride wouldn't let him because whether it was for a hookup or something more, Chains liked being the only man in a chick's life while they saw each other. When he picked a club girl to be his for however long, she never fucked any of the other members during that time. That was just the way Chains was wired, and that's why his ex-wife and best friend's betrayal hurt him deeply. After nearly seven years, he'd finally gotten over it, but not to the extent that he'd get seriously involved with another citizen.

Chains pulled over to the curb in front of his parents' house and turned off the ignition, then sauntered up the sidewalk to the front porch. He hesitated before he rang the bell and hoped his dad was at work since their encounters were never pleasant. It seemed like he always rubbed the old man the wrong way. As long as Chains could remember, his dad had never said anything positive to him. When he was a kid, the harsh words were like knives, cutting him to the core, and when Chains had been in high school, he'd dealt with it by cutting school, smoking weed, shoplifting, and spending more time than not in juvenile detention. He'd done everything he could to piss off the old man just so he could feel like shit, then maybe he'd understand how Chains felt. But his dad only grew angrier with him and increased the verbal and emotional abuse until Chains took off the day after graduation.

The door flew open, and the memories from the past scattered to the deep recesses of his mind.

"Why didn't you ring the bell? I thought I heard a motorcycle," his mother said as she unlocked the screen door.

"Hey, Mom." He walked inside, and the sweet aroma of freshly baked cake filled the living room, transporting him back to the kitchen of his childhood, where he'd sit at the table and watch his mother take one of her delicious vanilla cakes out of the oven.

"Aren't you even going to give your mother a hug?" She held out her arms.

Chains gave her a squeeze, then pulled away quickly. "How've you been?"

"Very busy. I've been baking cakes for three days straight."

A small smile ghosted his lips. "It smells great in here."

She held up four fingers. "That's how many quinceañeras I have to bake for. What was I thinking?" Regina shook her head.

"You love it." The smile widened. "And you're the best baker in Alina. For years, I've said that you should have your own bakery."

"I'm busy enough with the orders I get. The website you made for me has brought in so many customers—even some from Durango."

"Then you need to hire a few people and start selling around the country."

His mother laughed. "Your dad would throw a fit. He's already on my back for taking in too many orders."

"I bet he is." Bitterness laced his voice.

Regina's eyes found his. "You judge your father too harshly."

"He's the one who taught me how to do that."

"I'm just saying that you've never given him a chance—he's really a very nice and loving man."

A dry laugh. "Are we talking about the same person?"

She looked away. "Come into the kitchen and I'll give you a piece of cake. I have a fresh pot of coffee brewing. Emily gave me a coffeemaker for Mother's Day—it was when we all went out for lunch at Poppies." His mom rummaged through one of the cupboards. "You didn't show up," she said in a low voice.

"I called and told you I couldn't come," Chains said as he pulled out one of the kitchen chairs and sat down.

"Anyway, she'd be so mad if she knew I've only used it two times. I guess I should give it a chance, but I still like the sound of the coffee pot when it percolates."

"Then use what you like. Just 'cause Emily got you something doesn't mean you have to love it or use it."

"True, but I don't want to hurt her feelings."

"It's just a coffeemaker, Mom. I'm pretty sure Emily could deal with it." He picked up the fork, cut off a big bite, and shoved it into his mouth. Flavor exploded, and he chewed slowly, savoring the sweet and citrus tastes on his tongue. "This is so fuckin' good," he said.

"Chet! You really need to watch your language, especially at the brunch this Sunday. Try not to use vulgar language."

"That's right—the brunch is this Sunday," he said before taking a sip of hot coffee.

Regina stood in front of him, hands on her hips, eyes narrowed and deadly. "Don't you dare tell me that you're not coming. I've been reminding you about it practically every damn day."

"Watch your language, Mom." Chains deadpanned. "Don't break a blood vessel—I'm coming. I just thought it was next Sunday."

A grin slowly spread across her face. "You've always liked to tease your mother. Bret will be happy you're coming."

"I doubt that, but I know you are." He stood up from the table and brought his empty dish and coffee mug over to the sink. "Do you need me to bring anything?" he asked as he rinsed off the dishes before putting them in the dishwasher.

"What would you do if I told you to bring some quiches?" Her dark eyes sparkled.

Wiping his hands on a paper towel, he shrugged. "I'd swing by the store and buy them. I don't think you've caught on that people don't have to cook everything from scratch anymore."

"Oh you," she said, smacking him lightly on his arm.

After wadding up the paper towel, he threw it in the trash. "I've gotta get going. Are the boxes in the garage?"

Regina glanced at the clock over the stove. "I didn't realize it was so late. I have to finish decorating one of the cakes that need to be delivered later on."

"Do you want some help packing up the car?"

She shook her head. "Thanks, but your dad will be home before I leave and he can do it."

"Okay." Chains started walking toward the door leading to the garage.

"The box you want with your old textbooks and personal papers is on the right. It's marked *Chet*. Don't take any of the other boxes. I have to go through them someday, and I don't want you accidentally walking away with them."

"No problem. I'll close the garage door when I'm done. Did you change the code?"

"No, it's the same. Did you want to bring some cake back with you for your friends?"

"No, thanks." He turned the doorknob.

"I'll see you on Sunday, and try and be good with Bret and your father … and stay longer than fifteen minutes, okay?" Creases lined her forehead.

"I got it. Bye, Mom." He stepped into the garage, flipped on the light, then closed the door behind him.

When Chains spotted the box with his old name on it, he walked over and picked it up. Several other boxes surrounded it, and he kicked the lid off one of them and saw some of his old high school yearbooks. *Mom won't even miss these.* Deciding that he'd take a couple more boxes with him than he'd intended, Chains stacked two of them in his arms and headed over to the SUV.

When he arrived at the clubhouse, Muerto, Eagle, and Aztec were hanging out by the big oak tree drinking beer. Chains honked the horn at them as he pulled into a space.

"I need help carrying in some boxes," he said while opening up the trunk.

"Did you buy a bunch of shit in town?" Muerto asked as he walked over.

"Nah. I picked up some stuff at my parents' house. I'm thinking of taking that job offer to do an online web design class, so I wanted to look at some of my old textbooks and class notes."

"Doesn't that stuff become obsolete, like, in a week?" Aztec asked as he pulled out a box from the trunk.

"Not that fast, but yeah, the technology changes real fast, but the principles are the same," Chains replied.

"I hated school. Why the fuck do you wanna teach?" Eagle asked as he walked toward the front entrance carrying a box. "You're already too busy. When was the last time, bro, you were at the strip club? A few nights ago you didn't join us at Lust 'cause you had too much shit to do."

"My work goes in cycles—I'm in a busy one now." Chains pulled open the door and entered the main room.

"You're even too busy to fuck, if the club girls are telling the truth," Aztec said.

Chains looked over his shoulder. "How is my fucking schedule any of your damn business?"

Muerto laughed. "Nothing's private around here, you know that, bro, especially when you live on the premises."

"I don't give a shit who or when you fuck, I was just making a point about how busy you are," Aztec said.

Chains rolled his eyes and headed up the stairs.

"Does Steel know about you wanting to teach? That might cut in on club business. What if we gotta do something important and you've got a class going that night?" Eagle chuckled as he rambled on, "Do you tell your students that you have to reschedule 'cause you gotta give some fucker a beatdown?"

"Maybe you can fuck one of your sexy students." Aztec walked into Chains's room and put the box down on the floor near the dresser.

"The class is *online*, dude," Chains said. He regretted bringing up the teaching job in the first place. His friends were highly buzzed, and this quasi-sitcom routine could go on for hours.

"Dudes hook up with chicks all the time on the internet," Aztec replied.

"That's on dating apps, not a school," Eagle said as he leaned against the wall.

"I think you can pick up a chick in a school app." Aztec took out a joint and lit it.

Muerto guffawed. "What the fuck are you talking about?"

After moving and stacking the boxes in the corner of the room, Chains twisted his upper body from side to side, trying to work out a few kinks in his back.

"Thanks for helping out," he said, hoping to put the nonsensical conversation to rest.

Aztec looked at him through a veil of thick smoke. "So are you fucking your student or not?"

"I haven't even decided if I'm gonna take the job, but if I do, I'll let you know if I hook up with one of my online students." Chains walked over to the door.

"People have cybersex all the time. I heard it on one of those talk shows the club girls watch. I bet you can do that with your student. Those college chicks will do anything for a good grade." Aztec blew out a stream of smoke.

"Maybe I should teach," Eagle said.

"Fuck, Raven's pissed that I forgot to pick up her canvases when I was in town," Muerto said as he looked down at his phone.

"Sounds like something you need to take care of," Chains said, then pointed at Eagle and Aztec. "You two can finish your conversation downstairs. I have a lot of work to do right now."

"Do you think I'd be a good teacher?" Eagle asked as he walked out of the room.

"Yeah—a great one," Chains replied before closing and locking the door.

He glanced at the boxes and decided to go through them the following week. He had to complete a job for one of his clients, and begin another one for a new customer.

Thor padded over to him and nudged his wet nose against Chains's hand. He was back to normal, and Chains went over to the closet and took down a box of Milk-Bone treats. The dog barked and his bright blue eyes watched his owner intently.

"Here you go, buddy," Chains said as he opened his hand. Thor snatched the snack from the palm of his hand. "I'm gonna work for a while, then we'll go out." Thor barked again then padded behind Chains.

The biker settled into the chair and opened his laptop as Thor lay on the floor next to him. For a long moment, he stared at the computer screen as images of Autumn teemed in his mind. It wasn't rational or even logical as to why Chains was thinking of her at that moment, but it seemed that it happened whenever he was alone and it was quiet. He knew he should be working on the integration of the shopping cart tool on one of his client's website, but Autumn was on his mind, so he typed her name into the search bar instead. He saw pictures of her at the Highlands Animal Care Center, and those captivating eyes seemed to burn right into him. *Why can't I get you out of my mind? What the fuck's going on with you, woman?*

Thor's soft yelps in his sleep dragged Chains out of his thoughts. He rubbed the back of his neck, closed the window containing the photographs of Autumn, and clicked opened his client's folder.

Chapter Nine

IT WAS A beautiful fall morning. The trees lining Gaylord Street glinted with gold and red. Shafts of sunlight shifted and danced through branches and leaves. The air was crisp and carried a sweet aroma from the apple trees Chains passed as he rode to his parents' house. He'd debated about going to the brunch when he'd woken up and saw what a perfect day it was for a long ride around the countryside. Picturing the look of disappointment on his mother's face was the *only* reason he was showing up. Chains couldn't give a rat's ass about his brother or his upcoming wedding. The only thing that surprised him was that Bret had found a woman stupid enough to put up with his phoniness and bullshit.

Both sides of the street in front of his parents' house were filled with cars. He gritted his teeth and circled around the block a few times as he debated about going inside, but guilt niggled at the back of his mind, so he parked his bike several houses up from his parents'. Chains figured he'd give thirty minutes of his time, then cut out and hit the backroads. For the most part, he hated engaging in pointless small talk and answering inane questions about his life.

Chains's engineer boots thumped on the pavement, his muscular build casting a long, reed-like shadow. He slipped his hand into the inner pocket of his jacket and pulled out a joint. Stopping for a moment, Chains dipped his head and cupped his hand around the lighter as he lit the spliff. He inhaled deeply, held his breath for a few seconds, and then blew out a column of thick smoke.

He watched as a tall blonde with long legs in a short skirt rushed up the porch steps. The door opened, and his mother flashed a big smile, then stepped aside as the woman walked into the house. Chains finished the joint through a myriad of successive drags before tossing the roach to the ground; he stepped on it and let out a final stream of smoke. Jamming his hands into his pockets, he sauntered across the lawn.

The door opened just as Chains reached the porch. When he saw his father, he stepped back, his jaw tightening. Meeting his dad's eyes, he lifted his chin.

"Your mother didn't think you were going to come," his father spoke in a scratchy smoker's mumble.

"I told her I would," Chains replied.

"You've said a lot of things you didn't do." He reached into his dress shirt pocket and pulled out a pack of Winston. He tapped one out and lit it. "You should've dressed better—you look like a hoodlum."

"I am a hoodlum." Chains took the steps two at a time, brushed by his father, and entered the foyer.

The tantalizing aroma of bacon and cinnamon curled around him as he went down the hall and into the kitchen, avoiding the crowd in the living room. His mother stood by the stove, an apron dotted with pumpkins and topsy-turvy leaves wrapped tightly around her waist; she pulled out two quiches from the oven.

"Hey, Mom," he said.

Regina looked up and a large smile graced her face. "You made it." She put the quiches down on the counter and took off her oven mitts.

"I said I'd be here. How're you holding up?"

She blew a stray wisp of hair away from her face. "Okay. Can you bring the platter of potatoes and the basket of croissants into the dining room? Set them on the buffet table."

"Sure." He shrugged off his jacket and hung it gingerly on the back of a chair in the corner of the kitchen, then picked up the items.

People mingled in the dining and living rooms, and Chains set the two dishes on the table before he snagged a slice of bacon from a serving dish and gobbled it down.

"Chet," his sister Amelia said. "I'm so glad you came."

"I told Mom I'd be here." One corner of his mouth hitched up. "When did you get in?"

"Yesterday. I'll be here for a few days, then it's back to Denver. Let's get together and grab some lunch." Her bluish-gray eyes twinkled.

"I'll check my schedule."

"It's been ages since I've seen you. You missed Mother's Day and the Fourth of July"—she tapped a finger against her chin—"and the family barbecue … and Dad's birthday."

"Sounds about right," he replied.

"Emily said she hasn't seen you since last Christmas, and she *lives* here." Amelia reached over the table and picked up a cherry tomato, then popped it into her mouth.

"I've been busy." Chains glanced at the time on his phone. *I've only got twenty more minutes to go, then I'm fuckin' outta here.* He could feel the crisp air rushing around him already.

"Are you dating anyone?" she asked.

"Nope."

"You should think about settling down." Amelia snatched another tomato.

"So should you."

A large clap on his back had Chains turning around.

Bret shook his head. "I lost the fucking bet. Amelia and Emily said you'd come, but I said you'd do your usual no-show routine. Damn, dude—I lost fifty bucks."

Chains moved away from his brother. "I came for Mom."

"I know that—you'd never come for me, but then I wouldn't go for you either." Bret took a sip from the flute in his hand.

"You don't have to worry about that—I don't go in for this pansy-ass shit. Where's the booze?"

"I'll get something for you," Amelia said. "Do you want a glass of champagne?"

"Tequila—two shots."

"Okay." She squeezed his hand then scurried away.

"How's your web development business going?" Bret asked as he scooped up a handful of cashews.

"Good." Chains crossed his arms over his chest.

"It looks like you got some new tattoos. I got one on my upper arm. It's fucking awesome. Where'd you get yours done?"

"At the club's ink shop. One of the brothers did them for me."

"What's the name of the place?" Bret took another gulp of his drink.

"Get Inked."

"That's your club's business? I didn't think you guys owned anything but strip bars." He gave him a wry smile.

Before Chains could reply, Amelia walked in, drink in hand.

"Here you go," she said, handing him the tumbler.

"Thanks." Chains threw the tequila back.

"When are you gonna get married again?" Bret asked.

"Never."

"You'd think differently if you had a pretty and classy woman like mine." Bret raised his hand and gestured to someone behind Chains. "I want you to meet her."

"Is the drink good?" Amelia asked.

Chains jerked his head back. "It's tequila—of course it's good." When his sister's face fell, he shook his head. "I'm just messin' with you. Yeah, it's real good, and I could use another one."

"Okay." She snatched his glass from him and ambled away.

"Here's my sweetie," Bret said.

Chains turned around and his insides went cold as he locked gazes with Autumn. A gasp flew past her lips, and she quickly pressed a hand to her mouth.

"This"—she faltered, her eyes cutting to Bret—"is your brother, Chet?"

Chains leaned in slowly. "Yeah," he said in a low voice. He was so close that he could smell the fresh, clean scent of her hair and the seductive fragrance of her perfume.

Autumn's skin flushed pink and then red, and she stumbled backward, nearly losing her balance, but his strong arm reached out and supported her. Her gaze sliced to his, and it looked like she was going to pass out.

"You don't look so good. Are you okay?" Bret asked.

A few heartbeats passed before she spoke. "All of a sudden it feels so stuffy. I just need to get some fresh air." She looked away from Chains.

When Autumn ran her fingers up and down Bret's arm, sparks of anger ignited inside Chains, but he feigned indifference.

Bret wrapped an arm around her visibly trembling frame. "This pretty woman is Autumn." He neared his face toward hers, but Autumn turned hers away, and his lips landed on her jaw.

"Here's your tequila," Amelia said. Her eyes darted between the three of them as if sensing the mounting tension.

"Thanks, again." Chains drained the glass and put it on the buffet table. "I gotta go."

"But you just got here," Amelia said.

"Typical—just do the minimum. That's the story of your life." Irritation punctuated his voice.

In one swift move, he grabbed hold of Bret by his shirt and pulled him to within inches of Chains's face.

"Don't *ever* fuckin' disrespect me!" He pushed Bret away.

"What's going on here? His father's voice boomed. "Chet?"

Chains turned around and marched into the kitchen. Rage burned inside him. From the corner of his eye, he saw his dad approaching.

"I want to talk to you," he said sternly.

"What's going on, Stanley?" Anxiety laced his mother's voice.

Chains looked at his mom. "I gotta go. See you."

"Already? What's happened?" Regina rushed over to him.

"Don't coddle the fucker," Stanley said.

"Nothing's happened. I didn't plan on staying very long."

"You shouldn't have even come," his dad growled.

"Stanley!"

Chains stalked out of the kitchen. *I can't fuckin' believe she's that asshole's woman.* As he made his way down the sidewalk the *click-clack* of heels reverberated through his skull.

"Chains! Wait up," Autumn said breathlessly.

He picked up the pace, putting more distance between them.

"Please," she said.

He reached his bike and jumped on, but she'd caught up to him and gripped the handlebars.

"I want to talk to you."

Chains cocked his head to the side as he slowly took out a pair of sunglasses. "About what?"

"I had no idea you were Bret's brother."

"Why does that matter?"

Autumn let go of the bike and stepped back, her mouth parted as if startled by his response.

He slipped his shades on. "Welcome to the family." With the flip of a switch, the bike roared to life.

"You act like you're mad at me, and I don't know why," she said.

"I'm not mad."

Chains revved the motor and Autumn jumped back. Without another word, he pulled away from the curb and sped off.

Houses, trees, and storefronts blurred past him as he rode like the wind, all thoughts and feelings disappeared into nothingness. The cool air whipped around Chains, the smell of sage and damp earth filled his nostrils as the rumble of the engine and the vibration of the bike underneath connected him to the landscape, to the universe, and took him the hell out of his head.

After the three-hour solo ride, Chains walked into the clubhouse and held up two fingers to the prospect behind the bar.

"Where's Thor?" he asked.

Aztec glanced over at the couches where several of the club girls sat watching the big screen television.

"I think Ruby took him out for a walk. He kept looking out at the lot like he was waiting for you to get home."

"I went for a ride." Chains walked over to the bar.

"Didn't you have something to do with your parents?" Aztec said as he followed him.

Chains salted his hand then threw back the double shot of tequila. "I only stopped by." He sucked on the lime wedge, then tossed it aside. "It was too nice of a day to pass up a ride."

"Damn straight. Crow and me rode earlier. Where'd you go?"

"San Juan Mountains—Tecolote Pass." He looked over at the club women.

"You must've gone for a long ride. I fuckin' love that pass." Aztec picked up the beer bottle Vegas put in front of him.

"It was awesome." Chains pushed away from the counter. "I'm gonna see if the girls know where Ruby is."

He ambled over, and as he approached the women, he saw Lila painting her nails and Kelly swiping polish on her toes.

"Hey," he said.

Lila looked up and smiled. "Hey, cutie." She shook her right hand while blowing the nails of her left one.

"Aztec told me Ruby took Thor for a walk. How long have they been gone?" Ever since Thor had that episode with the poisonous berries, Chains had become super protective of him. He'd told the women not to take Thor into the woods, but sometimes they forgot.

"About twenty minutes," Fina said while staring at the TV.

"Where'd she take Thor?"

Fina shrugged.

"I think she took him on the road next to the club," Kelly said, looking up.

"Thanks," he said before leaving the clubhouse. Chains had told Ruby many times not to take walks outside of the MC's property unless one of the members was with her. The area around the club was desolate.

He started the SUV's engine, drove out of the lot, then turned left on the old highway. About a quarter of the way down, the road forked, and Chains turned right onto an unpaved street. He and some of the other members had found Ruby walking in that particular area in the past, so he thought it was the best place to begin the search.

Groves of scrub pines interspersed with sagebrush, cactus, and the occasional adobe bungalow. The SUV made a sharp left, kicking up dust as it bounced down a narrow road. Chains passed by a cement block wall with a broken bottle atop it, surrounding a stucco house that had a single strand of Christmas lights around it.

Slowing down to avoid a large dip in the road, he heard Thor barking. From the pitch and steady duration, Chains knew something wasn't right. He leaned over and took out a Glock from the glove box, then pushed his foot down on the accelerator and sped in the direction of Thor's barks.

As Chains came up on a path littered with stones, he saw a big four-wheel drive pickup parked to the side.

"Leave me alone!" A thread of fear wove through Ruby's voice.

Anger rippled through Chains as he pulled the car over and jumped out. The muscles at the back of his jaw pulsed as he walked with purpose toward the loud voices.

"Shut that fucking dog up!" a man yelled.

"I bet you like that, bitch," another man growled.

As he approached from behind, Chains saw a tall, skinny man wielding a baseball bat and a muscular man pinning Ruby to the ground. His pants were part down and he straddled her while punching her in the face. Thor's teeth shone in the afternoon sun as he snarled and barked at the man carrying the bat.

Chains quickly closed the distance, and without a word, he kicked the asshole in the back with his steel-toed boot, then dragged him off the club girl and stomped on the jerk's flaccid dick.

"Patton, get this fucker off me," he yelled.

The skinny guy stopped in his tracks, then turned around. His face blanched as he rushed over. Chains held up the gun and shot the bat, and the douchebag yelled out and dropped it. Thor rushed at the man and clamped down on the fucker's leg with his teeth, trying to pull him down.

"Get him off me," Patton yelled as he stumbled to the ground.

Chains watched as the asshole punched Thor and tried to tear him off his body, but Chains knew the pathetic jerk didn't stand a chance against the dog.

Ruby scrambled to her feet, then ran over to her attacker and kicked him hard in the shin. "That's for being a fuckin' asshole!"

"My car's parked by the road. Get inside and lock the doors. I'll be there in a minute," Chains said.

"Call your damn dog off!" Skinny ass yelled.

Chains glanced over and saw Thor biting the man all over.

"Looked to me like you were gonna use that bat on him," Chains said calmly as he raised his boot and slammed it back down on the muscular jerk on the ground.

"I wasn't. Fuck, he's gonna kill me."

Chains looked away and gave another blow to the jerk's dick. "You like hurting women, asshole? You're not so tough now, are you?" He added a few more blows.

The man closed his eyes and moaned.

"Shit! Help me! The dog's killing me!"

Chains whistled loudly, and Thor jumped away from the crying man and rushed over to his owner. He licked Chains's hand and sat next to him, his bright eyes fixed on the man he'd just been attacking.

"You did real good, buddy," Chains said as he patted the top of the husky's head.

Chains landed another hard blow—this time to the rapist's stomach, and glanced over at the skinny jerk who was curled up in a ball sniveling.

"Time to get going, buddy." Chains snapped his fingers and Thor barked, his tail wagging a mile a minute. Chains chuckled, then headed to the SUV.

"I know what you're going to say," Ruby said as he slid into the driver's seat. "I'm sorry, but in my defense, I was so paranoid about

Thor eating those berries again that I decided to go where I know he'd be okay." Her voice hitched and she blinked several times.

He gently pinched her cheek. "Don't sweat it. I appreciate you taking Thor out, but next time just keep your ass on the property, okay?" Chains looked over at her and winked.

Ruby scooted over and rested her head against his arm. "You're the best. I'm surprised no one has caught you. If I was the settling down type, I'd make a play for you, and I wouldn't let any of the other women around you." She craned her neck and kissed him softly on the jaw.

Chains kept his eyes straight ahead, hating that Autumn had slipped back into his mind. *Now that she's gonna be my sister-in-law, she's fuckin' off limits.*

"Thor was tryin' so hard to defend me." Ruby's voice broke through his thoughts.

"Oh yeah?"

"Yep. That fuckin' skinny ass had a bat so that's why Thor couldn't do what he wanted to."

"I'm just glad I came looking for you when I did."

"I'm not even sure where they came from. There's rarely anyone on that road except for Mr. Colombo, and sometimes, Mrs. Castillo. Mr. Colombo is a real sweet older man. He always gives me a plant when he sees me."

"So, he's the one responsible for all that shit in your room?" He chuckled.

"Don't you like them?"

"I'm just joking." He glanced at her and saw the red marks around her face start to darken. "When we get back, you gotta put some ice on your face. We got pain pills in case you need any. Did he hurt you anywhere else?"

"Not really. He was a little rough with my tits, but I bit him and that's when he started hitting on me. I swear I don't know where they came from."

"Motherfuckers like them go trolling for women. You were the perfect prey—alone in an isolated place. Don't do that shit again. If I hadn't come, who knows what they would've done to you."

Ruby visibly shuddered. "I know. It's just starting to sink in how bad it could've been. I've learned my lesson."

"Do you want a joint?"

Her blonde curls danced when she nodded.

He reached into the inner pocket of his cut and took one out. "Matches are in the glove box."

Ruby moved over and after lighting the joint, she blew the smoke out the window. For the rest of the drive back, they were both lost in their thoughts. Of course, Autumn had the starring role in Chains's musings, and as hard as he tried, she wouldn't go away. He figured in time, she'd be replaced by the next pretty and sexy woman who caught his eye, but deep down he knew it wouldn't be that easy. Autumn was the first woman who'd had an impact on him since his divorce. There was a connection between them that he couldn't explain, and he knew she felt it too. Why else would she run after him when he'd left his parents' house?

Autumn had acted like it was her fault that Bret was her fiancé. Most women who were happy and secure with their relationship wouldn't have given him the time of day, except for maybe a glance or two, and they certainly wouldn't have left their man to run after his brother like she did that day.

None of this shit matters 'cause she's Bret's woman. And even though there was no love lost between them, Chains wouldn't think of messing with his brother's woman. But a part of him was pissed and he didn't understand why. It wasn't like he and Autumn really knew each other or went out. She was Thor's vet and she saved his life, but then, that was what she was supposed to do, right?

Deep down inside him, the thought that his jerk brother didn't deserve her pricked at him, but he had no intentions of thinking further on that.

"Whatcha thinking about?" Ruby said, breaking the silence.

Chains turned onto the road leading to the clubhouse. "Not much."

"You're a pretty quiet guy sometimes. I think it's because you're so smart. I mean, you do all that computer stuff and make all that software. I dated a real smart guy once—he wanted to be a doctor, so he was in school studying all that. He was so serious and always thinking." She glanced over at him. "He wasn't as good-looking as you, but he liked being by himself and could be real quiet. I don't know—you kinda remind me of him—the smart and quiet stuff, I mean."

Chains nodded, then leaned out the window and punched in the code. The steel gates opened and he drove through.

"Let me know if you need some meds," he said before turning off the ignition.

"Will do. I just want a long hot shower."

"I'll let the guys know what's up so they don't bother you tonight." Chains opened the driver's back door and Thor jumped out of the car.

"Thanks. You're a real sweetie—just like the medical student." She giggled, then sashayed into the clubhouse.

Thor dashed toward the back porch while Chains sauntered after him. He filled one of Thor's bowls with water and watched the husky lap it up. The leaves on the oak tree rustled softly in the crisp breeze, and a few of them in warm colors of gold and red floated in the air until finally collapsing to the ground.

Chains leaned against the cool stucco wall of the porch and watched Thor run and bark while trying to catch the falling leaves. Then, in an instant, Autumn was in his head again. Images of her warm smile and the copper highlights in her auburn hair caused a deep yearning in his gut. For one fleeting moment, Chains regretted that he'd sworn off citizen women since his divorce.

The screen door slammed behind him, and Chains looked over and saw Aztec walking toward him.

"Ruby's singing your praises, dude," the biker said as he took out a joint.

"I wanted to kill those fuckers, but we don't need the damn badges up our ass," he replied.

"Did you hurt them at least?"

Chains nodded. "Thor and I made sure they were in a whole lot of pain. Motherfuckers."

"Yeah—assholes like that gotta be taught a lesson. I hope Ruby learned hers—this was bound to happen." Aztec blew a thin stream of smoke out of the corner of his mouth.

"I got a feeling she won't be walking alone anymore."

"We're headed to Brother's for some food—you wanna come?"

Chains pushed off from the wall with the heel of his boot. "Yeah—barbecue sounds real good." He whistled for Thor, who dashed over. "Let me feed him first."

"Sure." Aztec threw down the spent joint and snubbed it out with the toe of his boot. He held the screen door open for Chains and Thor, then went inside.

Chains had a ton of work to finish, but he didn't want to be alone with his thoughts that night. He'd rather lose himself in motorcycle talk, throw back a few shots of tequila, and check out the chicks at the restaurant. Maybe he'd join the brothers afterward at the club's strip bar. It'd been a while since Chains had been to Lust, and he'd heard that Army and Brutus had hired a few new dancers. It was about time he got back to his old ways and stopped acting like a fucking pansy. As a matter of fact, he was glad, no ... thrilled that Autumn and Bret were getting hitched—it kept him from losing his damn head.

"Ready to roll?" Eagle asked as he walked into the main room.

Chains pulled Thor close and nuzzled his face into the dog's soft fur. "Be good," he whispered. Rising to his feet, he cleared his throat. "Thor gets no more than two treats, and let him out in the back area only, not in the open space."

"Sure, baby," Alma said.

Kelly nodded, then threw a kiss at him.

The remaining members lifted their fists in the air, their eyes glued to a horror movie on the television screen.

Chains fished out his keys and walked slowly toward his motorcycle.

Chapter Ten

"SO, WHY THE hell did you go after Chet?" Bret shifted his eyes to Autumn, then back to the road.

"I didn't want the tension between the two of you. I thought if I could talk to—"

"Don't try and fix what's been broken for a long time. Chet's an arrogant asshole. He thinks that he's something because he rides a motorcycle and belongs to that outlaw gang."

"He's in the Night Rebels, right?"

"Yeah—loser all the way." Bret reached over and grasped her hand. "Don't waste any more time thinking about him. He rarely shows up at family functions, so you probably won't see him anymore. I doubt if he'll show up to the wedding. I told my mom that I don't want her pushing him—I'd rather he didn't come."

Autumn turned her head and stared out the window. She still couldn't believe that Chains and Bret were brothers. What were the odds that he was really Chet? *Astronomical for sure.*

"Did your parents have a good time?"

"What?" Autumn glanced at him sideways.

"You seem distracted, sweetie. I was asking if your mom and dad enjoyed today."

"Oh ... yeah, they had a nice time. They loved meeting all your extended family. I still can't believe my dad talked my mom into flying down here." Autumn chuckled. "He told me that she was clutching his wrist so hard during the flight, he thought she was going to break it."

"I don't understand people who are afraid to fly. Statistics show that more people die in car crashes than airplanes, yet I bet your mom doesn't think twice about driving."

Autumn shrugged and looked out the window again. "Phobias have no explanation, but they're real fears and we have to respect that."

"I'm just saying, it's kind of ridiculous, you know?"

A motorcycle's low rumble made her hold her breath as they approached a stoplight. She looked over, and for a brief second, disappointment pricked her gut when the rider wasn't Chains. Bret kept going on about phobias, his voice buzzing like a gnat in her ear. Autumn tuned him out and kept staring at the biker next to them. The man turned toward her, smiled, then revved the engine.

"Asshole!" Bret screamed.

The light turned green and the rider sped away.

"Does he think that makes him cool?" Bret said. "I hate jerks like that."

"Big boys with loud toys." Autumn chuckled. "I bet it's fun riding on something so powerful. I'm pretty sure it was a Harley-Davidson."

Bret looked over at her. "When did you become a motorcycle aficionado?"

"I've always admired them. Living in a small town, I notice them more."

"What's there to admire? My lowlife brother rides a Harley, and he went out of his way to make sure it's louder than hell. I should turn him in. There are laws now about noise levels on motorcycles. Those asshole bikers don't give a shit about anyone but themselves."

Autumn's stomach clenched and she exhaled a long breath. "I know your brother. He brought his dog, Thor, into the clinic and I treated him."

"Why didn't you tell me?"

"I didn't know you two were related. He didn't give a last name and simply said his first name was Chains."

"Figures—what a moron."

"I thought he was a nice man, and the way he loves Thor is amazing."

His lips flattened into a grim line. "I knew something was off when you two met. Do you want to tell me what's going on?"

Her composure faltered. "Nothing," she mumbled.

"Why didn't you say something when you saw him at the house? And what was the *real* reason you chased after him?" Bret fixed her with a steely gaze.

"When you introduced him, I was just too shocked to think, and I already told you I ran after him to try and make peace between the two of you. You have to admit that it was pretty tense, I mean, it looked like Chains was going to punch you."

"His fucking name is *Chet*," he grumbled.

When a car honked behind them, Bret flipped the driver off in the rearview mirror and drove forward.

"I'm sorry about all this. I wasn't keeping anything from you. When he was coming into the clinic, I had no idea he was your brother. If I had, I would've told you, so let's not fight about this, okay?"

"Okay." His eyes narrowed as he stared ahead, and she could see his jaw was as tight as a rubber band.

A tense silence descended upon them for the rest of the drive. When Bret pulled into her driveway, Autumn opened the passenger door and jumped out.

"I gotta go, sweetie," he said as he slid out of the vehicle.

"You're coming back, right? Remember, we have plans for dinner tonight."

Bret audibly sighed while running his hand through his short brown hair. "I'm fucking pissed right now because I have to be in Grand Junction for business early tomorrow morning. Since it's almost a four-hour drive, I want to leave today."

Autumn's eyes widened. "And when were you planning to tell me this?"

"I was debating about staying or getting up and leaving at around four in the morning. I didn't want to say anything until I made my decision. You know I'm not a morning person, sweetie." Bret walked around the car and pulled her into his arms. "Don't be mad. I'll make it up to you when I get back."

"And when will that be?"

"A few days." He bent down and kissed her. "Be good while I'm gone."

She jerked her head back. "Where did that come from?"

"I'm just joking, silly. Don't be so touchy."

Autumn pulled away. "Have a safe trip."

"I'll call you when I get there. Uh … I need to borrow a bit more money for the business venture."

She tilted her head. "Again? I just gave you four thousand dollars a couple of weeks ago."

"Yeah, and I appreciate it, but the other guy who was going to invest backed out. He sort of left me in the lurch. I'll pay you back for sure."

Autumn shook her head. "I don't have any more cash around."

"What about cash advances on your credit cards?"

"My credit cards are maxed with all the wedding expenses. I'm sorry. Maybe you can ask your parents."

"I don't want them involved in *our* business."

"Have you thought about taking out a small business loan?"

"That won't work. I had a problem before I met you and it kind of screwed up my credit. I got another couple of years before the negative shit falls off my credit report. What about the clinic?"

The blood in her veins ran cold. "What about it?"

"You could take out a loan on it. I'm on the deed right?"

At that moment, Autumn mentally kicked herself for letting Bret talk her into adding him to the deed of the property.

"I'm not doing that," she said coldly.

"Why the fuck not? There's a shitload of equity in the place. I checked it out."

"I'm not jeopardizing my business. I worked hard to come up with the money to purchase the building and property. I vowed I'd *never* borrow against it. I'm sorry, but you may have to put your business venture on the back burner until you can raise enough capital. You could try and raise money online through crowdfunding for startups. I did that when I'd decided to buy the clinic. I posted my business plan and goals on Kickstarter. I can help you with that."

Bret stood there glaring at her. "We're going to be a married couple in two months. Do you know what the fuck that means?"

"Yes," she said softly. "And I am supporting you. I raised more money than I imagined with the business campaign I posted. I told you I'd help you with that."

"You're unbelievable!" He stomped back to the driver's side of the car. "Fuck you." Bret backed the sports car out of the driveway and sped away with the tires squealing.

His actions left Autumn frozen on the lawn as she inhaled a sudden breath into her lungs. It seemed that Bret was always angry at her for some reason, and when she didn't give in to his demands, he'd act like a recalcitrant child throwing a tantrum. The sound of a car backfiring shoved Autumn into the here and now, and she hurried up the sidewalk and went into the house.

Cinder rushed over and rubbed against Autumn's legs, purring. She bent down and scooped the cat into her arms, cuddling Cinder close to her as she swallowed past the small lump in her throat. Refusing to cry, Autumn crossed the room and went into the kitchen.

"Are you hungry?" she whispered against Cinder's ear.

The cat meowed and squirmed a little in Autumn's arms, so she put her pet down, took out a can of food, and emptied it into Cinder's bright blue bowl.

A sudden surge of loneliness engulfed her. She chided herself for being foolish. For as long as Autumn could remember, she never liked leaving things on a bad or sour note. She walked into the family room and rifled through her purse, searching for her cell phone. When she found it, Autumn clicked on Bret's number as she held her breath.

She'd almost hung up when he picked up on the fifth ring.

"I'm packing," he said.

"I feel bad about our fight," she said.

"Did you call to tell me you can loan me the money?" His voice was terse.

"No, but I will help you to come up with a way to get it. How much do you need?"

"About fifteen grand."

Autumn suppressed the startled gasp aching to burst from her throat.

"I can earn that back threefold in a few months of launching the business."

"Let's talk about what we can do when you get back," she said.

A long pause. "I have to go. I'll call you when I get to Grand Junction."

The phone clicked off and Autumn held on to it for a long while before she rummaged through her purse again and pulled out Chains's phone number. She tapped in all but one of the numbers, then stopped.

"What the hell am I doing? I've got to get a grip on all this." Autumn put the phone down and jumped when it rang. "Hello," she answered tentatively.

"Hi, Autumn. I wanted to tell you that I had a great time at the brunch this morning. I loved meeting your parents," Sadie said.

A breath of relief escaped from her chest; for one crazy moment, she'd thought it was Chains on the phone.

"They enjoyed meeting you too. Regina put on a lovely brunch. I'll never be able to compete with her, that's for sure."

"Do you want to?" Sadie asked.

"Not at all." Autumn giggled. "What're you doing for dinner? Bret has to go to Grand Junction for business, and he's leaving tonight, so I'm free."

"He bailed out on you *again*?"

"I guess so, but he does have a drive ahead of him."

"Why didn't he have an early dinner with you?"

Sadie's question only made Autumn feel lonelier. "He had to prepare for tomorrow's meeting. Do you want to go out tonight?"

"Sure," her friend replied. "Where do you feel like going?"

"Spice Room. I've been dying to try it ever since it opened. Bret keeps promising we'll go, but we never do. I know he's just stringing me along because he's not keen to try Indian food."

"I'm game. I like gyros. Is it like that?" Sadie asked.

"Not exactly, but I know some of the spices are the same. You like bold and hot flavors, so I'm pretty sure you're going to like it," Autumn said.

"Sounds good. Does seven work for you?"

"That's perfect. I'll meet you there then."

Autumn put the phone on the coffee table then ran her hand over Cinder's soft fur. She was happy that Sadie agreed to go out for dinner because she really didn't want to spend the whole night alone with her thoughts. Autumn couldn't believe she was ready to call Chains, and for what reason? What would she have said to him? For some reason, she was drawn to the biker and wanted to know him better. *After all, he's going to be my brother-in-law,* but she knew that was a lie.

The truth was, she was attracted to him. Crazily attracted, despite all the reasons she shouldn't be. If Autumn told Sadie about it, her friend would clap her hands and tell her how thrilling and exciting it must be. But she didn't feel that way about it at all. She found her attraction … unsettling. Autumn felt something inside that could easily veer out of control, and she didn't like that at all. Her world and her life were orderly, but a biker had come into it, upsetting the balance and making her think all sorts of wild things.

For the first time ever, Autumn felt like her life was unraveling and getting out of hand, way past her comfort zone, and she didn't have a damn clue how to deal with it.

Sighing, she tilted her head back against the couch and closed her eyes.

Chapter Eleven

Two weeks later

CHAINS CURSED UNDER his breath and ignored the ringing phone as he tried to figure out why the code on his client's website wasn't working. Pushing back from the desk, he stared at the screen as if the answer would jump out at him. His eyes were dry and achy, and he rubbed them with the heel of his hand.

The phone rang again and again and *again*.

"What the fuck," he muttered, frowning at the cell. He picked it up and glanced at the number on the screen. With pursed lips, he slowly brought it to his ear.

"I'm in the middle of something." Irritation laced Chains's voice.

"Sorry, but I had to talk to you," Bret replied.

For a nanosecond his chest tightened. "Is Mom okay?"

"Yeah, everyone's fine."

"What is it then? I'm trying to finish up something for a client, so I don't have a lot of time."

"Okay. We haven't spoken since the brunch, right?"

Chains leaned forward and typed on the keyboard. "Uh-huh."

"I don't even know why the hell we were mad." Bret let out a dry chuckle.

"'Cause that's the way we roll—we're always pissed at each other." He shook his head and closed the laptop. "Cut the bullshit. Why did you call?"

"Autumn told me that she knew you from the clinic she owns."

"So?"

"Nothing. I just picked up that you two seemed comfortable with each other."

Chains stiffened against the chair. "What the fuck does that mean? I brought my dog in because he was sicker than hell. She fixed him up. End of fuckin' story."

"Hang on there … I'm not saying anything bad about it, so don't get so defensive," Bret said.

"You got five seconds to tell me why the hell you're calling before I hang up. I don't have time for this bullshit." Chains massaged the back of his neck with his free hand.

"I've changed my mind," Bret said in a low voice.

"About what?"

"Getting married. I'm not ready to settle down just yet." A long sigh came through the phone.

Chains jerked his head back. "What the hell? You just figured that out *now*?" He laughed dryly.

"I've been feeling it for a while, but Mom was so happy and she loved planning everything that I just didn't know how …" his voice trailed off.

"Why the fuck are you telling me this? I'd think you should be talking to your fiancée about it, not me." Chains stretched his legs out in front of him, and Thor raised his head and looked up.

"Yeah, so that's the thing. I'm not real good at doing this type of stuff. Chicks get all teary-eyed before breaking down in sobs and causing a real scene. I'd prefer to bypass that."

"I'm sure you would, but you need to tell her." Anger shot up Chains's spine; he was getting more pissed as the minutes ticked by. He didn't want to be dragged into his brother's drama.

"I want you to tell Autumn for me."

Chains jumped to his feet. "Are you fuckin' serious? Why the hell would I do *that*? For once in your pathetic life, be a man and take responsibility. I'm not getting involved in this."

"Responsibility? *This* is coming from someone who lives like he's in a criminal frat house and rides around on a damn motorcycle?" Bret snorted.

"And owns a business and doesn't ask Mom or Dad for a fuckin' dime. I've been on my own, supporting myself since I was eighteen. You're thiry and still looking for handouts."

"Asshole," Bret said with a hiss. "Don't worry about what I said. I'll just do a no-show at the wedding. I don't give a fuck!"

The thought of Autumn standing at the altar in a packed church waiting for Bret to show up pierced his mind … and his heart. He couldn't let his moronic brother humiliate her that way. *Fuck!*

"I'll tell her, but you better stay away from me, because if I see you, I'm beating the shit outta you." Chains hung up and threw the phone on the bed. "What a sonofabitch!"

Thor pushed up from the floor and sat on his haunches, then looked up and whined.

"It's okay, buddy," he said calmly, even though anger still seethed inside him. He walked over to the closet and plucked out a Milk-Bone. Thor's ears lifted and his tongue hung out as he looked eagerly at Chains's hand. "Here you go." Chains tossed the treat into the dog's waiting jaws. He then picked up the phone and looked at the time: 5:45 p.m. He crossed back over to the computer and did a search for Autumn's home address. If he was going to do this, he thought it wouldn't be a good idea to do it at the clinic.

"You fuckin' asshole," he muttered as he called the clinic to see whether Autumn was still at work.

"Highlands Animal Care Center. May I help you?" a woman said.

"Is Dr. Stanford in?" he asked.

"Who's calling, please?"

He scrubbed the side of his face. "I was just wondering if the doctor is in."

"Is that you, Chains?" A high-pitched giggle. "This is Sheila. How are you?"

He rolled his eyes. "Good. Is the doc still there?"

"No, she just left about ten minutes ago. Is Thor not feeling well? I can get Dr. Jenkins on the phone."

"Thor's fine, but I had a question. I'll call back tomorrow."

"Are you free tonight? I made a huge pot of chili last night that'll take me forever to get through. The kids think it's too hot." Another giggle.

"Thanks, but I've got something going on at the clubhouse. One of the members is calling me now."

"Oh …" Disappointment weaved through her voice. "Maybe tomorrow night?"

Chains tilted his head from side-to-side, cracking his neck. "That won't work either. Actually, Sheila, I'm not into dating right now."

"Dating"—she laughed a bit too loud and long—"who said anything about *that*? I thought we could be friends."

"I'm not friends with chicks." That was the truth. The whole notion of a man and woman hanging together without having sex was foreign to him.

"Why not? That's ridiculous." Sheila huffed.

"That's just the way it is. I gotta go. I'll see you around." Chains slipped the phone into his jeans pocket, then picked up the keys on the dresser. "I shouldn't be doing this shit at all," he said as he walked out of the room. But there was no way he could let Bret hurt Autumn any worse than he already was. Chains wasn't sure if Bret was just bluffing, but he didn't want to take the chance with her feelings, so he petted Thor, high-fived the members in the club, and strode out into the chilly fall air.

Brushstrokes of pomegranate pink and sherbet orange painted the fading blue sky. In the distance, the mountain peaks turned a shimmering gold in the light of the setting sun. Chains straddled his motorcycle, then slowly rode toward the old highway.

By the time he'd arrived in town, the colors streaking the sky earlier had disappeared into the dark ashes of nightfall. Chains took his time getting to Morning Glory Circle, half hoping Autumn wouldn't be at her house.

He took a right and cruised down the street as he looked for her address. The cul-de-sac was quiet except for an occasional car pulling into a garage. The homes and yards were well-kept, and several oak and maple trees dotted the neighborhood. Lights glowed in the windows, and in a nearby house, he could see a man seated in a chair near the fire, reading what looked to be a magazine.

Chains stopped in front of a two-story white stucco home with a red barrel-tiled roof and dark shutters on its windows. There was a large porch across the front, and he craned his neck to read the address: 14225. He killed the engine and hopped off the bike, then walked up the sidewalk. Yellow light from inside glowed against the lawn. He pushed the doorbell and leaned against the wall as he waited for Autumn to answer. She didn't come. He tried again. For a few minutes he stood on the porch and stared at the stars visible through the almost bare branches of the weeping willow tree on Autumn's front lawn.

A chilly breeze picked up, and the rustling of the leaves on the branches sounded like whispers in the night. Chains zipped up his leather jacket, and as he started to walk down the porch steps, a pair of headlights flashed across the front lawn. A car turned into the driveway, and the sound of the garage door opening had him sprinting toward it.

He walked inside just before the door began to close and watched Autumn slide out of the car carrying two bags of groceries. She hadn't noticed Chains standing in the shadowed corner, and he stuffed his hands into his jacket pockets and slowly approached her.

"Autumn," he said in a low voice, not wanting to freak her out.

She whirled around, and her eyes widened as her face paled. "Who is that?" she asked, a slight tremor in her voice.

"Chains."

"*Chains?* You scared the hell out of me." A nervous laugh reverberated around the garage, bouncing off the concrete walls.

"Sorry. I was on the front porch and then saw you pull in. You didn't see my bike parked in front of the house?" He offered her a weak smile.

"No, I didn't. I've got so much on my mind that I'm pretty much zoned out after work. It's freezing in here, let's go inside."

Chains followed her and found himself in a bright kitchen with white cupboards, gray and charcoal granite countertops, and graphite slatted blinds. He stood off to the side, watching Autumn put the two canvas bags filled with groceries on the island before bending down and picking up a bluish-gray cat.

His gaze languidly ran over her body, admiring the way her tight skirt hugged her hips and her snug top molded over her breasts. A hint of cleavage had him wanting to lick all the way from her neck to her pussy with a few stops along the way.

"Why're you here?" Autumn said, her voice slicing through his thoughts.

He glanced up at her face and noticed she was flushed, and the fine line between her brows had deepened a bit.

"I need to talk to you."

She petted her cat for a second or two before gazing back at Chains. "About what? And how do you know where I live?"

"Can we sit down?" he asked, ignoring her questions.

"I have to feed my cat and put the groceries away." Autumn placed the cat down on the floor, then gestured to one of the chairs in the family room. "Have a seat."

"Okay, I'll wait for you to finish."

He settled on the multi-colored couch that had a Native American pattern running through the fabric. A large stone fireplace was the focal point in the room, and two cushy chairs in a solid rust fabric sat on either side of the couch. A flat screen TV hung over the fireplace, and books, framed photographs, and knick-knacks filled two built-in bookshelves that were on either side of it.

"You got a nice place here." Chains stretched out his legs.

"Thanks. I still don't know what you're doing here."

He heard cupboards opening and closing behind him.

"Come on in here when you're done putting stuff away and I'll tell you." He blew out a breath, and his muscles tightened in anticipation of the news he was about to divulge. *After I'm done here, I'm gonna find Bret and kick his ass real good. Stupid sonofabitch.*

"Do you want something to drink?"

"You got any beer?" *A bit of booze will make this go a lot easier.*

"No beer—I don't drink the stuff. I do have tequila and vodka. Will either of those work?"

"Tequila straight is good."

A few seconds later, Autumn handed him a tumbler, then went over to the fireplace and flipped a switch. Tall orange-yellow flames danced and flickered around logs that looked like the real thing, replete with glowing red embers. A mix of warm air and radiant heat filled the room.

"That's better." She crossed the area and sank down into one of the cushy chairs. "You can't beat the ease of a fire that lights with a flick of a switch. No clean-up either," she said with a smile.

"It's cool." He threw back the clear drink, then ran his index finger up and down the side of the glass.

"So, what did you want to tell me?"

"I need to talk to you about Bret." His voice came out gruffer than he'd intended.

Autumn clutched the base of her throat. "Is he all right? He got in a bad car accident, didn't he? That's why I haven't heard from him. Oh, God … He's in the hospital, right? Or is he—"

"It's not that … Bret's fine." His brother hadn't mentioned he was out of town, and that fact pissed Chains off even more.

"That's a relief." She settled back in the chair. "So what is it?"

Chains pulled his legs up and leaned forward slightly, his gaze fixed on hers.

"You're making me nervous. Just tell me." She stared down at her hands, fidgeting in her lap.

"Autumn, Bret's …" Chains looked away. *Fuck!*

"Bret's *what*?" she whispered.

He clenched his jaw and locked eyes with hers. "The fucker's breaking off the engagement. He doesn't want to get married. The sonofabitch didn't have the balls to tell you himself, so he called and asked me." Chains shook his head. "If it's any consolation, I'm gonna beat the shit outta him for doing this to you when he gets back in town."

"Is this for *real*?" Autumn whispered. Her hands were clasped together so tightly that her knuckles had turned white.

"I wish it weren't, but... yeah, that's what he said." Chains scrubbed his jaw. "I'm sorry my brother's such a fuckin' asshole."

"I can't believe it," she mumbled. "Why would he do this to me? I mean, things have been tense between us for the last few months or so, but to call off the wedding? I was feeling stressed about the wedding too, but to call it off... and like *this*? It's awful." A ragged sob escaped and she lowered her head, her shoulders shaking slightly.

He sat watching, her soft sobs tearing through him. Chains rose to his feet and came over to her. "Fuck, Autumn, don't cry." He reached out and gripped one of her arms. "The asshole doesn't deserve you. Come here." Chains pulled her up from the chair and she fell against him as he wrapped his arms around her.

"Why would he do this?" she mumbled over and over.

Chains didn't say anything; instead, he stroked her hair and held her close, breathing in the scent of her perfume. She was so soft, so beautiful, and she fit perfectly in his arms. A warm hand reached up and touched the side of his face. He tilted his head back and his gaze moved to hers as he felt an unexpected jolt of need and desire roll over him. Instinctively, Chains dropped his arms and stepped back.

Autumn turned away, her cheeks blooming, and she plucked out a tissue from a box on the corner of the coffee table and wiped her damp face.

"I'm okay now." She sighed loudly and smoothed her hair back. "I'm sorry for getting so upset."

"You don't need to apologize." Chains stood rooted to the spot. "Do you want me to get you anything, like a drink or something?"

A weak smile. "I could use a shot or two of vodka, but I'll get it myself."

"No way. Sit down and I'll bring it to you. Where do you keep the bottle?" He was glad to be doing something; he needed to distance himself from the situation and from *her*.

"Top cupboard to the left of the fridge."

"Got it."

Chains bounded into the kitchen and went straight to the cabinet. After he had the bottle in hand, he looked around for a glass. He glanced over at Autumn, who was now sitting on the couch and hugging her cat. Chains spotted the tequila on the counter and poured a couple of shots in a tumbler, then he brought both glasses into the family room. There was no way he could just take off now; if he did, he'd be no better than his selfish-ass brother.

"Here you go," Chains handed Autumn her drink.

"Thanks. Sit over here," she said patting the couch.

He plopped down, then brought the tumbler to his lips and took a big sip.

"I guess I'm not really surprised that Bret's called off the wedding," she said, her voice trembling on the words *the wedding*. "We weren't getting along all that well, and he always seemed so preoccupied. I guess he just got tired of me." Autumn shrugged, then took a drink of vodka.

"My brother's always been the restless type—changing jobs, cars, and apartments all the time." He drained his glass. The last thing he wanted was to have Autumn start crying again; he wouldn't be able to stand it. A woman crying made him go all soft and twisted inside.

"Then, I guess he wants to trade me in for a new model." There was a small hitch in her voice.

"He's an asshole."

"Bret's been less attentive lately so I knew something was up, even though he kept denying it. My friend Sadie kept telling me I was just having pre-wedding jitters." She shook her head. "I *knew* in my gut something wasn't right. Do you think he wants to go back to his ex-girlfriend. I'm pretty sure her mother's trying to get them back together.

Barbara—that's her mom. She's a total bitch, and Bret *insisted* that I have her at the kitchen shower. Can you believe that? And he wanted her and the ex-girlfriend at the wedding. Isn't that insane? How stupid I've been." Autumn breathed in deeply and let it out slowly. "Do you know Barbara and her daughter, Teresa? Do you think Bret wants to go back to her?"

Chains shifted uneasily in his seat; he didn't go for talking about women's feelings and other stuff. It seemed that few men could grasp what women *really* wanted them to say, and getting involved with all that was like walking in a field full of landmines.

"I don't know much about Bret's life. I haven't been around the day-to-day family shit for about fourteen years."

"So you don't know Barbara or Teresa?" Desperation flashed across her face.

"No, I don't. Uh … do you have a friend you can call to be here with you?"

Her jaw slackened and she looked away. "I'm sorry. I'm putting you in the middle of all this—Bret's your brother, after all."

He jerked his head back. "I'm more concerned about you than him. What he did to you is unforgivable. It's just that I think you need a girlfriend to talk to about all this."

Autumn took another sip of her drink. "I can call Sadie."

"Will she be able to come over? You probably don't want to be alone tonight."

"I'm sure she can." A faraway look came into her eyes. "I just don't have luck with men. Bret's the second guy who dumped me before the wedding."

Chains raised his eyebrows slightly. "No shit."

A small, dry laugh. "Yeah … pretty pathetic, huh? I found my ex-fiancé, or should I now say my ex-ex-fiancé, banging a friend of mine. And now Bret … This is all such a fucking pathetic joke. Why do men keep leaving me? What the fuck's wrong with me?" She sank her fist into the cushion.

"It's not you, it's them—they were both assholes. You just haven't found the right one yet."

She reached out and touched his hand. "Thanks for that. Why haven't you gotten married?"

His muscles stiffened. "I was once, but it didn't work out."

Autumn's eyes widened. "That's a surprise. Bret told me he was the first one to get married in the family."

"He's not only an asshole, but he lies a helluva lot. I know you don't feel this way now, but you're lucky you're not getting hitched to him. You would've had a shitty life."

"It's just that I thought I was finally settled with a nice guy. All this wedding planning has consumed me for more than four months. What am I going to tell people?"

"That you and asshole have called off the wedding. It's better like this than to go through a divorce." Chains rose to his feet. "You want another vodka? I'm gonna have some more tequila."

Nodding, she replied, "Half of what you poured me before. Do you want to eat something? I'm starving. I've been trying to be real good about carbs and such because Bret thought I needed to lose a few pounds, but I'm famished."

Chains looked over his shoulder at her. "You don't need to lose anything. My brother's an idiot."

"Thanks. See, you are good with this woman stuff."

"I could go for a pizza, or whatever else you want."

"I'm craving cheesy enchiladas and a shredded beef burrito and a full order of sopapillas with a scoop of ice cream."

Chains laughed as he poured the drinks. "Sounds good. You want me to pick it up?"

"I can order through Door Delivery. Have you used their service?"

"Nah. No one comes to the clubhouse to deliver shit except for the mail."

"Are you sure you're good with staying? I mean, you don't have to babysit me."

He walked back over to the couch and put the drinks down on the table. "I'm good with it. I'm just really pissed off at my brother, and I don't want you to be alone."

"I'll call Sadie to come over later. I know she's working late tonight."

"I'll stay until she comes," he said.

"You don't have to. I'll be okay, really," she replied.

"Let's see how it goes after we eat."

Chains stared at the fire as she placed the order online. Autumn was too close to him and she smelled way too good, and he had to remember that she was in a very vulnerable position. His jerk brother had just broken this wonderful woman's heart, so if Chains showed her any attention, she'd probably do something she'd regret the following day. Even though Autumn had been engaged to Bret, Chains knew she was attracted to him, and there was no denying that he was damn captivated by her. He should just leave, and under normal circumstances he would, but Chains didn't want her to be alone because that's when dark thoughts crept in and loneliness became pervasive.

After the divorce, recriminations and raw emotions had swallowed up Chains, leaving him with nothing but bitterness and anger. He knew only too well what demons lurked in the still and shadowed corners of the mind long after the heart was shattered.

"Done." Autumn put down the phone, her voice pulling him from the recollections of the past.

Chains looked up at her. "When's the food coming?"

"In about thirty minutes or so. Is that okay?"

He nodded. "Look, I know this shit hurts, and it's gonna for a while, but I hope you don't spend too long crying over Bret—he just isn't worth it. People like him do their damage and then move on without a backward glance. They don't care about the heartbreak they've caused."

"Are you speaking from experience?" she whispered.

"Yeah. You don't want this to eat you up inside." He walked back into the kitchen and poured another drink. "You want another one?"

"I'm done with the vodka, but I'll have a glass of red wine when our dinner comes. How long did it take you to get over your divorce?"

Chains paused, then picked up the bottle and glass and sauntered back to the couch. "Too fuckin' long. The whole time I was filled with hate and anger, my ex was living her life, not giving a shit about the chaos she left behind. I was a fuckin' fool."

Autumn shifted so she faced him. "Why do people who are supposed to love you treat you so shitty? I'm sorry you had to go through that." She tucked her legs under herself. "Bret told me he loved me. He just told me that before he left on business a few days ago."

"People lie—they're full of shit. Love is such an overused word. It's easy to say but tough to live." He poured more liquor in the glass, then brought it to his mouth.

"You're so right. There're too many selfish people around—they take but never give. It seems like nowadays, loyalty isn't very fashionable."

"For the most part, citizens don't know shit about loyalty and strong bonds."

Autumn cocked her head. "Citizens?"

Chains smiled. "You and all the others who aren't in the biker world."

"That's right—you're in the Night Rebels. Bret told me that recently," she said.

Autumn lightly touched his arm, and he clenched his teeth. *Down, boy—fuckin' behave.* He dragged his gaze away from her tits and focused on the dancing flames in the fireplace instead.

"What's it like to be in a biker club?"

"Cool." Leaning back, he stretched out his legs, crossing them at the ankles.

"Bret made it sound awful."

"I'm sure he did. My family doesn't approve of my lifestyle choice, and I don't give a damn. I never gave a shit what people thought, even when I was young. I live my life the way I want to, and there's no fuckin' way I'm gonna apologize for it."

"I think that's admirable."

Autumn touched his forearm again, but this time she didn't pull away. Chains groaned inwardly and kept his gaze on the fire.

"So, you're from Denver?" he asked, changing the subject.

"Yes. I went to the veterinary school at CSU in Fort Collins after I graduated from college. I was with a practice in Denver, but after my breakup with Dylan, I needed a change of scenery, so I came here. I love Alina. When I was a kid, my parents and I spent a few weeks in this area. We went to Mesa Verde and camped in the San Juan Mountains."

"The trails and passes kick ass for riding. Now that Bret's proven he's a jerk, you gonna take off?" Chains glanced over at her.

She shook her head. "No. I'm here to stay."

He nodded and looked away.

"Should I call Bret and ask him why he did this?"

Chains cocked his head and gazed at her. "I wouldn't—but I'd definitely ask him to reimburse you for the money you lost. He's the fucker who broke it off—he needs to pay up."

"I'm pretty sure he's not going to do that." She looked down at the diamond ring. "I could hock this—that would piss him off."

"Then do it."

"I threw my last ring at Dylan and told him to go to hell. My parents lost money on that one. I've paid for most of the wedding this time around." She covered her face with her hands and groaned. "I can't believe this is happening *again*."

Before he could answer, the doorbell rang, and Autumn leaped up from the couch and scurried out of the room, saying, "It's our food."

Autumn came back into the room with two large bags as the aroma of chili and cumin swirled in the air.

"Damn, woman, how much shit did you order?"

"A lot. Remember, this is make-me-feel-better and fuck-you-Bret food. We can eat on the coffee table. I'll get some forks and hot sauce," she said, walking into the kitchen. Her cat followed behind, meowing.

Chains laughed as he pulled his phone out of his pocket. He called

Eagle and told him to feed Thor and keep an eye on him, then he hung up.

"Is Thor doing well? I couldn't help but overhear your conversation," Autumn said as she put the round foil takeout containers down on the table.

"He's back to his old self. What do you need me to help you with?"

"Nothing. You can start eating." She put the hot sauce down on a coaster. "I'll grab some extra napkins after I put the side of ice cream in the freezer."

When Autumn came back into the room, she plopped down next to Chains, and her cat jumped up to snuggle against her other side.

"This is my cat, Cinder. She loves to cuddle." Then, she asked, "Do you have enough room? I can push her over a bit."

Autumn's legs were brushing against his.

"I'm good," he said, then cut into the beef burrito supreme with a fork.

"I can't wait to try the enchiladas. I've been craving them all day." When she reached over to snag her foil container, her arm touched his.

Autumn's closeness felt good—comfortable and familiar. It had been a long time since he'd found himself so attracted and intrigued by a woman. Part of him wanted to embrace it, relish in it, but the part deep inside him that was still raw from Krystal's betrayal held him back.

After dinner, Chains helped Autumn clean up, then he stayed and watched a mindless sitcom on one of the channels. During the show, he glanced over at Autumn and saw that she was fast asleep. Her head was on the armrest and her feet were bent at the knee and lightly touching the side of his right thigh.

He couldn't drag his eyes away from her body—the outline of her tits and the curve of her waist. Licking his lips, he stared at the auburn strands of hair cascading past her shoulders, the smooth skin tinged with a golden glow from the floor lamp, and her softly heaving chest. Autumn's lips were slightly parted, and he was seized with the overwhelming urge to slip his tongue in between them.

Chains gripped the arm of the couch and pushed up to his feet. He looked around and noticed a blanket on top of a chest near one of the windows, and went over and grabbed it. Gingerly, he placed the blanket over her body; she sighed and gripped it, then tucked it snuggly under her chin. He picked up one of the decorative pillows from the couch and carefully placed it under her head so as not to wake her.

After turning off the television, Chains dimmed the kitchen lights and made his way to the front door. Trying out a few bump keys, he let himself out and then locked the door. The air had turned icy as the nighttime temperature dropped. He breathed in deeply, and the cold burned his lungs and made his eyes water.

Straddling the bike, Chains glanced at Autumn's house and narrowed his eyes. He was drawn to her, pulled by something deep inside him, something that craved her in a way he'd never felt before.

"That can't happen," he muttered under his breath. "No fuckin' way."

Chains turned the keys in the ignition and pressed the starter. The bike roared to life, and he squeezed the clutch, clicked the gearshift lever, and twisted the throttle as he pulled away from Autumn's house and sped down the road.

Chapter Twelve

Autumn tried to sit up, but the pressure in her head made her sink back down. It was like an axe had been planted in her brain. She tugged the blanket closer and burrowed deeper into the couch. Then a moment of panic hit her. *I have to get to the clinic! What time is it?* She glanced at the clock on the bookshelf, then bolted up. It was nearly one o'clock in the afternoon. How could she have overslept this long?

Ignoring the pain in her head, Autumn pushed up from the couch and shuffled into the kitchen to get a glass of water to wet her parched throat. When she spotted the half-full vodka and the two empty bottles of red wine on the counter, she groaned.

Cinder meowed and rubbed against her legs, then padded over to the pantry.

"Oh, God. Did I forget to feed you last night?" Moaning with every step she took, Autumn opened the pantry door, pulled out a box of dry food, and poured it into Cinder's bowl. She glanced at the shelf and counted ten cans of wet food, then let out a breath of relief: she hadn't forgotten to feed her sweet cat the night before.

After downing two glasses of water, Autumn trudged up the stairs. She turned on the faucet in the master bathroom and splashed cold water on her face just to feel something refreshing. Glancing in the mirror, she groaned at the reflection of her eyes—a lattice of pink over the white.

"You're a total mess." She turned away and shuffled to her bed. "How am I going to function today?" Without thinking, Autumn picked up the receiver of the landline phone and dialed the clinic. There was no way she could properly do her job, so for the first time since she'd bought the clinic, she'd have to call in sick.

"Dr. Jenkins," Mark's voice said.

Confusion stabbed at her brain. "Uh ... sorry, Mark. I thought I called the clinic. This is Autumn." It felt as if her mouth were full of cotton. She glanced at the bathroom and wished she'd brought a glass of water with her. The room was spinning a bit, and Autumn didn't think she should try and stand up.

"Hi, Autumn. Are you okay? You sound a bit funny," Mark said.

"I'm not feeling very well today. I won't be able to come to the clinic. Can you and Marian handle my patients?" Autumn scooted back on the bed until she hit the headboard.

"The clinic's closed. I'm the doctor on call." A small hesitation. "Do you have a fever?"

"Why's the clinic closed?" *If only I could get this fucking drum to stop beating in my head.* She pressed her fingers against the right temple.

"*You* are out of it." A small chuckle crackled through the phone. "It's Saturday—we close at noon, remember? I picked up two of your patients this morning, and Marian spotted the other three. I was actually going to give you a call to check up on you. Marian said you were probably doing wedding stuff."

The wedding. Autumn's stomach lurched. *Bret called it off—he dumped me.* "I overslept, but I'm actually feeling pretty sick now. I really have to go."

"Do you need anything? Kim can drop by if you want some help."

Kim Jenkins was a sweet woman and always willing to help. With two small kids and another one on the way, she seemed to have oodles of time to devote to her husband and keeping a well-organized home. Autumn didn't know how Kim did it all and still maintained her cheery disposition.

"I'll be okay. It's probably a twenty-four-hour *something or other*. I gotta get to the bathroom."

"Uh ... okay. I'll call you later to make sure you're all right."

"Thanks," she managed to get out of the bed and stumbled into the en suite.

A short while later, she lifted her head from the toilet and dragged herself over to the sink and washed up. Three aspirins later, Autumn lay on the bed, trying to summon some small amount of energy. The events of the night before blitzed through her mind, and she couldn't believe Bret wasn't man enough to break off the engagement in person … or even in a damn text. *The jerk sent his brother over to do the dirty deed. His brother—Chains.* The corner of her mouth tugged up a little. Chains had tried to be so supportive in a very awkward situation. Autumn could tell that he hadn't wanted to be in the middle of their relationship, but he'd come over to console her anyway. The brother *in the outlaw club* had done that, whereas the brother with the white-collar job who owed her an explanation had passed the buck.

She grabbed the phone and typed a quick text to Bret.

Autumn: *What the hell?*

It seemed like forever until the small response beep sounded.

Bret: *Things just haven't been working between us.*

Autumn: *So u sent ur brother to break off the engagement???*

Bret: *U seemed to have a rapport with him.*

Autumn: *But u and I were the couple. U should've been man enough to talk to me.*

Bret: *I just don't want to be married.*

Autumn: *Why the fuck didn't u tell me that b4 I put deposits on everything!*

Bret: *I thought I wanted this. I don't.*

"So, that's it?" she said at the phone.

Autumn: *U owe me for the deposits and the money I put into this.*

Bret: *The woman's the one who pays for the wedding. It's always a risk.*

She clenched her teeth and growled in exasperation.

Autumn: *And u owe me the 4k I loaned u for ur business.*
Bret: *I have to go.*
Autumn: *Ur a fucking coward!*

Tears stung her eyes as she threw the phone across the room. In the distance she heard a bell chime and at first wondered if she was imagining it, but the ringing didn't stop. Groaning, Autumn swung her legs over the side of the bed and slowly stood up. At least the room had stopped spinning in front of her.

When she was halfway down the stairs, she figured out that someone was ringing the doorbell and had no plans on stopping.

"I'm coming," she said.

Autumn paused at the door to look through the peephole and froze when Chains came into view. She glanced down at the pair of baggy shorts and the small black T-shirt she'd thrown on, and moaned.

The bell chimed again, and she quickly ran her fingers through her hair, then swung open the door.

"You could wake the dead with all that damn ringing," she grumbled as she unlocked the screen.

"Good to see you too." Chains stepped inside and shut the door behind him.

"What're you doing here?" Autumn asked.

"Making sure you're okay." He walked past her into the family room.

"You don't have to check up on me," she said, following close behind.

"I know."

Chains stood in the middle of the room, looking at her, and Autumn felt her face flush as his warm brown eyes dropped to where the swell of her breasts peeked out above the scooped neckline of her T-shirt. She folded her arms across her chest and shifted in place.

"I'm doing fine, all things considered."

"That's good." He cocked his head to the side, his gaze tracking up and down her body.

Autumn cleared her throat. "Why don't you sit down. I can offer you juice or water." She glanced at the empty bottles on the coffee table. "I pretty much killed the wine and vodka last night."

"And I took care of the tequila. Water's good."

Grateful for an excuse to get away from his stare, she scurried to the kitchen and opened the cabinet. The way Chains looked at her made her nervous, excited, and irritated all at the same time. She couldn't be thinking about him in that way, or *any* way, especially since she should be nursing her wounds over the breakup.

"I bet you had a helluva hangover this morning," he said.

"This *afternoon*, and it's a doozy." Autumn handed him a bottle of water. "I unintentionally played hooky this morning—a first for me."

Chains chuckled. "You gotta do shit like that once in a while. Always playing it straight sucks." He brought the bottle to his lips.

"I guess I'm the epitome of 'playing it straight.' I've always lived in life's safe zone."

"I gotta change that," he said.

Autumn shifted her eyes away from his. "How do you plan to do that?" She picked up Cinder and nestled the cat onto her lap.

"First thing is to get you on a Harley."

She smiled. "I guess that would be a start. A lot of people don't like the noise motorcycles make, so I'd be going against the norm by riding on one, I suppose."

Chains nodded. "There's nothing like it. When you got the wind rushing around you, and the smell and taste and feel of the landscape, nothing else matters. It's like fuckin' meditation for a biker. As far as the sound goes, I get a kick outta revving the engine at stoplights. It's my way of saying, 'Fuck you' to a world of noise, rules, and regulations."

"You're quite the rebel. What do you do besides ride your motorcycle and piss off people?"

"I have a web development business, but that's definitely secondary to the club and my bike"—he took another drink of water, then smiled—"and to irritating citizens." He laughed.

"Wow, I never would've thought you'd be into computers. You don't fit the stereotype."

"I'll take that as a compliment." Chains winked at her.

"How long have you had the business?" She ignored the warmth spreading through her.

"Seven years. It's been good. I could hire some people to take care of the orders I have to turn down, but I'm cool with where it is. I need time for the club."

"And for riding your motorcycle."

He nodded. "You catch on fast."

She stroked Cinder's coat with both hands. "I've got a question. Did you clean up the place last night?"

Chains leaned back against the cushion and stretched out his legs. "Yep. I also draped a blanket over you before I left."

"So that was you. I wondered how it got there when I woke up. How did you lock the door after you let yourself out?"

He shrugged and looked away.

"Okay … I guess I don't *really* want to know."

Then a silence fell between them.

"I contacted Bret," Autumn blurted out.

"Yeah?"

"By text. I knew the coward wouldn't pick up the phone."

"You got that right."

"He told me he just didn't want to get married anymore. Can you believe *that*?"

"Actually, I can," Chains replied.

"I don't even know what that means. He was acting like everything was cool with us, and then this out of the blue?" She shook her head. "Anyway, I told him he'd have to reimburse me for half the wedding, and he said something stupid—I can't really remember what it was." She reached over and grabbed her cell phone.

"Bret always says stupid shit. You don't have to find the text."

Autumn tossed the phone. "And when I told him he has to pay back the four thousand I loaned him, he stopped texting *pronto*. What an asshole. What did I see in him anyway?" *Security, companionship, the American dream.* The words looped through her mind.

"I've got no idea. And why the fuck is he borrowing money from you? To hear my dad tell it, Bret's making a shit-ton of money at his job."

"He said he wanted it for a new business he was starting—a software something … He was sketchy about it, and when he wanted more money from me and I didn't give it to him, he got real mad at me." Autumn tapped her upper lip. "Now that I think about it, it wasn't all that long ago when he asked for more money, and now he's broken the engagement. I wonder if the two events are related."

"Could be. I don't buy the shit about starting a business," Chains said.

"Why not?"

"'Cause my old man would've rubbed it in my face at the brunch."

"Maybe Bret didn't want to tell him until he got the business off the ground."

"Nah. He and my dad are real tight—he'd have told him."

"Does your dad know that you have a business?" she asked softly.

"I don't know, and I don't give a shit if he does or doesn't."

"Did you tell anyone in your family?"

"My mom. I'm not really close to my blood family—they really haven't ever been there for me. I consider my true family the club. You know, the term *brotherhood* gets thrown around a lot in today's society, but none of the citizens have a fuckin' clue as to the real meaning of the word. We take it to a life-and-death level. There's no fuckin' way I wouldn't take a bullet for my brothers or they wouldn't for me. There's a closeness we got born outta loyalty, strength, and love that you don't see in most families." Chains crushed the water bottle, then tossed it on the coffee table. "I've never had one iota of that kind of trust, support, or closeness with my blood family."

The hurt that seeped from Chains when he talked about his "blood family" squeezed at her heart. From the way Bret had spoken of his parents, she'd gathered that they showered him with praise, love, and support his whole life, but Chains had a different experience in the same household.

"You're lucky you found the club," she whispered.

"Damn straight. I felt outta sync with my siblings and parents when I was growing up. Being a biker is more than riding a Harley."

"I'm sure it is," she replied.

Chains hit his fist against his chest. "I feel it in my heart and soul. That's what the citizens don't get."

His words resonated with such passion and conviction that even Cinder popped her head up and stared at him.

Chains's gaze latched on to hers. "There's something about you that makes me tell you things I don't want to think about."

The husky roughness of his voice made a sudden shiver race up her spine. Immediately, she chastised herself for feeling attracted to Chains when it hadn't even been twenty-four hours since *his* brother broke up with her.

"I've had other people tell me that too," she said flippantly, even though every nerve in her body snapped. "I should call my friend Sadie. I meant to last night, but I fell asleep." She rolled her eyes. "Well, *passed out* before I could give her a ring."

"So you want me to go?" He rose to his feet.

"I don't want to keep you from doing what you usually do. I'm really okay, but thanks for caring."

"No worries."

Chains walked toward the hallway, and she jumped up from the couch and followed him over to the door. Autumn turned around, and for endless moments they stared at one another until the air was thick with sexual tension.

"Autumn," he said in a low, husky voice.

Her heartbeat raced as he took a few steps, his gaze lowering to her mouth.

Suddenly, a car alarm went off across the street, the blaring siren piercing through their arousal. Regaining her composure, Autumn gripped the knob and flung open the door. A rush of cool air burst in, and she wrapped her arms around herself.

"Thanks again," she mumbled.

Chains tipped his head and then stepped out onto the porch. Autumn checked out the way he swaggered over to his motorcycle and pulled a muscular leg over the leather seat, then without another glance in her direction, he put on his sunglasses. Across the street, Mrs. Harrison sat in the driver's seat, waving her arms around while Mr. Harrison looked under the hood of the Cadillac.

The bike's engine drowned out the alarm, and she watched Chains pull from the curb and ride away. When Autumn couldn't see him any longer, she immediately felt his absence. After closing the door, she went back into the family room and flipped on the fireplace. As warmth started to radiate from the flames, Autumn crossed over to the couch and sank down, pulling a Sherpa blanket around her shivering body. She glanced at the phone, and instead of picking it up and calling Sadie, she just sat there with her brain numb and her heart broken.

Cinder jumped up on the sofa and snuggled next to her, softly purring until she stuck her hand out from under the blanket and petted the cat.

"You're so beautiful," she whispered as tears spilled down her face. Cinder meowed and cuddled closer.

A sob escaped Autumn's throat, and she pulled Cinder up against her and buried her face into the cat's soft fur.

And as she cried, she realized that the tears weren't for Bret or her broken engagement ... they were all for Chains.

What's wrong with me?

But she knew. It was Chains. He had come into her life and shook it up like no one ever had.

And for the first time since she'd agreed to marry Bret, Autumn suddenly felt free ... and *alive*.

Chapter Thirteen

THE MEETING WITH the Wichita buyers had been set, and Chains was one of the members who would accompany Paco, Diablo, Eagle, Army, Crow, Aztec, and Shotgun. The plan was to meet the following night at the old adobe off Yellow Feather Road. The place was owned by an aged biker, Rocky, who'd been like a father to Paco ever since his dad was sent to prison for murdering Paco's mother when he was a teen. The old biker had helped the club out many times if they needed an alibi or had to dispose of evidence. Rocky was anti-establishment and didn't trust the badges any more than the Night Rebels did, but he had friends in important places and was an asset to the club.

"Tomorrow night should be an easy transaction. We've never dealt with high society criminals before," Jigger said.

"Should be, but we can't count on anything," Crow replied.

Chains nodded. "We'll be packing assault weapons just in case the fuckers try and cheat us out of any money. I don't trust anyone."

"I don't either," Jigger said.

"Same here," Crow added.

"None of us trust anyone outside the brotherhood," Aztec said.

"And sometimes you get fucked over by a brother." Eagle pulled out a chair and sat down. "Look at what Skeet did to the Insurgents. They shoulda killed the asshole."

"At least they took care of Tigger," Chains said. "A member betraying the brotherhood is like a stab in the back in the worst possible way. That's something you never forget."

"Or forgive," Eagle added.

The members nodded, and Chains pushed his chair back and stood up.

"I'm gonna take Thor for a walk," he said to the brothers.

Upon hearing the word *walk*, Thor jumped up and began barking, his tail wagging.

"Let's go, buddy." He gave a chin lift to the guys and left the room.

As Thor sniffed every patch of grass, Chains took out his phone and sent a quick text to Autumn, not expecting to hear back from her until she was done at work. A wide grin spread across his face when the phone beeped.

Autumn: *Hi. I was just thinking of u.*

His grin grew larger.

Chains: *How r u?*

Autumn: *Hanging in there. Busy as hell at work. That helps.*

Chains: *U wanna join me for dinner?*

Autumn: *Sure.*

"Fuck yeah," he said aloud. For the past week, Chains had asked her a couple of times to go out to dinner, but she'd always had an excuse. One time he'd ordered a pizza and brought it over while they watched a chick flick. After he'd left, it had taken an hour of late-night riding in the cold air to get his dick to calm down. Yeah … he had it bad for her.

Autumn: *How about Leroy's? Craving chocolate cream pie. :)*

Chains: *Thinking Chianti's. Lasagna's great. We can get pie at Leroy's after.*

Autumn: *I've never been, but Italian sounds good.*

Chains: *Does 7 work?*

Autumn: *I'll meet u there.*

His impulse was to tell her that he'd pick her up—he was the man and that's what he did, but this wasn't a date—he didn't go out with citizen women. They were only two people getting together for dinner, and he was helping her through a tough time because he felt bad about what his dick brother had done to her.

Chains: *K. Later.*

He slipped the phone into his back pocket then traipsed after Thor. Chains was looking forward to that night. Since he'd told her that Bret had called off the wedding, he had gotten to know Autumn better as a person and was able to look past her sexy curves. That didn't mean Chains still wouldn't check her out or fantasize about her riding his cock—after all, he was a red-blooded man, but he genuinely thought of her as a woman *and* a friend. Never did he imagine he'd be able to have a platonic relationship with a chick, especially one as pretty and hot as Autumn. It just went to show that life was full of surprises.

When it came down to it, Chains was pretty damn cocky about the control he exercised whenever he was around her. After the divorce from Krystal, he'd made a vow to never get involved with another citizen, and he was keeping to that promise. Once Autumn got through all the shit his brother had caused, she and Chains would go their separate ways. Very civilized and modern—that's what he'd say about their relationship.

Thor stood by a patch of brown grass, sniffing, and when Chains snapped his fingers, the dog raised his head and looked at him.

"Time to go, buddy," Chains said.

Thor's ears pricked up and he barked a few times before dashing in the direction of the clubhouse.

CHIANTI'S WAS A family-owned restaurant that had charm and a homey feel to it. Boasting a bar that could rival any big-city restaurant, customers gladly waited for their tables around the hand-carved cherry wood counter, sipping liqueurs and brandies from around the world.

Watercolors of windswept shores of Capri and enchanted evenings in Rome covered the eatery's brick walls.

"It smells awesome in here," Autumn said as they squeezed into a spot at the bar. She cocked her head and smiled at Chains. "Good selection."

Her eyes sparkled and her smile warmed him. The urge to kiss her deep and hard irked him. Autumn was melting the ice wall he'd put around his heart, and he didn't like that.

"Wait 'til you taste the food. It's the best in the county. What do you wanna drink?"

"I'll have a white wine spritzer."

A guy with curly hair and glasses pushed his way to the bar, a credit card dangling from his fingers. Autumn scooted toward Chains, filling the small space between them.

"It's so crowded," she said.

He could feel her breath on his cheek. "It's always like that here."

As more people came up to the bar to place their orders, Autumn stood right next to him, her arm pressed against his. She was so close that he could smell the honey-almond scent of her hair and feel the heat of her body.

"What're you drinking?" the ruddy-faced bartender asked as he slapped two cocktail napkins down on the counter.

"White wine spritzer and a double Jack," Chains said.

The man nodded before rushing away.

"I'm glad I decided to meet you for dinner," Autumn said, those mesmerizing eyes gazing up at him.

Chains shifted a bit, so instead of their arms touching, her rounded tits pressed against his chest. *Yeah … that's a lot better.* His dick stirred. "Me too. It's good to get away from your thoughts once in a while."

"You do that when you ride."

"Yeah." He held her gaze—there was no way he could turn away—until the bartender put their drinks down on the small napkins.

"That'll be fifteen dollars," the man said before taking an order from another patron.

Autumn laughed. "We're packed in here like sardines. I can't get my purse open."

Chains laid a twenty on the bar. "When you're with me, you don't need to open your purse for anything. I got it."

"I owe you one."

He shook his head. "You don't owe me anything."

"Okay … thank you. And for your information, at some point, a woman *always* has to open her purse. I may want to freshen up my lipstick."

His gaze slid down to her mouth. "Your lips look good to me."

"Really?" The tip of her tongue skimmed over the top.

"Fuck, woman." Chains pushed against her, and she jerked her head back and tried to take a step, which proved to be fruitless as a tall blonde stood plastered against her.

Autumn gripped the stem of the wineglass and brought it to those full lips. She looked at everything but *him*.

Chains was hard as fuck. He couldn't help it. She captivated him like no other woman ever had. He pushed back a bit and ignored the irritated mumbling of the person behind him. He picked up his drink and took a gulp, then watched some men at the bar hovered over girls in tight skirts and dresses, talking and slipping their arms around the women's shoulders.

From his peripheral vision, Chains saw Autumn stealing sidelong glances at him. He cut his gaze to her and smiled inwardly when streaks of red darkened her cheeks.

"You hot?" he asked.

"What?"

"I'm asking if you're hot 'cause your face is red." He enjoyed the way she brought the empty wineglass to her mouth and a took a sip of nothing. Autumn was nervous as hell around him, and that was a good thing. He figured if she wasn't interested in him, she wouldn't be fidgeting and ripping up the cocktail napkin and acting like she wanted to jump out of her skin.

"Oh ... that." Autumn's hand flew to her face and pressed against her cheek. "It's so crowded in here that I feel like I can't breathe."

Chains threw back the rest of the whiskey. "You wanna wait outside?"

"Maybe that would—"

Suddenly she fell against him, and without thinking, he wrapped his arm around her waist and pulled her closer. She felt perfect in his arms, all soft and warm and damn sexy.

Autumn gripped his shoulders. "Someone fell into me."

"Yeah."

That sweet tongue licked those tempting lips before she looked up into his eyes.

The din of voices, clinking glasses, and music faded away as Chains stared at the full mouth just begging to be kissed. Pressing his thumb underneath Autumn's chin, he gently tilted her face upward. As he lowered his head, she leaned in and stretched up to meet him.

Then someone crashed into them while drinks spilled and glasses shattered. Groups of people stumbled away from the bar and a swarthy, stocky man slammed down onto the shiny hardwood floor.

Chains wrapped both arms around Autumn in a protective hold and led her away from the fight. In a few seconds, two tall, beefy men started yelling, and one of them picked up the man from the floor like he was a feather and dragged him to the front door. The other bouncer grabbed the back of the neck of a thin man in his early twenties and pushed him toward the lobby.

"What was that all about?" Autumn asked as she pulled out of Chains's arms.

He tipped his head to a stacked blonde in a tight leather dress with a plunging neckline. "She's the prey the two dudes were fighting over."

Autumn looked over. "Fighting is so juvenile, but I can see it. Do you think she's pretty?"

Chains shrugged. "She's all right, but you got her beat in the looks and curves department."

She shook her head. "Have you always just said whatever's on your mind?"

"Yeah—that's the way I roll. There's no reason to bullshit."

The slender brunette hostess approached them with two menus and an amicable smile.

"Your table's ready. Did you have a tab at the bar?"

"No," he replied.

Chains stepped back and let Autumn go in front of him as they followed the woman to their table.

"Your server will be here shortly. Enjoy your dinner." The hostess turned and walked away.

For the first ten minutes Autumn seemed to be uncomfortable, and Chains suspected it was because they'd almost kissed. If it wasn't for that damn fight he would've tasted her, and he was pretty sure it would've been sweet.

"It wasn't too bad of a wait," he said, breaking the silence between them.

Autumn nodded. "Not bad." She looked down at the menu, running her finger along the edge. Chains watched her as she pored over the selections, front teeth biting into a glossy lower lip.

She looked up. "What?"

"Nothing," he answered.

"Why are you watching me?" Autumn glanced back down at the menu.

"Am I making you nervous?"

"Do you already know what you're going to order?"

"Lasagna and a salad. You didn't answer my question."

She put the menu down and folded her hands on top of it. "Look, this thing we have going on between us is not real. I mean, I'm vulnerable right now, and you're a player. You can't help chasing whatever new woman makes a blip on your radar. Whenever another woman piques your interest, you'll switch gears and start laying on the charm with her."

"Are you done?" he asked, slightly amused. "I get that you're vulnerable right now, but this attraction between us started before my jerk brother broke off the engagement."

"Maybe …" her voice trailed off as she took a sip of water.

"And I'm not a player."

"Aren't you?"

The smug look on her face made her more beautiful and desirable. He wanted to lean over and grab a handful of Autumn's hair, then yank her closer and kiss her, but instead, he sat back and shook his head no.

"I'm sure women throw themselves at you."

"Throwing and taking are two different things. Are women attracted to bikers? Hell, yeah. Do they want to spread for a guy in leather who rides a Harley? Damn straight. Do I fuck every chick that wants it? No way."

"You're a very confident man with a bit of cockiness thrown in."

"And that means I fuck every chick who's into me? You're too smart to think that, Doc."

A ghost of a smile whispered across her lips. "I didn't mean that. I guess I've been taken in by the stereotype of the 'bad boy biker.'"

"I'm a lot of things, baby, but a stereotype isn't one of 'em."

"I didn't mean to offend you."

"No offense taken. Anyway, I'm not looking to hook up with a citizen, so don't sweat it."

"Why not?—I mean the citizen part."

"Been there, done that." He picked up the tumbler the server had just put down and took a swig.

"Then, who do you date?" she asked.

"I don't date, but I hook up with"—he paused, then looked at her over the rim of the tumbler—"biker chicks."

"What does *that* mean?"

He downed the whiskey. "Women in the biker scene."

"Where do you meet them?"

"Parties, clubhouses, bike rallies, motorcycle shows—they're part of the lifestyle, and they embrace it. Do you know what you wanna eat?"

"Does that mean this conversation is over?" She smiled, then picked up the wineglass.

"There's nothing more to talk about on that topic. We now understand each other a bit better."

"I guess." Autumn pressed the glass to her mouth and took a drink, all the while her gaze fused with his.

There was something intimate about watching the way her tongue licked her lips before she set down the wineglass that made Chains want to pursue her. The chase would be exhilarating and something new for him, and there was no doubt that he'd catch her in the end.

"You seem like you're a million miles away. What're you thinking about?"

"That I'm enjoying being with you. I spend so much time at the clubhouse and with the brothers that it's nice to have dinner with a pretty and smart woman. It's a change of pace for me."

"I'm having a nice time too," she whispered.

"Are you ready to order?" the waiter asked.

Chains glanced over at Autumn and gestured for her to go first.

"I'll have the gnocchi with pancetta and pumpkin cream sauce."

"An excellent selection," the server said as he jotted down the order on a pad. "Minestrone soup or salad?"

"Salad with balsamic vinaigrette." She handed the menu to him.

"And for you, sir?" the waiter asked as he glanced at Chains.

"Lasagna. Salad with ranch."

"Very good." The server took Chains's menu. "I'll be back with more bread and water. Would either of you care for another drink?"

"I'm good, thank you," Autumn replied.

Chains picked up the tumbler. "Another Jack, and bring me an Alpine Glacier Lager."

The waiter nodded, then walked toward the kitchen.

"Is that a local beer?" Autumn asked.

"Yep. It's one of my favorites."

"Besides whiskey." Her lips held a hint of a sly smile. The light from the candles reflected in her eyes, making them shimmer.

Chains let his gaze slowly slide over her: he loved the way her skin glowed and how the auburn locks looked like fire-spun threads. *Yeah ... she's gorgeous.*

"Actually tequila's my vice. It's my go-to, but salt and lime have to be part of the equation. What do you like besides wine?"

"Margaritas are good. I'm not a big drinker, so I'm a lightweight if I have strong drinks like martinis or"—she pointed at the empty tumbler—"straight whiskey ... Really, straight *anything*." She laughed. "I guess I did more studying than partying in college."

"That's cool. I know my limit, and for the most part, I stay within it. Being sloppy drunk is never attractive, but it happens."

Autumn leaned forward. "I want to let you in on a secret, but you can *never* tell your mom, okay?" Intrigued, Chains nodded. "A while back, your mom threw me a kitchen shower. That alone is ridiculous because I don't cook. Anyway, I was so nervous about the shower and the whole wedding thing that I got totally smashed with my friends the night before. The next morning, I was so damn hungover that all I could manage to do was smile and say thank you for a bunch of gifts I was never going to use."

Chains laughed. *Damn, I like this woman.* Autumn wasn't a poser. She didn't say shit to make him like her or think she was cool. So many women molded themselves to be what they thought he wanted, including his ex-wife. *If Krystal had been herself, I'm sure I wouldn't have hitched up with her. Her true colors came out after I slipped the damn ring on her finger.*

"I'm pretty sure your mom would be disappointed if she knew I was so hungover at the shower."

He winked. "Your secret's safe."

"I was starting to have doubts about marrying Bret. Deep down I knew he wasn't the one, even though I kept convincing myself he was. My friends also would tell me that I was just having pre-wedding jitters."

"Salad with balsamic vinaigrette," the waiter said, placing the dish in front of Autumn as she leaned back in the chair. Then, he put Chains's salad down and sprinkled some cracked pepper on the dishes before scurrying away.

"Going with your gut is always the best. I learned that a long time ago." Chains buttered a slice of bread, then picked up a fork and dug into the salad.

"I agree with you, but a lot of times our rational mind talks us out of listening to our instinct. Does your mother know about the broken engagement? She hasn't called me." Autumn popped a cherry tomato into her mouth.

Chains shrugged. "I don't talk to her that much."

"She hasn't called you about it?"

"No, but she never would. I'm not involved with the family. The first time I found out that Bret was getting hitched was when my mom called and told me to come to the brunch."

"I'm surprised you came since you're so removed from all of them."

"I did it for my mom. She rarely calls and asks me to do shit with them. I was gonna back out, but I knew she'd be hurt, so I went."

"You're a good son," she said, a smile in her voice.

"Not really, but then, my mom wasn't the best mother in the world."

Autumn put her fork down and stared at him. "Are you serious? Your mom's like June Cleaver and Carol Brady rolled together."

He busted out laughing. "That's why my childhood sucked."

She reached over and lightly smacked his hand. "I'm serious. Your mom is a whiz in the kitchen, she's a great housekeeper, she dotes on Bret to the point where it's annoying, and she adores your dad."

"And she favors my sisters, never stood up one fuckin' time for me when it came to my dad, and all her housekeeping drove me nuts."

"I can see your point about the housekeeping. The few times she came over to my place, I saw her do the dust test—swiping a finger over the bookcase shelves and the buffet. I never found out if I passed or not." She giggled.

"Bret would've told you if you hadn't," he said wryly.

"You're right about that. Did you guys ever go out to eat when you were growing up? Going out to dinner, takeout, and ordering pizza were pretty much the staples in my house when I was young. Actually, my parents still do it."

"We rarely went out unless it was over to a relative's house." He shook his head and pushed away the empty salad plate. "When I was at home, I couldn't wait to get the hell outta there. I just didn't belong—that's all."

"Who has the lasagna?" a teenage busser asked as he lowered a round tray.

"Right here," Chains said.

The teen put down the plate, then he placed the gnocchi in front of Autumn, cleared the empty plates and glasses on the table, and sauntered away.

"This is *so* good," Autumn said as she put another forkful of food into her mouth.

"Glad you like it. I've never had a bad meal here." Chains cut into the lasagna. "Did you always want to be a vet?"

She dabbed the corners of her mouth while nodding. "Yeah. When I was eight years old, I found an injured bird in the backyard and put it in a cardboard shoebox; then, I read everything I could about how to care for the bird and nursed it back to health. Eventually, the bird was strong enough to fly away. After that, I was hooked."

"You're real good with animals. Thor took to you real fast, and he's not too good with people he doesn't know. You saved his life—I'll never forget that."

"Thor's a great dog. I'll admit that I loved seeing the way the two of you interacted with each other." She took another bite, then suddenly her face grew taut and her hand flew to her chest.

"What's wrong?" Chains asked.

Autumn didn't say a word, but her gaze was fixed on something behind him. He looked over his shoulder and scanned the room, and then he saw Bret sitting at a table near the kitchen with a woman. Chains turned back around.

"Don't let it bother you that the fucker's here." He reached out and put his hand on top of hers and squeezed it lightly.

"He's with his ex-girlfriend—Teresa. I wonder if he'd been cheating on me this whole time. Maybe *she's* the reason he broke it off with me. What an asshole."

"Are you okay being in the same room as the jerk?"

Nodding, Autumn's lips pressed together to form a straight line.

"All right, but if you wanna leave, just give me the word. We're still going to Leroy's for pie, even if it's take out."

Another nod, but this time, it was more relaxed.

Chains motioned to the waiter, who rushed over. "Another glass of red wine and another one of these," he said, pointing to the empty beer bottle.

"I'm good," Autumn said.

"You look like you need one," he replied.

She let out an audible sigh. "Just one—that's all."

"I'll be right back with your drinks," the waiter said.

As they finished their dinners and sipped their cocktails, Autumn seemed to have forgotten about the bastard being in the restaurant. Even though Chains acted nonchalant about Bret's presence, inside he was seething. He wanted nothing more than to drag the whiny fucker out of the eatery and into the alley for a well-deserved beatdown. Chains was pretty sure Autumn's heart was breaking, and he hated Bret for being the cause of it.

While he was taking out his money clip to pay the bill, he heard the familiar voice.

"Autumn—I thought that was you," Bret said. "How are you?"

Chains glanced up and glared at him. The woman Bret was with clung to him like a fucking leech. The smug expression on Bret's face told him that his stupid brother loved that Autumn saw him with another woman. Without thinking, Chains reached over and grabbed Autumn's hand, tucking it into his. Bret's gaze darted from Autumn to Chains, then back to Autumn.

"You two look like you're having a good time," he said between clenched teeth.

"We are." Chains's jaw tightened.

Bret's gaze cut to his. "I was talking to Autumn."

"You need to be talking to me 'cause we got something to settle."

Autumn squeezed his hand as if to calm him down, but Chains was chomping at the bit to deck his brother right then and there.

Bret stepped back from the table. "How's business at the clinic, *Autumn*?"

Chains felt her stiffen, and before she said anything, he leaned forward and spoke, "Stop with the stupid questions. There's no reason for you to be standing here, so move your ass and get the fuck away, or I'll make sure you do."

Bret whispered something into the brunette's ear, and without another word, he pulled her behind him as they left the restaurant.

You always were a fuckin' pussy. When they were young, Bret always ended up running to Daddy whenever Chains whooped his ass, even though most of the time his brother had started the fight. Of course, Chains was the one who always got punished—because in the eyes of their father, Bret could do no wrong, and Chains couldn't do anything right.

"Thanks for that," Autumn said as she pulled her hand out of his. "The only reason that asshole came over to the table was to flaunt that bitch. Did you see the way she looked at me—like she won. Won what? A selfish bastard? She can gladly have him." Autumn's voice hitched.

"My brother never had any class. And the chick he was with can't hold a candle to you."

"Thanks. He said he'd loved me, and he does *this*? Bret acts like I did something horrible to him. I don't get it. I still don't know why he broke up with me."

"'Cause he's a fuckin' moron."

A small chortle escaped through her lips. "I don't mean to be a downer, but can I take a raincheck on that slice of chocolate cream pie?"

"Sure. Do you wanna go home?"

"If you're ready. All of a sudden, I'm exhausted."

Chains stood up. "Let's go."

Every star stood out sharply in the clear, cold air. An icy wind brushed across Chains's face as he walked Autumn to her car. The sound of their footfalls echoed slightly off the gravel lot for a few seconds.

"Here I am," Autumn said as she opened the door to the car.

"I'll follow you home, and this isn't open for discussion."

She reached out and put a hand to his cheek and caressed it. "I wasn't going to argue about it. You're such a sweet man, even though you pretend not to be. I saw that gentleness inside you with Thor, and now with me. I appreciate all you've done for me."

"Autumn, fuck," he said in a low voice before grasping her hand and bringing it to his mouth.

She immediately snatched it away. "I better be going."

"Whatever," he mumbled. "Let me trail behind you on my bike."

He stalked away, wondering why the hell he kept fucking up with her. *Maybe it's because she keeps giving me mixed signals. Dammit!* Chains blew a breath he didn't realize he'd been holding and took out the keys to his Harley.

When he arrived at her house, he stayed on the driveway and watched her get out of the car.

"Do you want to come in for a while? I can make some coffee—I actually know how to do that." A small laugh bounced off the garage's concrete walls.

"I should head back. I want to take Thor out for a walk."

She tilted her chin down and frowned. "Okay then. Goodnight."

"Night. Make sure to lock up."

"I always do. I've been living alone for years." Annoyance laced her voice.

Chains almost weakened and took her up on the offer, but he didn't want to look like an ass when she shot him down. He'd already made a fool out of himself over a woman a long time ago, and he may be a lot of things, but getting duped more than once wasn't one of them. There were plenty of women out there, those who wanted nothing more than a few hours or nights of pleasure. They were the ones who were safe and uncomplicated, and Autumn was anything but that. Yeah, he'd stick to the club girls. From what Eagle had told him, another sweet piece was interviewing to join the ranks, and he may just be interested enough to try her out for a month or two.

"Thanks for dinner. I had a nice time." Autumn's soft voice sliced through his thoughts.

"Me too. I'll call you about that raincheck," Chains said as he backed out of the driveway. He waited until she closed the garage door before taking off.

The darkness engulfed him as he headed to the clubhouse via the back roads. Along the way, he saw shadowy clumps of cacti and sagebrush, small hillocks, and large rock formations.

The evening flashed through his mind and he had to admit that he'd had a real good time. He couldn't remember the last time he'd enjoyed an evening with a woman, and they hadn't even hooked up. Chains accelerated and embraced the icy wind as it stung his face and whipped around him.

He didn't need a citizen, especially Autumn, who was reeling from the breakup with his brother. Seeing Bret hadn't seemed to push her over the edge, which was a good sign—it meant the healing had begun.

So it was time for him to back the fuck away—as far away as possible.

Chapter Fourteen

AUTUMN BALANCED A cup of caffè mocha and a slice of chocolate chip pumpkin bread in her hands and weaved through the stream of customers until she reached the table in the corner. Just as she plopped down onto the paisley blue-and-green cushion of the wooden chair, she heard Sadie call out her name. Looking up, she waved her friend over, then pushed aside her purse and the basket of creamers to make room at the small table for two.

"It's freezing outside," Sadie said, setting her oversized handbag on a chair. "Sorry, I'm late—work has been crazy all week." Then, she checked out Autumn's coffee and sweet bread. "What did you get?"

"The usual. I'm so predictable." Autumn rolled her eyes.

"How's the pumpkin bread?" Sadie shrugged off her down coat.

"Delicious and decadent as always." Autumn broke off a piece and popped it in her mouth.

"Looks good, but I'll probably go with my usual—a double chocolate brownie. I'll be right back."

As Autumn waited for her friend to return, she glanced out the window and saw a motorcycle parked across the street. Her pulse raced as it had a tendency to do whenever she heard or saw a bike. Before she'd met Chains, Autumn hardly noticed motorcycles unless they were loud or cut in front of her in traffic.

Of course her thoughts were filled with Chains—that, too, had become a habit. What the hell was she going to do about him? As much as she rationalized the disaster her life would become if she pursued anything with him, her body and gut told her to throw caution to the wind. And what type of relationship would they have? *Friends with benefits? I could never do that. And I'd probably be one of many he'd share his bed with. Damn, why can't I find a normal guy? I thought I did. Bret seemed normal at first.* But her gut twisted with that thought. Remembering the multitude of times that Bret had canceled their dates due to work or to hang out with his buddies came back with a startling clarity. *And what about that time when he took me out for a romantic dinner for my birthday and all he did was look at his fucking phone.* No, the truth was that Autumn had ignored the signs until she didn't, and she'd dealt with the troubling aspects of their relationship, sometimes gracefully, often haltingly. Soon afterward, Bret had broken it off, and relief had been the lingering feeling from the fallout.

And there was Chains: rugged, sweet, brooding, and sexier than any man had the right to be. *I'm just on the rebound. That's it. But he's so damn nice. Why does he have to be so nice and dangerous at the same time?*

The roar of an engine followed by the slight rattle of the windows cut through her musings, and Autumn watched the man on the black Harley. He was decked out in black leather and denim, and by the way he pushed into traffic, she figured he was a Night Rebel—an outlaw … *just like Chains.*

"Those guys purposely rev their engines," Sadie said as she put her cup of coffee piled high with whipped cream, along with a decadent-looking brownie down on the table.

"It's their way of saying, 'Fuck you' to the citizen world," Autumn replied, her gaze fixed on the disappearing rider.

Sadie laughed. "Where the hell did *that* come from? Have you been watching those documentaries on the History channel about the biker gangs?"

Autumn shifted her attention to Sadie. "I didn't even know they had documentaries on outlaw clubs."

"They do, but they're pretty one-sided—I mean, the cops always come out as the super good guys and none of the bikers has one redeeming quality. So, what's new with you?" Sadie scooped up some of the whipped cream with her finger.

"I bumped into Bret last night and he was with his ex-girlfriend." Autumn smiled as the memory of Chains putting his brother in his place on her behalf flitted through her mind.

"What a bastard! Why aren't you pissed as hell?"

Autumn shrugged. "I guess I'm dealing with it all pretty well."

"Do you think he was cheating on you?"

Autumn shook her head. "No. I think he ran to her because Bret can't be without female attention."

"So he runs to this skank? I remember how obnoxious her mother was at the bridal shower. I hope you smashed that stupid cup and saucer she gave you as a gift. Believe me, you're so much better off without him in your life."

"I think so too," she said.

Sadie chewed on a piece of brownie. "This is so good—it's worth every calorie, every gram of carbs and sugar in it."

Autumn laughed, then took a sip of her coffee.

"Where did you bump into him? God, I still can't believe what a schmuck Bret is. I mean, who the fuck asks his brother to break up for him? I still can't wrap my head around *that* one."

"I was at Chianti's"—she put her elbows on the table and rested her chin in her hands—"with Bret's brother." Autumn groaned.

Sadie's eyes sparkled. "This is getting good. What were you doing with his brother?"

"Having dinner," she replied weakly.

"Duh ... but *why* were you having dinner with his brother?"

"Because I'm stupid and on the rebound and so fucking mixed up about all this." Autumn stifled a smile as she sat back in the chair.

Sadie giggled while pointing at her. "You've got the hots for Bret's brother. I fucking *love* it! How long has *this* been going on?"

"Since I met him at the clinic. I ignored it because I was still with Bret, but I felt some kind of connection with Chains right off the bat."

"*Chains*? That's his name?"

Autumn looked down at her half-eaten pumpkin bread. "That's his nickname. His real name's Chet, but he goes by Chains. The name suits him much better."

"Uh … it's kind of strange, but the whole family's a little odd, right? I mean Bret's mom is like some Nazi homemaker, the sisters are like replicas of mommy except they wear better clothes, and the dad has 'mass murderer' written all over his face with all the suppressed anger he's got going on."

Autumn laughed. "You are *so* bad, but I love it. No matter what's going on in my life, you always bring humor to it."

"I just say it as I see it. So tell me more about *Chains*." She giggled. "It sounds so funny."

"He's in a motorcycle club—a scary one."

Sadie's eyes widened. "It has to be the Night Rebels, and that just fits into my description of the family."

Autumn nodded. "The Night Rebels. Fuck … He's the guy my parents warned me about when I was growing up."

"And that makes him even more exciting. I'm guessing he's gorgeous and sexy as sin."

"Totally, but he's sweet too. He loves his dog—"

"So we know he's not serial killer material since he likes animals," Sadie cut in with a chuckle.

Autumn smiled. "And he's been super supportive during this whole breakup. He's so pissed at Bret for doing this to me"—she held up her hand—"*and* he went to the engagement brunch because his mother asked him to. I think that's commendable, especially since he doesn't get along with his dad or Bret."

Sadie's forehead crinkled and she cocked her head. "Was he the tall guy in tight black jeans who didn't have an ounce of fat on his muscular body? The one with a hint of a beard?"

"That's Chains."

"He's hot. I noticed him, but he didn't stay very long. Why the hell are you even debating this?"

"That's the problem—he's hot. No problem getting a woman, you know?"

"Bret was a major flirt. Is he like that?"

Autumn thought for a minute. "I don't think so. He's never looked at any women when we've been out. The hostess at Chianti's was very pretty with a cute shape, and he didn't give her a second look. Bret would've been all over her."

"In that case, the only way you're going to get to know him better is to go out with him. Just because a guy's good-looking doesn't mean he's going to cheat. Mitch is handsome, and I don't doubt him for a minute."

"But Chains is a biker—I think that makes it different. Women are always throwing themselves at those guys."

Sadie shook her head. "Look at some of the rockers or actors who've been in long-term marriages. A lifestyle choice doesn't change who the person is inside."

"That's true. But how can I date my ex-fiancé's *brother*? That's too weird, isn't it?"

"I'll admit it'll be awkward at family functions."

"Chains isn't really involved with his family. I was with Bret for over a year, and I never even met him until the brunch."

"Then you don't have a problem. I say go for it. What's the worst that can happen—you have great sex and awesome memories?"

"Or that I fall hard for him and suffer one of the worst heartbreaks of my life."

"Could you keep it casual, like an arm's distance thing and not get too emotionally involved?"

"Not with him," Autumn whispered. "There's something exciting and dangerous about Chains on a deep level. It's much more than how hot he is. Dating him would be putting my heart at stake, and I don't know if I can take that risk."

"If you don't, then you'll always wonder what could have been. I've know you for several years, and I've never seen you this into a guy during all that time, and that includes Bret. I'm just saying, you should listen to your inner voice—your gut, and stop over analyzing it. Sometimes taking a risk is what brings ultimate love and happiness." Sadie picked up the last piece of her brownie and brought it to her lips. "I'm just saying," she said again before popping the bite into her mouth.

"I hear you … I just don't know." Autumn glanced at her phone. "Crap, I have to get back. I have a full afternoon." She drank the last of her coffee, then gathered up her things. "Let's have dinner sometime next week."

"Sounds great. I'll walk out with you—I have to get back to the office."

The two friends parted ways after setting a dinner date for the following week. Autumn rushed to her car, and within minutes she was pulling up in front of the clinic.

The afternoon was so busy that it didn't give her a chance to think about Chains, Bret, or anything except giving the best care to her furry patients.

By the time Autumn finished checking on them in the recovery room, she was exhausted and grateful that Marian was the vet on call for the night. She said goodnight to Rodney and Lauren, then traipsed across the parking lot to her car.

Frost covered the windshield and she cursed under her breath as she scraped it away, making a mental note to keep a pair of gloves in the car. It was a cold night, and the chill reached into her bones. She couldn't wait to get home and curl up on the couch and enjoy the steady warmth of the fire. Autumn loved watching the flames—they were hypnotizing. It wiped out all thoughts and was a type of meditation for her.

The sky was a matte black canvas with little to no stars painted on it. The smell and feel of snow was in the air, and frost had also covered the bare branches of the trees, making them look like waving alabaster arms.

Autumn pushed the remote for the garage opener and pulled in. She switched off the ignition, jerked the door open, and slid out of the car. With one hand on the roof, she opened the backseat door and pulled out a large tote and her purse. Shoving both straps on one delicate shoulder,

Autumn closed the door with her hip, the sound echoing through the garage. An empty water bottle fell from the tote to the ground and she picked it up. Just as she straightened up, someone grabbed her around the waist from behind.

Autumn screamed out, but a hand clamped around her mouth. She struggled, then lifted one leg and kicked back hard.

"Fuck, Autumn!" Bret cried out. "I just want to talk to you."

She yanked out of his hold and spun around. "What the hell's wrong with you? Why did you grab me like that?"

"I should be the one asking the questions," he growled as he bent down and rubbed where she'd kicked him.

"Get out of here. I've had a long, hard day, and I don't want to deal with you."

"I said I want to talk to you."

"You should've done that before you broke off our engagement. You're not part of my life anymore, and I don't have to put up with you." With one hand on the car, she walked backward.

"I just have one question—were you fucking my brother when we were together?"

White anger shot through her, and she stopped in her tracks. "I told you to get out!"

"I'll take that as a yes. What kind of a slut are you? Whoring around with Chet and acting like the perfect woman with me. You disgust me."

"And you're nothing but a whiny, selfish coward. You weren't even man enough to breakup with me face to face. I'm actually surprised you didn't send your mommy to do it. And even though I don't owe you anything, I wasn't sleeping with your brother."

"Lying bitch! I sensed something was off with you, but I never imagined you were betraying me with my brother. No wonder you didn't want to help me out and support my business venture. How do you think I could ever be married to a woman who didn't support me and who cheated on me?"

"I never cheated on you. And you're telling me you broke up because

I didn't hand over fifteen thousand dollars to you? Do you hear how ludicrous that sounds? I offered to help you set up an account to raise the money, but you didn't want to hear of it."

"If you loved me you would've wanted to work for our future, but you were just playing me."

"And if you loved *me* you would've talked to me about the problems we were having like a normal person. Chains is the one who came over and told me about the breakup. He's been the one to support me. Where the hell have you been? Not even a fucking phone call after all the time we were together? You're like a little boy. Your brother is more of a man than you'll ever hope to be in fifty lifetimes."

Bret's face contorted and turned red. He rushed up to her, his shoulder rolling back. "You fucking bitch!" He punched her in the face with his fist.

At first she was stunned, even as her head lulled and everything went from black to white. When the white receded, the side of her face exploded in pain. As soon as he delivered the second blow she tasted blood, and rage engulfed her. Without thinking, Autumn swung back, clipping him in the throat. Satisfaction rushed through her when she heard him cry out, and she wildly grabbed the nearest thing on the shelf beside her—an empty paint can.

"Fucking slut!" Bret reached out and pulled her hair.

The pain seared through her scalp, but Autumn ignored it, and when he came in closer for another blow, she clobbered him as hard as she could with the empty can and sprinted to the door leading into the house.

Momentarily stunned, Bret cried out, "Get back here. I've got shit to settle with you!"

Autumn pushed the door open, then slammed it and hurriedly bolted it. For extra measure, she dragged one of the kitchen chairs over and secured the back of it under the doorknob. With a pounding heart, Autumn pressed her ear against the door.

Nothing.

A small breath of relief escaped through her bloodied lips.

Cinder stood next to her, the cat's copper eyes glued to the door and tail thumping against the floor.

"It's okay, honey," Autumn whispered. "He's gone now."

Bang!

"Shit!" Autumn's hand flew to her chest as she jumped back.

"Open this fucking door or I'm going to break it down!"

"I'm calling 9-1-1."

"I don't give a fuck," he said, pounding on the door again.

"I already called Chains. He's on his way over." Faster than a speeding bullet, she fished out her phone from the tote.

"Fucking bitch! I never should've touched you!"

Autumn heard crashing and commotion in the garage, and she suspected Bret was destroying the place.

Then, it was quiet.

In the distance, the low rumble of an engine penetrated the silence.

She stood by the door and waited for a long time, then sank to the ground and sobbed. Cinder rushed over to Autumn and nuzzled against her. She grabbed the cat and held her close.

After what seemed like hours, Autumn pushed up from the floor and walked around the house, checking all the locks on the windows and doors. Her head pounded and her face was on fire. She trudged up the stairs and went into the bathroom, then gasped when she saw herself in the mirror: a swollen face dotted with angry red marks, a bruising eye, and dried blood at the corner of her mouth.

"I can't believe this." She turned on the faucet and started to clean the blood from her battered face. No man had ever struck her before, and this certainly was the first time Bret had hit her. It was still unbelievable. He'd never exhibited any violent behavior during their relationship. *What the hell happened tonight? He was like a different person.*

After Autumn had taken care of herself and changed into a fleece nightshirt, she curled up on the couch and stared at the fire. Cinder snuggled in her lap after having been fed, and the images of the beating kept flashing through Autumn's mind. *What if he comes back? What if he's watching and sees that the cops or Chains haven't come yet?* A shudder of fear crept up her back. Without thinking, she tapped in Chains's number.

"Hey." His deep voice soothed and caressed her.

"Hi. I'm sorry to bother you—"

"Don't ever apologize for calling me."

She pressed her lips together, then winced as pain shot through her. Debating on whether to tell him about Bret, she simply said, "I've got the jitters tonight."

"You want me to come over?"

"Yes," she whispered.

"I'm on my way—hang tight."

"Thank you."

"I'm always there for you, baby."

Tears trickled down Autumn's cheeks as she put the phone on the coffee table. How could Chains be so selfless and kind, and Bret—so selfish and cruel? *How could they come from the same parents?*

The warm fire made the house toasty and cozy, and knowing Chains was on his way gave her a sense of security. Before Autumn knew it, her eyes had closed and she drifted off to sleep.

THE LOUD ROAR startled her awake and panic seized her with thoughts that Bret had broken down the door and was in the house. Then Autumn recognized the familiar sound of Chains's motorcycle, and she jumped off the couch and rushed to the front part of the house and looked out at the street. Seeing him get off his bike, she flung the door open and rushed down the walkway.

Chains looked up and lifted his chin at her; then, she ran to him and collapsed in his arms. He caught her, and they stood there like that, frozen into a promise: he'd catch her, shield her, no matter what the world threw at them. Autumn buried her face in his chest as tears streamed down her face.

"What is it, darlin'?" he asked, his hand running through her hair.

"I feel so lost and alone," she said between sobs.

"No reason to—I'm here. What's got you spooked?"

"Just hold me," she whispered.

"Okay, but let's go inside. You're shivering real bad."

With his arm wrapped around her, he guided her into the house and gently sat her down on the couch. She kept her head bent, fearful of what he might do to Bret when he found out what had happened.

"Do you want me to get you a drink? How about something warm?"

She shook her head, and he sat down and pulled her into his embrace.

"Why don't you tell me what's going on?"

Autumn nestled into him, inhaling the scent of leather, wind, and soap. Tingles shot through her when she felt his lips press against her head.

"Are you freaked out from seeing Bret last night?"

"No. He came by tonight, and we had an awful fight."

Chains pulled away a bit. "Tell me about it." He placed two fingers under her chin.

At first she resisted when he tried to tip her head back, but then she went with it.

"What the *fuck*?" The look of shock, then anger and, finally, hatred burned in his eyes and frightened her. "Did that fucker do this to you?"

Not able to answer, she nodded. Autumn felt his body stiffen and icy chills danced over her skin.

"Don't do anything impulsive," she croaked out before coughing up a storm.

Chains jumped up and was back in a couple of seconds with a glass of water. She gulped it down, hoping to ease the dry spot in her throat.

"Better?" he asked.

"Yeah. The dry air in the fall and winter seems to settle in my throat." She smiled, hoping that would dissolve the fury in his eyes.

Chains sat back down and turned to her. "Has the asshole ever hit you before?"

"Never," she said. "I don't know what happened. He seemed enraged that you were with me last night. He kept accusing me of having an affair with you behind his back when we were engaged. The whole thing is crazy and unbelievable. I was shocked when he struck me."

Chains ran two fingers over her eyes, cheeks, nose, and jaw. "Nothing's broken. I'm gonna make the sonofabitch pay for what he's done to you."

"Don't … please. I don't want the police involved in this."

"Baby, I have outlaw status. I play by my own rules."

"I'm pretty sure he won't be back or try this again. When he was pounding on my door, I told him I'd called you. It did the trick and he left. I think he's scared of you."

"Yeah, I bet he is," Chains muttered. "When did this happen?"

"Almost two hours ago."

"You gotta ice your face right now. Do you have an ice pack?"

"No." She groaned. "I know all this and can't believe I didn't think of it. I guess I'm still in shock." Autumn started to get up, but he stopped her.

"Stay here—I'll get something for you."

"I have a package of frozen berries in the freezer, and there's a dish towel in the bottom drawer next to the sink."

In less than five minutes, she held the frozen fruit against her face while Chains cradled her in his arms.

"How's your work going? I know you had to finish up for one of your clients," she said.

"Good. I got it done after I left last night. Do you need anything for the pain?"

"I'm good. I have a pretty high threshold." Autumn put a hand on one of his. "I talked about you with my friend Sadie. We met for coffee today." She wanted to steer Chains's thoughts away from Bret so he would cool down.

"And?"

"She remembers you at the brunch. She thought you were totally hot, but I don't think I'm telling you something you haven't heard a ton of times."

He let out a low chuckle. "What did *you* say about me?"

"That I thought you were hot too"—she ran a finger up his arm—"and sexy and sweet."

His arms tightened around her. "Is that all?"

"No," she whispered. "I told Sadie that I feel a pull toward you—something I've never felt with any other man." Autumn held her breath.

"Is that good?" he asked, his voice thick.

She exhaled. "Very."

"The connection thing is real—I feel it too."

Tilting her head back, she looked up at him. "You do?"

The heat in his eyes chased goosebumps up and down her arms and shivers across her back.

"Yeah." His gaze lowered to her mouth.

The bag of berries dropped to the floor as Autumn twisted in his arms and looped hers around his neck, tugging him toward her.

Chains lowered his mouth to hers.

"Autumn," he whispered, the sound of her name on his lips unfurled a desire deep inside her.

She melted into him when he tangled his fingers in her hair and pulled her closer. Autumn trailed her hands around his body, feeling each line, each ripple of his perfect physique. Chains trailed his hands down her neck; then, he ran fingertips over her breasts as she arched into him.

"Oh, Chains," she murmured.

He brushed his lips gently across hers. "I want you so fuckin' bad," he rasped.

"Take me," she whispered, holding him tighter.

Chains softly pressed his mouth to hers, the kiss searing her lips. He raised his head. "Are you feeling okay?" His eyes narrowed. "Your face is pretty swollen."

"I can't kiss you the way I want to, but the rest of my body is just fine. I'll give you a raincheck on the kissing." She smiled.

"That's your second raincheck, baby. Where's your bedroom?"

"Upstairs." *Holy shit! This is really happening.* Nerve endings crackled and arousal surged through her senses. *Wait! What the hell am I doing? Don't overthink this like you always—*

In one fluid movement, Chains stood up and swooped her into his arms, cradling her close. Autumn's pulse was racing, and she clung to his neck as he took her up the stairs, two at a time.

Chapter Fifteen

CHAINS'S LIPS WERE soft and warm as they trailed feathery kisses down her neck. The roughness of his stubble added to the sensations spreading through Autumn like warm melting chocolate.

"You like that, darlin'?" he whispered against her skin as he hovered over her.

"Feels wonderful," she murmured.

"I'm gonna make you feel even better."

She inhaled sharply as he nipped at her earlobe while his fingers pushed up the hem of her nightshirt. Chains's hands skimmed over her skin as he tugged the fleece shirt up over her hips. Autumn sat up and pulled it over her head, then tossed it on the floor. Cool air swept over her body, making her nipples harden.

"Fuck," he rasped. "Your tits are more beautiful than I imagined." One of his thumbs slowly brushed against the stiff buds, and she jumped as a jolt of lust seared through her.

With her hands at his waist, Autumn pushed up his T-shirt and slipped them beneath. Warm skin and taut muscles made her gasp, and she leaned in and pressed her lips against his. Immediately, he held her flush to him, his tongue thrusting deep into her mouth as his fingers roamed down her back and rested right above her butt.

When Chains deepened the kiss, pain shot through Autumn, and she groaned and pulled away.

Resting his forehead against hers, he said, "Fuck, baby. I got carried away. Did I hurt you?"

"I got carried away too. It's just a bit sore."

"When it's not, I'll kiss you the way you deserve it," he said while lightly peppering his lips over her face.

"Take your shirt off," she whispered.

Chains lifted it above his head, and her breath caught as her gaze wandered over his smooth, chiseled chest. She reached out and slowly ran her fingers over defined biceps and steel corded pecs.

"You're gorgeous," she murmured.

"Never had anyone call me that, but I like it coming from you."

His muscles rippled as she stroked every inch of his chest, the ridged abdomen, and lower. In her fantasies, she'd *imagined* what he looked like, but the real thing just blew her away. When she brushed her palm across his hard dick, he pulled away and perched at the edge of the bed. One at a time, Chains pulled off his boots and then his socks.

His smoldering eyes caught and held hers, and heat seared through every part of her body. While he undid the belt and zipped down his jeans, she struggled to breathe as need engulfed her. Chains tugged off his pants and boxers and kicked them aside. Autumn's gaze shifted downward, and a nanosecond of panic zinged through her when her eyes feasted on his dick—large and thick—standing straight out from a patch of trimmed dark hair.

"Fuck," she whispered. She watched in fascination as he straddled her. Without thinking, she reached out and curled her fingers around his shaft; the skin was smooth and soft.

"That's all for you," he whispered in her ear, his warm breath teasing her senses.

A whimper escaped from her throat as hot breath fanned her skin. Autumn's flesh tingled wherever Chains kissed her as desire surged through her body and landed between her thighs. Autumn reached for his dark hair, relishing the short, wavy strands slipping through her fingers. His soft tongue and warm lips quickly found their way down to the hollow between her breasts. Arching her back, moans whispered from her parted lips.

"So pretty and tempting," he said against her skin, his voice roughened by passion.

She took a hissing breath as Chains pulled one beaded nipple into his mouth and covered the other breast with his hand. As he squeezed and kneaded, he sucked, licked, and bit her other nipple all the while rubbing against her. Heat pulsed between her legs and felt so good that she never wanted him to stop.

"I've been wanting to do this for a fuckin' long time," he said before moving his mouth to the other hardened bud.

Autumn locked eyes with his and watched as he kissed the tip, then pulled it hard between his teeth until she gasped at the delicious pain. The intensity of it, the hunger and desire, consumed her as she writhed underneath him.

Chains slid a hand past her ribs, down her belly, and lower to the front of her panties. He cupped her sex, and she groaned as he palmed hard against it.

"Are you wet for me?" he rasped.

"Yeah," she panted.

"That's what I want to hear." Chains scooted down and softly bit and licked his way up her legs to her thighs, then back down as one hand kept pressing against her throbbing sex. His lips skimmed over her hips, then peppered kisses around her navel and quivering belly.

Autumn squirmed and shivered under his touch, and when he looped his fingers on either side of her magenta lace panties, her hips bucked and she cried out.

Chains let out a deep, oh-so sexy chuckle. "You're on fire—I fuckin' love that."

Then he slowly slid them down past her feet and kissed his way up to her thighs, gently spreading her legs. Chains sat back on his knees as his gaze traveled over her nakedness before settling on her wetness.

"So fuckin' perfect." One finger slipped into her slick folds while his thumb grazed over her hardened nub in a teasing circle that made her delirious with want.

"Please," she murmured.

"Please *what*, Autumn?" he asked, his voice raspy as he continued to play with her.

At first, she felt a bit timid; none of the men she'd been with were talkers during sex. But Chains liked to talk dirty, and even though it tantalized her, it made her feel exposed.

"Tell me what you, baby." Leaning forward, he planted kisses across her breasts and throat, then brushed warm lips against hers. "No reason to be shy."

Autumn sucked in a breath, then slowly released it. "I need to come—to feel you inside me."

"See ... that wasn't so hard." Chains bit down on one breast and sucked hungrily. Lifting his head, he caught her eye and winked. "I'm gonna let you come ... in time. And we're gonna fuck real good." Another swipe of lips across hers.

"What you're ... uh ... doing feels so good," she said tentatively.

"That's good," he bent down and placed his mouth right above her sweet spot and sucked gently.

"Fuck!" she cried as her hips bucked off the mattress.

Chains straightened up, his heated gaze fixed on her. "You're fuckin' hot," he said, "and very, very wet."

"I am?" she croaked.

"Oh yeah." He spread her legs wider, then settled in between them. "You're so sexy," he said as his thumb moved over her burning nub. "So soft." He circled it again while he kissed and bit and licked her inner thighs.

"Oh ... Chains," she said, grabbing and then pulling his hair hard.

"There are so many dirty things I want to do to you," he breathed against her soft skin as he ran a finger from her tight slit to the pulsing button.

A shudder of raw passion passed through her at the sound of his hoarse voice and the touch of his hot breath spreading over her skin. Autumn clutched his tatted bicep, loving the way his muscles flexed as his fingers moved over her throbbing clit. Then, with the tip of his thumb, he stroked her with a feather-light touch. A groan escaped her, followed by a gasp as he shoved a finger deep inside.

"Oh, fuck," she panted.

"You like that?" he asked thickly before adding another one.

"Oh yeah," she said, her hips rocking as she rode his hand.

Autumn arched into him, gripping his shoulders hard as the tension mounting in her threatened to explode. With one long swipe Chains ran his tongue from her slick opening to her clit, then forged a wet trail, flicking around her belly button up to the points of her nipples. He removed the two fingers from her heat and slid them into his mouth, licking off her juices. "You taste real good, baby," he said roughly.

He worked his way back down between her legs and rotated one finger around her clit, over and over, while thrusting his tongue inside her and pulling in and out in quick succession.

"Fuck, Chains," she gasped and ran her fingers through strands of his hair before taking a fistful.

As those skilled fingers played with her clit and that wicked tongue plunged in and out, a surge of heat burned through and the tension inside her grew tighter and tighter.

"Come for me now, darlin'." His lips vibrated against her pussy, bringing the delicious sensations within her to a fevered pitch.

Unhinged, she drew in a ragged breath as her muscles clenched around his tongue, and a low groan rumbled from his throat. Chains removed his mouth and inserted a finger inside, then sucked on her sweet spot with purpose. Right away, he started relentlessly pumping and pushing into her deeper until he touched *that* spot. And then her mind went totally blank and a giant flood of sensations rushed through her entire body, engulfing it with an intensity she'd never experienced before. All at once, she dissolved into tears and giggles, unable to control herself. The climax was so profound that it was the most wonderful sensation she'd ever felt. *Holy shit, he's amazing.*

Chains gave her clit an affectionate kiss and lifted his head over her heaving body, wiping his glistening mouth with his hand as he held her gaze.

When her body had finally stopped spasming, Autumn let out a satisfied sigh and reached out and stroked his arms lightly.

"Thank you for *that*."

The corner of his mouth turned up. "It was hot as hell watching you come."

Autumn looked at his hard-on and licked her lips.

"Yeah, I need to fuck you," he whispered, his voice steeped in so much emotion that it surprised her.

"Okay," she rasped.

Chains turned away briefly, fumbling with something on the floor. She noticed the foil packet and looked on as he ripped it open with his teeth, then rolled the condom on faster than she could blink.

Spreading wide, she watched him climb up her body leaving a trail of hot kisses and bites in its wake until burying his mouth in the crook of her neck.

"Every part of you tastes amazing," he said, easing into her a bit at a time. He lifted his head and latched gazes with her. "You doing okay?"

"Yeah … I'm doing great."

"Tell me how you want it."

Confused, she shook her head. "I'm not sure."

"Do you want it nice and slow or rough and fast?" He tilted his head back and hissed out a breath. "Fuck, you feel good," he grunted, finally pushing in all the way.

Autumn closed her eyes as she felt her insides fill with Chains's erection: it was an indescribable feeling—one in which she was afraid of becoming easily addicted. Never having experienced anything but ordinary sex, she opened her lids and whispered, "Rough and fast."

Chains bit each nipple hard, and before she could cry out, he'd pulled out and slammed back into her. The breath *whooshed* out of her and just as she was about to inhale, he pushed back in again. Autumn's heated walls molded around him, craving him more and more with each thrust.

"You're pussy's fuckin' perfect for my cock," he grunted between pants.

Chains's fingers dug into Autumn's hips, and she locked her ankles around his waist and rocked her hips forward, meeting his rhythmic thrusts. He drove deeper with each plunge, and she savored every minute of it, watching the ink on his arms dance while he fucked her fast and rough. Every time Chains slammed in farther, fire surged through her veins, and the coil in her core tightened even more.

"You like that, baby?" he growled, beads of sweat dotting his hairline.

"Yes." She felt taut muscles flex under her fingertips as she ran her hands up his back and gripped firm shoulders.

The room was filled with their grunts, moans, and pants, and as they moved together faster and harder, the headboard banged into the wall from the force of their coupling.

"Chains," she breathed, shuddering.

"Autumn, fuck," he grunted as he kept pounding into her.

When his finger touched her clit, she exploded into a shattering, mind-numbing climax that rocked her entire body. It was like an intense roller coaster ride picking her up into the stratosphere, then dropping her down over and over until her head was spinning. He pulled all the way out, then rammed his cock in so deep that a multitude of colors erupted behind her eyelids. A moment later, he was joining her with a chorus of growls, grunts, and groans as he shuddered his release deep within her.

Chains stayed, panting, the musky scent of sex filling the bedroom. He nuzzled her neck and slowly pulled out, threw the used condom in the waste paper basket next to the nightstand, then lay down on the bed, drawing her to him. Their legs intertwined on top of the crumpled, damp sheets.

"That was fuckin' good, baby," he said while running fingertips up and down her arm.

"It was amazing. I just wished I didn't look like a damn gargoyle."

A deep chuckle from his chest vibrated against her ear. "You're one helluva beautiful gargoyle." He squeezed her tight, then she felt him stiffen. "How's the pain?"

"It's really starting to throb. I'm going to take a pain pill."

"Tell me where they are, and I'll get one for you."

Tilting her head back, she met his eyes. "See … you are sweet, but it'll be our secret. I'll get it, though. I want to freshen up a bit."

Leaning down, he kissed the tip of her nose tenderly. "It better be—I got a reputation to uphold," he replied and winked.

A giggle burst through Autumn's lips, but as she pushed up from the bed, the pain on the side of her face immediately shot needles through her. Gritting her teeth, she shuffled to the bathroom and closed the door.

She looked in the mirror and gasped. "I look awful! I can't go to work like this—makeup won't cover the swelling." Wincing as she touched the bruising around her right eye and cheek, she opened the medicine cabinet and took out a pill.

After cleaning up and splashing cold water on her face several times, she wrapped the robe hanging on the back of the door around her and returned to the bedroom. Autumn smiled when she saw Chains sitting back against the headboard, speaking in a low voice to someone on the phone. She'd expected him to be dressed and ready to leave.

"So we'll roll tomorrow night. Um … let me know what you find out. Later," Chains said. Then he moved the phone from his ear to the nightstand. Looking up at her, he asked, "Are you hungry?"

"A little." Autumn glanced down and saw copper eyes staring at her. "I know Cinder is. Who were you talking to?"

Chains stood up. "One of the brothers. Something we had planned for tonight got rescheduled." He bent down and picked up his clothes. "I'm gonna take a shower, and you figure out what you want to order for dinner. I'm good with anything."

"Okay. Shampoo and soap are on the shower shelves. Let me get you a towel."

Chains leaned against the door jamb, his gaze fixed on her every move. "Thanks," he said, gripping the bath towel. He yanked her to him and crushed her against his chest. "I'm gonna spend the night if that's cool with you."

Warmth spread through her. "I was hoping you would."

Placing his fingers under her chin, he lifted her face to him. "Glad we're on the same page," he said, brushing his fingers across her mouth.

She kissed each one, and sucked the last one between her lips. A low growl rumbled from his throat and he pressed her closer.

"Fuck, Autumn." He ground against her, and placed her hand on his stiff dick. "See what you do to me?" he said huskily.

Cinder meowed, then dashed over and rubbed several times against Autumn's legs until she laughed and tugged out of Chains's arms.

"My cat is calling," she said.

Chains smacked her playfully on the ass. "That's another raincheck, but I'm collecting on that one tonight."

He turned around, and Autumn stood there for a few moments admiring the firmness of his butt and how it flexed when he moved. The bathroom door shut and Cinder bumped her head against Autumn's ankle.

"I'm sorry, sweetie." She bent down and scratched the cat under the chin. "Let's get you some dinner."

An hour later, Autumn snuggled beside Chains as they watched an action movie. Empty takeout cartons and beer cans littered the coffee table. With one fuzzy-socked foot, she moved a cardboard carton out of the way.

"Cinder! Down," she said.

Chains pulled his arm away from her shoulder and pushed up from the couch. "Let me get this cleared up."

Autumn pressed the *Pause* button on the remote. "I'll help."

He shook his head. "Stay right where you are. I got this." He stacked the boxes inside themselves, then scooped up three crushed beer cans and ambled to the kitchen.

Autumn couldn't believe that Chains had been cool with ordering from the Spice Room. On his way to pick up the food, he'd stopped off to grab a twelve-pack of Coors and a pint of Ben and Jerry's New York Super Fudge Chunk. The ice cream was a once-in-a-while indulgence, but after what Bret had done to her, Autumn needed the pint in the worst way. And the super cool thing was that Chains didn't even bat an eye when she'd asked him to pick it up for her. All he wanted to know was how many she'd like. Autumn couldn't believe that he didn't give the tiniest bit of shit about her wanting the calorie laden dessert. *Bret would've harped on it for days, always reminding me that I could stand to lose a few pounds. How can these two be brothers?*

"Do you want anything else from the kitchen?" Chains asked, slicing through her thoughts.

"Just you." She laughed.

"You got that, baby. You don't want the ice cream?"

A huge grin spread across her face. "Maybe later."

Chains came back with two beers, which he put on the end table next to the couch. Settling back down on the couch, he circled his arm around Autumn and tugged her close.

"Would you eat Indian food again?" she asked before hitting the *Play* button.

"Yeah. It was really good and spicy." Gently, those wonderful lips pressed against hers, soft and strong all at once. "Good choice," he whispered against her mouth.

Autumn leaned further into him and cupped his cheek. He captured her hand and brought it to his mouth, kissing each knuckle and finger.

"I really want to thank you for everything—being there when the wedding was canceled … Tonight … Everything."

"No worries, but don't think I fucked you because of what my asshole brother did to you tonight. I've been wanting to be with you for a while now."

Autumn swallowed, then smiled weakly. "You're very direct. I've never been with a man who just says it quite like you do."

"I don't play games. I told you that before."

"I like that—it's refreshing."

"I'll tell you what you want to know, except for club business. That's off-limits to everyone but the members. Anything else and you'll get a straight answer from me."

"Good to know. I'll give it to you straight too."

Chains quirked his lips and nodded. "I hate what my fuckin' brother did to you—as far as the wedding, but most of all, what he did tonight. I'm not talkin' about it 'cause I don't wanna upset you or make the anger that's bubbling beneath the surface explode inside me. Just know—I haven't forgotten what the fucker did earlier."

Her stomach churned, and she bounced a curled knuckle against her leg. "It's okay … well, it really isn't, but what I mean is that I don't want you to fight Bret over this."

There was a long pause and Autumn began to wonder whether he heard her, but then he locked his gaze on hers. And those eyes filled with care and kindness and desire. *All for me. What do I do with that?*

"I don't want to talk about *him*"—Chains spat the word out like it was poison on his tongue—"anymore." Two fingers ran from the hollow of her throat down between her breasts, skating over them, then tweaking her hardened nipples as the other hand untied the sash of the robe.

Autumn moaned and arched her back, and he groaned deep in his throat as he opened her robe and then gently eased her down on the cushions, those soft and skilled hands still touching everywhere. His tongue circled a path around each breast before his teeth bit the pebbled buds and pulled them into his mouth.

"So beautiful," he murmured.

Fire rushed through her veins and the swell between her legs ached like hell. She practically fell apart when his hand palmed her, and she ground against him like a dog in heat. Chains chuckled deeply, and slipped a finger into her slit.

"Fuckin' wet," he whispered.

"Take me upstairs," Autumn mumbled, her mind reeling, her body pulsing.

With a soft sweep of warm lips across hers, he lifted her up, and for the second time that night, he carried her up the staircase.

THE TANTALIZING AROMA of frying bacon and rich-bodied coffee woke her. Autumn burrowed deeper into the warm, soft sheets, tossing the duvet over her head to block out the morning light trickling in through the blinds. Fitfully, she turned on the other side, but nothing stopped the gnawing in her stomach. She threw off the covers, pushed away some auburn strands from her face, then gingerly rubbed the remainders of sleep from her eyes.

Autumn sat up but flopped backward onto the mattress, slayed by the rush of pain to the right side of her face. Squinting at the sunlight, she turned away and let her lids close. An electronic ring scrambled her brain as she groaned and cussed under her breath. Eyes still shut, she groped around on the nightstand until she snagged the cell phone.

"Hello?" she answered, her voice dry as tumbleweeds, her mind a fog.

"Are you okay?" Sadie asked.

"I just woke up. I'm under the weather." Autumn would tell her friend what that asshole had done to her, but she didn't want to get into it at that moment.

"That came on fast. You were good when we met at the coffeehouse."

"Yeah, well, that's the way it goes sometimes. Can I call you back later?"

"Sure—I was just calling to see if you wanted to do a girl's night out next week with Rachel and Alicia. We haven't done one in a while."

"Yeah … sure, that'd be great."

"I'll let them know it's a go. We were thinking Wednesday after work?" Sadie said.

"That's fine." Autumn placed a finger over her right temple and massaged it gently.

"Great. Do you need anything?" Concern laced Sadie's voice.

A new head and face without any swelling or bruises would be good. Oh … and punching Bret in the face a few times would be a great bonus. "Not really. Thanks for asking."

"If you do, let me know. Now go back to bed and get better," Sadie said.

"Thanks, we'll talk soon."

Autumn dropped the phone back on the nightstand and inhaled. The delicious aromas filled her nostrils, making her stomach growl loudly. Pushing up slowly from the bed, she rubbed her good eye and shuffled to the bathroom.

When Autumn came downstairs, she heard the clatter of pans in the kitchen and paused to listen, then smiled broadly. *He can cook too.* Memories of the night before flickered through her mind, making her heart beat fast. She'd never experienced anything in bed like she had with Chains, but their time together was about so much more. Apprehension crept through her. *What does this all mean? Was last night a hookup or more? Do I want more?* Yes, she did. Chains did something to her; it was like they were made for each other. Autumn had never felt as strong of a connection with any of the men in her life. *That has to mean something. And I felt it from the first day. I'm not imagining this.* But she had no idea how *he* felt. For all she knew, the night before was just a fun time and nothing more. After all, he was a biker—an outlaw one, to be exact, and they lived a very different lifestyle from the average person.

Again her stomach growled and gnawed, prompting Autumn to go into the kitchen. Chains stood at the stove, flipping something in a frying pan, his muscular back turned to her. Cinder slipped from the mud room door, scurried around Autumn's feet, and purred.

"Hey, sweetie," Autumn whispered as she scratched Cinder under the chin.

Chains turned and grinned at her, his light brown eyes lingered on the neckline of her pistachio-colored knit top before they skimmed over her breasts, down her hips, then back up to her face. Autumn's muscles twitched and she covered her nervousness by rearranging the napkins in the holder on the granite island.

"How're you feeling?" he turned his back and flipped what looked like tortillas onto a large plate, then covered them with aluminum foil.

"Better. What're you making? It smells delicious."

Chains looked over his shoulder and winked. "I hope you're hungry—I got carried away. We're having huevos rancheros, but I put bacon in them instead of chorizo 'cause I wasn't sure if you liked it or not."

"I like chorizo."

"Good to know for next time." He turned back to the stove.

So there's going to be a next time. She suppressed a giggle, then shook her head: she was acting just like a teenager. But there was this vibe in the air between them she couldn't quite put into words. It was electric and made her feel like high school all over again. Whenever she thought of Chains or if he was near, her stomach constantly fluttered. It was insane, thrilling, and scary all at the same time.

"Don't tell me you made homemade tortillas," she said, pushing the napkins away.

"I won't," he quipped.

"But you did," she said.

He turned around with a platter in one hand filled with sunny-side-up eggs. "Make up your mind, baby. Do you wanna know or not?" There was a glint of humor in those mesmerizing eyes.

"Smartass," she said, pulling out a chair at the table.

Soon they were both eating huevos rancheros with avocado, bacon, cilantro, and chopped tomatoes. Autumn dipped a tortilla into the runny yoke, and an explosion of flavor burst in her mouth.

"Where did you learn to cook like this?" she asked before taking a drink from her coffee mug.

"Supermom." He chuckled. "There was no fuckin' way I didn't pick up something from her. I was always in the kitchen trying to stay outta my old man's way. I learned to make the corn tortillas from my *abuela*—

grandmother—when we lived in New Mexico. Her home was a safe house when my old man was having a bad day and wanted to use me to relieve his frustrations. Abuelita would have none of that shit, so I spent a lot of time with her. She taught me to make homemade tamales—hers were the best in the world. She'd always make them for special occasions, like Christmas … or my birthday." Chains took a sip of coffee. "Fuck, I haven't thought about her in years."

"Bret never talked about her or living in New Mexico. Your mother told me she was raised there and that the family moved to Alina because your dad got a better job, but she didn't say too much about growing up there, or her Mexican heritage. All Bret ever said was that he wanted me to learn how to make homemade tortillas from your mother, but now you're saying your … what did you call your grandmother?"

"*A-buel-ita*," he said.

"Your abuelita's tortillas were better."

"My mom learned from her mom, but … yeah, my abuelita's fuckin' rocked. I'm not surprised my asshole brother never said anything about our Mexican half. As I told you, he was close to my old man, and the old man wasn't fond of the Mexican culture so he slowly extinguished it from our lives, especially when we moved to Colorado. Bret never gave a shit about our heritage and neither did my sisters, but it's always been a part of me"—he tapped a fist on the left side of his chest—"in here. My abuelita and I were real tight."

Sadness for the little boy he once was flooded through her, and Autumn looked down and began tracing geometric patterns with the fork on her empty plate.

"So, how do you like it?" he asked.

Blinking rapidly without raising her eyes, she replied, "It's very good. You've put me to shame."

Chains laughed. "There's no shame in not knowing something. If a person's interested, he'll learn, if not, then he won't. Either way, that's cool."

Smiling warmly, she met his gaze. "I'm just trying to figure out where you got all this stuff to cook. I know it wasn't from my kitchen."

"I went to the store while you were sleeping. And this time"—he grabbed her hand and squeezed it—"I used your key to get in and out."

"As opposed to what?"

"You don't wanna know." He winked and leaned over and kissed her softly.

"I'll trust you on that one." Autumn stood up and picked up their plates. "I'll do the dishes and you relax in the family room." She glanced down at Cinder, who was curled up at Chains's feet. "I think you have a new friend," she said, pointing at the cat.

"Yeah, we bonded this morning. By the way, I filled her bowl with dry food—it was pretty low."

"Thanks."

From under the sink, Autumn snagged and tied on an apron before rinsing the plates and stacking them in the dishwasher. The scent of leather and soap swirled around her, then Chains slipped his arm around her waist, drawing her back into him.

"You look sexy in that apron, baby," he whispered in her ear. "I'd love to see you in it with nothing but a thong." He nuzzled her neck, and her stomach flip-flopped while her skin buzzed.

Autumn leaned back into him and wiggled her butt against his erection. "Nice and hard," she muttered.

"All because of you, darlin'," he replied in a thick voice.

"And did you want me to do something about it?" she whispered, turning off the faucet.

"What did you have in mind?"

Autumn twisted around and pressed close to him, then began to rub against him, the friction driving her wild.

"Fuck, baby," he rasped.

She dug her fingers into his T-shirt and frantically tugged it upward. Chains bit her neck and shoulder, then his mouth took a lower path toward her breasts. His warm hands slid beneath her top and across her bare back, his touch sending a rush of tingles through her. When his hands cupped her breasts, Autumn arched into them, and he lowered his head and peppered kisses across her chest. Through the fabric of her sheer bra, he flicked at her nipples, driving them to hardened points as arousal surged through her senses.

"Chains," she murmured as he fastened his mouth on one of her nipples, sucking hard at the thin fabric. He bit and nipped and she moaned, pulling him tighter to her. It felt so good that Autumn feared she'd explode right then and there.

"Your tits ... fuck, baby. I just can't get enough of you," he said. Then he pulled away and dragged her to over to the couch.

As she lay on the sofa, shivers rushed up her spine while she watched him undress, his gaze never leaving hers. He bent over her and lightly kissed the good side of her face while those talented fingers tweaked her nipples hard.

"We've got all day," he whispered against her ear. "And I plan to take advantage of every fuckin' second."

As he peeled away her clothes, sprinkling the exposed skin with kisses and nips, Autumn closed her eyes and let herself get lost in the delicious sensations.

Chapter Sixteen

THE CLOUDS WERE blackened shadows that shifted with the wind, and Chains rode fast under a sky devoid of the moon and stars. The rage inside him was like fire lacing through his veins and creeping up his spine. He needed to ram his fist into Bret's face and make him *feel* what *he'd* done to Autumn.

Chains revved the engine at the red light, flipping off an angry driver who shook his fist at him. If the guy had said just one word, Chains would've lost it and most likely smashed in the windows of the jerk's car and then beat the crap out of him. Every one of his nerves snapped and crackled under the fury that threatened to explode.

After Chains had seen Autumn's battered face, it took all the strength he had not to run after his brother and beat him to a pulp. But Autumn had needed him, so he pushed down the anger, but it never left him—it just simmered under the surface, and now it was ready to boil over.

When Autumn had been in the bathroom the night before, Chains had called Eagle and asked him to scope out Bret's apartment to find out whether the pussy was there. He wasn't, but that didn't surprise Chains: Bret knew he'd come for him. Ever since they were kids, they'd competed with each other, egged on by their dad. Chains was always the victor when it came to women and kicking his brother's ass. But what Bret had done to Autumn was inexcusable, and Chains would make sure he paid for it.

The bike rounded the corner and then veered left on a dark street. He knew one of Bret's best friends, Matt, lived in a townhouse at the intersection of Sparrow Way and Concord, so he pulled over a block away and continued on foot.

The night was silent except for the rhythm of biker boots on asphalt, and the street was deserted, which surprised him since it was only six o'clock in the evening. As he walked on, Chains tried to rein in the fury swirling around inside him. If he didn't get a handle on it, there was a very good chance he might kill his brother. Pausing for several moments, he jammed his hands inside his leather jacket and took several deep breaths, exhaling slowly. Scorpio had taught him that technique. He had once told him he'd used it during his tours in Afghanistan when he'd been in the Marines, and then later when he'd been incarcerated. Scorpio swore by it, so now Chains implemented the method in hopes of calming the fuck down and avoiding a stint in prison.

One time, a few years back, Bret had called Chains to pick him up at Matt's house because he'd crashed his sports car when he was drunker than hell. Bret didn't want their parents to know, so Chains had helped him out. Now he was returning to this house for a second time, but it wasn't to help his brother out, it was to kick his ass.

He glanced around the area but didn't see his brother's car; however, knowing what a coward he was, Chains figured the car might be in the garage or that Bret had his friend pick him up. He went around to the back of the house and heard voices. Light spilled out onto a patch of grass, the scent of smoky hickory swirled in the air, and the filtered clang of metal against metal rang through the quietness.

Chains flattened himself against the stucco wall and peeked around its corner. He saw Matt in shorts and flip flops, standing by a large grill and drinking a beer. Pressed to his side was a skinny blonde in tight jeans and a T-shirt. The chick was sipping something in a tall glass. There was no sign of Bret.

"Do you want another drink?" Matt asked.

"Are you trying to get me drunk?" the blonde answered, then a string of giggles filled the small patio.

"Maybe." Matt bent down and kissed her, then opened the sliding glass door and escorted her to the couch.

Anger and frustration gnawed at his gut like a hungry rat, and Chains stood for a long time in hopes he'd see Bret inside the house, but his brother never materialized. *Fuck!*

The creak of the door sliding open had Chains back against the cold stucco wall.

"The steaks are almost ready, babe," Matt said.

Chains came out of the shadows and approached the unsuspecting man—like a lion does its prey.

"Is Bret here?" he asked in a low voice.

Matt's sharp yelp added to the din of aluminum utensils dropping on the concrete floor with a shrill *ping*. He glanced at the slightly ajar door and took a step toward it.

"I don't wanna hurt you, dude. Stay the fuck where you are and answer my question."

"Hey, Chet." A nervous laugh burst through his lips. "You startled me. How've you been?" Matt bent down to pick up the spatula, tongs, and large fork, his hands trembling.

Chains narrowed his eyes into slits. "This isn't a fuckin' social call. I'm looking for Bret."

"I don't know where he's at. I haven't seen him since he went away on business."

He stalked over to him and grabbed Matt by the front of his shirt. The utensils crashed to the floor again. "Don't fuckin' bullshit me."

Eyes wide with fear, Matt shook his head vigorously. "I'm not—I swear. If he's not at his place, then I don't know where he is. I've been kind of busy with this chick"—he glanced at the blonde on the couch—"that I started going out with a couple of weeks ago, and Bret's been out of town a lot. I swear, dude—I'm not lying to you. I wouldn't do that." His gaze rested on Chains's one-percenter patch. "I'd be crazy to do that, right?"

"Yeah—real stupid. I don't like citizens lying to me." He threw Matt against a small table piled with foil, plastic wrap, and spice bottles.

"I'm not. Maybe he's at his girlfriend's house."

At the mention of *girlfriend,* Chains nearly punched Matt in the stomach, but reminded himself that he didn't have any grudge with the guy.

"What's her name?"

"Teresa. He used to go out with her before he met Autumn. I guess they broke off their engagement."

"Where does this chick live?" Rage began to engulf him, and he bit the inside of his cheek hard, the taste of blood calming him.

"I don't know her exact address. Somewhere in the southeast side of the town. I think the name of her complex is Windbreaker. I'm sorry I can't help you. Do you want me to tell Bret to call you if I talk to him?"

"No, and don't say a fuckin' thing about *this* 'cause I'll be real pissed if you do." He cocked his head and glared at Matt. "And you don't wanna see me pissed."

"I definitely won't say anything to him."

"Hey, baby, who's your friend?" the blonde said as she opened the door.

"Tell your bitch to get back inside," Chains gritted.

"Go back in. *Now.*" Panic punctuated Matt's words. "I'll be in real soon. Fix yourself another drink."

"But who's your friend?" She hiccupped then giggled.

"Please, Chloe, go inside." Matt pushed her back, then grabbed the handle and slid the door closed.

"What's Bret's sweet piece's last name?" Chains asked.

Confusion raced across his face. "You mean his girlfriend?"

"Yeah—his slut."

"Uh … Shit … I can't remember." Matt tapped his chin over and over. "I know it, but I don't remember it now."

"I've got time to wait."

"It's … uh … let me see. I know it'll come to me."

The strong scent of burning meat filled the small space. Matt glanced behind his shoulder, then cleared his throat.

"Do you mind if I take the steaks off the grill?"

Chains gave him a chin lift.

As Matt put the black meat on a platter, he shouted out, "Singer! That's the last name," and let out a nervous laugh. "I knew it would come to me."

Without a word, Chains turned around and walked away. He hoped Matt wouldn't do anything stupid, like call Bret, because he really didn't want to hurt the guy. If Bret's friend squealed, Chains would have no choice but to teach him a hard and painful lesson: when a person messed with an outlaw, he incurred his wrath.

While straddling his bike, Chains called Crow and asked him to try and find out where a Teresa Singer lived. Besides him, Crow was the other member who was good with computer intel, and the two of them often worked together on club business.

As Chains was ready to start the engine, his phone pinged, and the corner of his mouth tugged up when he saw Autumn's name on the screen.

"Hey, baby," he said.

"Hi." The melody of her voice washed over him.

"What's up?"

"Nothing."

"You missing me?" he asked.

"Yes," she whispered. "Are you coming over later?"

In three hours, the drug deal was going down. "I don't know what time I'll be done. It may be real late."

"That's okay."

"I'll have to wake you up."

"I won't take a pain pill." There was humor in her tone.

"Okay, darlin'. I'll be over. I'm gonna bring Thor. I'm sure he's madder than hell at me about now."

"Aren't you at the clubhouse?"

Chains quirked his lips. "No. I had something to do."

There was a brief pause and he could hear her soft breathing. "I'd love to see Thor again."

"Is your cat cool with dogs?"

"Cinder gets along with my parents' terrier. She was the first pet in the family until Scruffy came along. If it was up to Scruffy they'd be best friends, but Cinder prefers an amicable but somewhat distant relationship. Is Thor okay with cats?"

"He doesn't have a problem with them when we come across them on walks, but I don't know how he'd do one-on-one."

"I guess we'll have to see how it goes. I'm willing to try."

"Me too, baby. If I get done sooner, I'll let you know." Chains appreciated that Autumn hadn't asked any questions when he'd told her he had club business that night.

"I'll see you later."

"You can count on it."

"Be careful," she whispered.

"I always am, so no worrying, okay?"

Her "uh-huh" didn't sound too convincing, but there was nothing Chains could do about it. The world he lived in was fraught with danger at every turn, and being aware of his surroundings at all times was how he dealt with it. Life wasn't permanent, so he made the most of each day, cognizant of the fact that it could be his last. Life and death were intricately woven together, and even more so in the one-percenter world: that was just the way it was.

Chains stared at the screen long after Autumn had hung up. The time they'd spent together had been amazing, and he couldn't wait until her face healed so he could get a better taste of her sweet lips. He'd only been gone from her a couple of hours, and he was already hungry for more. The thing with Autumn was that she made him feel things he hadn't felt—hadn't wanted to feel—in a long time. And as hard as he tried not to, Chains was falling for her—hard. *How the hell did this happen?* He'd sworn off citizens, and it hadn't been a big deal until that day he'd brought Thor to the clinic. Meeting Autumn had thrown him on his ass. A part of him kept saying that it was all too soon, but another part recognized that there was something deep and almost magical between them. And that's what blew him away because he never fell for all that bullshit, but Chains couldn't deny the magnetic pull that drew them closer, against their better judgment.

Not knowing where Bret was irked the hell out of him, but if there was one thing Chains had learned it was that patience was an asset, especially when stalking prey. The fact that Bret wasn't at his condo meant the douchebag was on high alert and running scared. He knew Chains would come after him, but what he didn't know was that Chains would wait until the right moment to strike, even if it took a week, a month, or a year. It didn't matter because he had every intention of teaching Bret a lesson. The club's menacing motto God Forgives, Night Rebels Don't was the way the brothers lived their lives. They didn't start fights or get into anyone's business unless someone disrespected them first, then they'd right the wrong no matter what. They were a no-holds-barred brotherhood, and people who fucked with them fell into two categories: brave to the point of being delusional or dumber than hell.

Chains pulled into the club's parking lot and killed the engine. Music, mixed with voices, carried toward him, becoming louder as he approached the clubhouse. A group of brothers milled around outside with beers in hand, most probably engaged in a serious conversation about engines and chrome. Motorcycle talk ranked higher than booze or women.

"Jester, how are you, bro?" Chains said as he walked over to a tall man smoking a cigarette. Jester was a member of the Devil's Cannibals MC. The club was based in Carlsbad, New Mexico. They were a small group, and the Night Rebels helped them out with gun smuggling and selling pot so the club could up their revenue. Since Deadly Demons MC—bitter enemies with the Insurgents MC in Colorado—claimed New Mexico, the Devil's Cannibals' bottom rocker didn't bare the name of the state, only the city—Carlsbad.

"Pretty good. It was a great ride coming here. What've you been doing? You missed the last couple of rallies in New Mexico."

"Been working my ass off," Chains replied.

"That's no fuckin' fun, dude." A deep laugh turned immediately into a crackling cough.

"How's life been treating you?" Chains asked.

"Not bad. My old lady and me keep fighting, but that's nothing new." Another cough. "Fuck! This shit's gonna kill me," Jester said, waving the cigarette in the air before bringing it to his lips and taking a few puffs. Smoke billowed around them as he jerked his head toward a group of scantily dressed women in very short shorts and skirts, and way-too-tight tops. "Looks like some of the bitches are gonna need some warming up."

Chains nodded. The women were what the club referred to as hang-arounds: women who partied with the members on the weekends. These wild women threw caution to the wind and embraced life with abandonment. They were there for the weed, the booze, and the men. They'd come and go—some partying hard for several weeks in a row, then disappearing, only to pop up again months or even a year later. It never ceased to amaze Chains how many women wanted to come party with them. Of course, the hang-arounds knew the game: they were there for sex and if a brother wanted it, they gave it. If some of the women had second thoughts, the Night Rebels respected that, but then the chicks wouldn't be allowed to party with them anymore. It was the way their world worked, and every player—member, hang-around, club whore—knew their roles.

"I heard you got a sweet piece of ass in your harem," Jester said. "Aztec was telling me I gotta fuck Lila, but"—he glanced around at several hang-arounds teetering in high heels—"there're so many chicks and so little time."

Chains laughed and clasped Jester's shoulder. "I know you can handle a marathon, bro. Lila's a club girl—she'll be here in the morning, but the hang-arounds are temporary."

"Good point. I'll try them out and Lila tomorrow."

"How long are you guys here for?" Chains asked.

"Through the weekend. We're heading back Monday morning."

"Fuck, dude, you got all the time in the world." Chains chuckled. "I'll be back to drink a beer with you." Chains lifted his hand and bumped fists with Jester.

"I'm pretty sure I'm gonna be busy," the biker said as he headed toward three hang-arounds.

"Then, I'll catch you later."

Walking into the clubhouse, it took Chains a minute to adjust his eyes to the low light. The place was packed, and the smell of whiskey, pot, and pussy washed over him. Several of the club girls walked around the throng of men, giving them a sneak peek of what they wore underneath their tight clothes. On full-house party nights, the club women were extremely territorial with the brothers and the club in general. They were the women who lived at the clubhouse, and they resented hang-arounds who acted like they owned the damn place. Many a party included a few knock-down, drag-out fights between the club girls and the hang-arounds—the club women usually winning.

Chains chatted briefly with bikers from other clubs around Colorado and New Mexico, and then he headed to his room. Normally, there wouldn't be a party on a night when a serious business deal was going down, but because the meeting date had been changed from the night before to that night, the brothers from other clubs had already come to Alina to party with the Night Rebels.

Thor started barking the second Chains slipped the key into the lock, and when he swung the door open, the Siberian rushed over to him, jumping up on Chains, licking his hands and then running around in circles.

"Did you miss me, buddy?" Chains asked as he dropped on one knee and drew the dog to him, stroking his soft coat repeatedly. "Did you eat?" He glanced over at Thor's empty dish.

A soft knock at the door had him up on his feet in a flash.

"Hi, stranger," Ruby said as she slipped inside his room. "I tried to get your attention as you walked through the big room, but it's so loud that you didn't hear me calling your name."

"No, I didn't. What's up?"

"I wanted to tell you that I fed Thor before the party started. I also spent last night in your room because he didn't want to sleep anywhere else. Was that okay? I hope you're not mad."

Chains smiled. "I'm not mad. Thanks for taking care of him. I appreciate it."

Ruby looped her arms around his neck. "I've missed you, baby," she said softly.

Gently, he pulled away. "Tonight's crazy down there. If any of the out-of-towners don't treat you right, tell me or one of the other brothers, okay?"

Confusion glazed her face. "Sure. Don't you want to relax before you have to go out on club business?" She stepped toward him, but he walked away.

"I'm taking Thor for a walk, then decompressing before I head out with the others." He looked over at her. "Nothing personal, okay?"

Ruby slowly nodded and shuffled to the door.

"Thanks again for watching Thor. I'll take you to Leroy's one night next week for some chow."

A smile as bright as the morning sun lit up her face, and she rushed back over and hugged him, planting a soft kiss on his chest. "I'd love that." She bounced out of the room, closing the door behind her.

Chains slumped against the window sill, looking at the mountains in the distance. Thoughts of Autumn filled his mind, and he couldn't wait to be with her again. He felt a nudge and looked down, smiling at Thor as he put his paw on Chains's knee.

"Hey there, buddy," he said, giving Thor a good head scratch before bending down and hugging him close. "Your doc's got a hold on me." Thor whined. "Yeah … I can't fuckin' believe it either." He stood up and snapped his fingers. "Let's go."

As they stepped into the hallway, a cacophony of noise enveloped them: laughter, squeals, moans, hard-punching metal music. Not wanting to take Thor through the great room, Chains walked to the back of the club and went out into the yard. Several men and women were fucking in the open while others were dancing to the beats of the music coming from large speakers attached to the fence. He hurried through the area, and soon they were far away from the madness behind them.

"Dude, wait up."

Chains heard footsteps pounding behind him. Thor barked, his tail wagging briskly.

"Hey," he said to Eagle as the biker came up to Chain's side.

"You out for a walk?" Eagle handed Chains a joint. "This is the premium stuff we're selling tonight."

Nodding, he put the joint between his lips, and Eagle flicked the lighter and held it out to him. Chains bent forward, cupping his hand around the flame, then pushed back as he sucked in the smoke.

"After we get shit done tonight, we can party. I need to stay focused." Eagle blew out a column of smoke. "I've got a bad feeling about the meeting."

Cocking his head to the side, Chains said, "Why's that? Those dudes are pretty straight. I checked and double-checked them out."

Eagle ran his fingers through his light brown hair. "I don't know, but I've learned not to ignore this shit when it hits me. We gotta go in easy and slow."

"Agreed. We need to be there at least an hour before to scope out the area and take our positions."

"Having some more members would be a good thing. I spoke to Paco about it." Eagle tilted his head back and stared at the sky. "No moon or stars helps."

"Always does, that's why we plan it this way."

Looking sideways at him, Eagle said, "Where the fuck were you last night? Thor was going crazy until Ruby slept in your room."

Chains stubbed out the roach between his index finger and thumb, then shoved it in his pocket. The grass was pretty dry since the first snow hadn't yet fallen, so he didn't want to take any chances of a wildfire. "I got tied up."

"With a citizen? Who the hell is she?" Eagle faced him, arms crossed over the chest.

"Just a chick," he replied.

"Bullshit. It's been so long since you hooked up with a citizen that I've lost track. So this—"

"Why the hell are you even keeping track?" he said, annoyance lacing his voice.

"'Cause I'm always looking to win some dough on different bets we have going on." Eagle chuckled. "I lost a chunk of change on you—Paco, Goldie, and Army did too. We didn't think you'd go as long as you did without fucking a citizen, especially at Sturgis last year. This sweet piece must be pretty special to have brought you down."

"Don't fuckin' call her *that*," he grumbled.

Eagle's eyes widened. "Fuck, dude, you're in deep."

"No, I'm not. I'm just having fun." But as he said the words, he knew he was full of shit, and by the way Eagle looked at him, Chains knew Eagle thought he was full of crap too.

"You planning to bring her around?" his friend asked.

Chains shrugged. "Not thinking that far ahead. What time do you got?"

Eagle snapped his fingers. "I bet you're screwing around with Thor's doc." He busted out laughing. "Jigger was fuckin' spot on. Am I right?"

"I asked what the damn time was, not whether you wanted to play question and answer."

Chains whistled between his teeth and Thor came running.

"This doc must be a looker for you to piss all over your 'no citizens' rule." Eagle glanced at the phone in his hand. "It's nearly eight."

"We should get going."

Suddenly, Eagle's ribbing stopped, and Chains saw his jaw clench. A serious and dark mood descended upon them as they made their way back; the only sound were boots crunching down on dried grass and leaves.

Chains lifted his chin at Paco and nine other Night Rebels—four more than had been originally scheduled to go. Three members from Fallen Slayers MC were standing by Paco's SUV.

"Hey." Knuckles, Fallen Slayers' sergeant-at-arms, drew Chains into a bear hug. "It's been too long, bro."

"How've you been?" Chains asked.

"Good. We just sold a bunch of bike parts to a fence over in Larkspur. He did good by us. We made a mint."

"It's fuckin' awesome to steal bikes from those damn weekend warriors," Tats said. Another Fallen Slayers' member, Tats was known to be precise and ruthless in executing a mission.

"They're nothing but a bunch of wannabe outlaws," Goldie said, disgust lacing his voice.

"Damn pussies—the lot of 'em," Army added.

"It's time to roll," Paco said. He pointed to a black minivan. "I can fit nine in there"—he waved his hand at a brown SUV—"and the rest can go in Diablo's cage."

"I'll be right back," Chains said as he rushed into the clubhouse with Thor at his heels.

Once he gave Thor his treats and settled him down, he weaved through the crowd until he was back outside, then hurried over to the waiting cages. Jumping into the back seat of Diablo's car, Chains slammed the door shut and the vehicle drove out of the lot into the darkness.

Chapter Seventeen

THE CARS BOUNCED down the rough dirt street before turning onto Yellow Feather Road. Diablo and Paco killed the headlights on their cages, and the cars slowed down to almost a crawl as they approached the adobe.

Chains held the assault rifle in his hands as he scanned the area for any movement other than black-tail bobcats, lizards, and cactus mice. The adobe was on flat ground, but mountain lions were known to wander down from the nearby mesas and San Juan Mountain range when looking for food.

Diablo stopped, and Chains jumped out to pull open a large door, then the two cars drove into the garage. The bikers slid out of the cars and walked out of the garage after having shut the door. The wind—a biting, icy one—nudged them forward. Chains listened to the rhythm of boots on the gravel and to his breathing. *Eagle's right—something feels off.* Chains felt his gut tighten, and a sixth sense whispered across his skin, raising the hair on the back of his neck. Darting his eyes around for the umpteenth time, he fell in beside Aztec.

"Do you feel it?" he asked in a low voice.

"Fuck yeah—something's not right," Aztec replied. "The others have gotta sense it too."

Paco gestured for Chains, Aztec, Eagle, and Knuckles to go around back as he pointed to the others to cover the sides and front of the adobe.

The house, the yards, the surroundings ... everything was seeped in darkness. Chains carried the assault rifle over his right shoulder and the Kill Light—a large industrial flashlight—in his left hand as he trudged gingerly over the small rocks and sand.

Slowly, Eagle opened the back door, hinges creaking loudly in the inky quiet. Adrenaline surged through Chains as he followed his friend into the house; Aztec and Knuckles were so close behind him, he could feel their breath on his neck.

Once inside, the men paused and listened for movements in the adobe—the click of a gun, shuffling footsteps, low whispers—but they heard only silence. Chains motioned with his light that he was going to check out the room to the left. Eagle gestured that he'd join him; Chains nodded, then ventured into the space.

Fuck, it's dark in here. He wished he could use his flashlight, but Chains didn't want to risk it. Something about this transaction was off kilter. His gut—rarely wrong—told him that this deal would go very bad. No matter how hard he tried to shake that thought, it stuck like fly paper.

"I'm gonna clear the closet," Chains whispered to Eagle, who softly clucked his tongue.

Standing to the side of the door, his rifle pointing toward it, Chains raised his foot and kicked it open. Eagle switched on the flashlight, illuminating the empty closet.

"Clear," Chains said in a low voice.

From the sound of heavy boots on the floor and against the wood, Chains knew the other members were simultaneously checking the nooks and crannies of the house.

"Nothing's fucked up here." Paco's voice echoed through the adobe.

The men gathered in the main room, and Diablo and Knuckles stood sentry by the front windows that looked out at the road.

"Tats, Crow, Brick, and Shotgun are gonna stay hidden in the brush to watch the outside. I want Diablo, Chains, and Eagle with me in this room." Then, Paco directed Army and Knuckles, "Take the back room"—he pointed to Muerto, Goldie, Sangre, and Aztec—"and two of you in each of the other rooms. I got a feeling shit isn't gonna go down the way it should."

The men mumbled their agreement, then dispersed to the positions the vice president had assigned. Fifteen minutes later, the crunch of tires on gravel rang out.

"The fuckers are early and driving without headlights," Diablo said as he stared out the window.

"Definitely planning to rip us off," Chains said.

"Damn straight," Paco replied as he stood by the side of the window. "We'll check 'em for weapons when they get inside. I'm not takin' any fucking chances." He looked over his shoulder at Chains. "These assholes checked out okay?"

Chains blew out a breath. "Yeah. The only snag was that the old man has a son." He snapped his fingers as he tried to remember the guy's name, then it hit him. "Eric, that's it. Anyway, the take on Eric is that he's a greedy fucker who doesn't negotiate straight. I brought this up at church, and Steel said that the old man was gonna be the one making the deal tonight."

"I got a feeling the old man pussied out and sent in the heavy," Eagle said.

"If it's this asshole Eric, he's gonna be in for a big surprise," Diablo replied. "There're three more cages coming. Fuck, they're looking for a fight."

Every muscle in Chains' body stiffened as he walked over to the window and peeked out. Four SUVs approached the adobe.

"Fuck, we shoulda brought more brothers," he said.

"We can handle them. No doubt the fuckers got strong firearms, but I brought some grenades just in case we have to use them," Paco said. "We can't check all of them for weapons since we're outnumbered, so we only let three people in. The others will have to wait in the car. If they don't want to, I'll give the signal to Crow and Shotgun to nuke them. I don't want to lose any brothers."

The doors to one of the SUVs opened, and three men filed out and walked right up the steps to the front porch.

"Are they that fuckin' stupid? Maybe this is gonna be real easy,"

Eagle said.

"And they only had three people in the cage. What the fuck's that all about?" Diablo said in a gruff voice.

"Maybe they don't know those cages can fit seven assholes," Paco said, and the bikers chuckled. "They're almost at the door, so let's take our positions."

Diablo stayed in one corner of the room, Eagle took the opposite one, and Chains and Paco stood at the back; all men had their weapons drawn. Muerto, Goldie, and Army stood in the doorway of each room with assault rifles ready to fire.

The door creaked open.

"Fuck, it's dark in here. The old man's losing it," a deep voice said as a medium-sized man walked into the room. "Put on some fucking lights."

One of the other men groped along the wall, but before he found the light switch, Chains flipped on the solitary bulb overhead.

"What the fuck?" the medium-sized man said, his deep-set eyes scanning the room.

"Where the fuck's Gary?" Paco growled.

"My dad's sick. He sent me. I'm Eric." The man extended his hand, but none of the bikers took it, and he let it drop limply down by his side. "Did you bring the weed?"

"The rest of your people keep their fucking asses in the cars. If anyone gets out, the deal's off," Paco said.

Eric's eyes narrowed. "No fucking way. I'm not sticking around here without some backup."

"Why do you need backup?" Chains asked.

The vein in Eric's right temple bulged. "Because I've never done business with you guys. I don't know if you're going to rip me off."

"If you did your fuckin' homework, you'd know our reputation," Diablo grumbled.

"This isn't negotiable—either they stay out or we're done here," Paco said.

Eric glared, his gaze bouncing around the room as he fidgeted in place. "At least put those guns down."

Chains grinned. "No fuckin' way."

"We're here for business, not talking. Do you have the money?" Paco asked.

"Yes, but I want to see the product first."

Paco nodded, then bent down with his gaze still fixed on Eric and the two men behind him and unzipped a duffel bag, taking out several large bags of pot. "We got four hundred pounds of pot, a hundred and fifty pounds of edibles, and fifty pounds of hash oil. That's what the old man ordered." Paco stood up, his gaze narrowing. "Now show us the fucking money."

Eric licked his lips. "It's in one of the SUVs."

Paco's remote radio crackled, and he brought it to his ear. "Yeah?"

Crow's deep voice hissed over the remote. "There're about ten fuckers getting outta the SUVs."

"Hang on." Paco turned to Eric. "Tell them to get their fucking asses back in the cages, or things aren't going to turn out so well."

Eric paused.

"Do it *now*, asshole," Chains said.

"And you better show me the fucking money, or this deal is off," Paco gritted.

Eric held up his hands. "Okay, take it easy. I just wasn't sure what was going down so that's why—"

"What the fuck does *that* mean? We made a damn deal with Gary. Your old man was cool with it. What the hell are you saying?" Chains took a few steps toward Eric. "You're stalling and that can only mean one thing—you don't have the fuckin' money."

"Or *all* of it," Eagle added.

Beads of perspiration rolled down the stocky man's face. "I think I'm going to be sick," he groaned as he bent over.

The light caught the shine of a gun as Eric took it out from under his jacket. Suddenly the two other men whipped out their weapons as well.

"It's war!" Paco said in the remote before throwing it down on the duffel bag.

Four burly men busted through the front door, and Chains noticed that they wore the colors of the Pueblo, Colorado, gang, Los Malos. Outside, the sound of gunfire punctured the silence of the night.

"You fuckin' asshole! You're dead," Chains yelled to Eric.

The bikers dropped to their bellies and slithered out of the room while Muerto, Goldie, and Aztec had their backs. When Chains saw Eric slip out the front door, rage burned through him.

"The fucker's trying to leave. I'm gonna get him. You okay without me?" Chains asked Paco as bullets lanced in the air around them.

"Go get him!"

The rounds of ammunition flying around the house sounded like a war zone. Shotgun and Tats were running toward the front door, while Crow and Brick had guns pulled as they grabbed three guys out of one of the SUVs. Chains saw several downed Malos writhing on the ground, their weapons nowhere to be seen.

Dust scattered beneath Chains's boots as he ran toward his brothers. He saw Eric point a gun at Eagle. Chains's heart raced and his breath quickened.

"No! Eagle drop down—the fucker's got a gun on you!" Chains screamed, but it was too late. The first bullet hit the biker in the chest. Eagle looked up, surprised, then the next bullet hit him, and he crumpled down to the ground.

"Eagle! Fuck!" Chains yelled.

Eric then aimed at Crow, and with the strength of a panther, Chains leaped and fell on top of the asshole, knocking the gun out of his hand. Eric bucked and pushed up, but Chains backed him against the door of a silver SUV.

He grabbed the front of Eric's polo shirt and slammed him against the car door several times while screaming, "Brother down!"

Eric tried to kick Chains, but the biker hit him in the groin—hard.

The man's breath rushed between his lips in a *whoosh* of spent air.

"You fuckin' double-crosser," Chains gritted.

"I … I got the money!" Sputtering and panting, Eric gasped for air. "I was going to get it—I swear."

"You shot a brother, motherfucker! A *brother*!"

"I thought he was going to kill me. It was self-defense."

"Fuckin' liar! You ambushed him—he didn't even see you."

From the corner of his eye, Chains saw several brothers rushing out from the adobe, after that it started raining bullets.

Eric pushed against Chains, and the biker loosened his grip, letting the scum think he was getting away. All around him was a downpour of gunfire, and bodies hit the ground with a *thud*. Bikers and gangsters ran in every direction in a storm of movement and noise.

Chains grabbed Eric by the neck and pulled him back, then pounded his head against the car window, shattering it.

"I have the money," he said, his voice high and thin with panic.

The image of Eagle—one of his best friends—getting shot by this fucker filled Chains's mind. He stepped back, aimed the gun at Eric, and pulled the trigger. Eric's eyes widened as he grabbed his belly. Blood squeezed through his fingers as he took a few stumbled steps, then collapsed on the cold, hard ground. The red pool underneath the downed man's body slowly spread around him.

Chains heard an engine start up and saw one of the SUVs hauling ass out of there. Paco, Diablo, and Knuckles chased after it, shooting at the tires. Chains dashed over to Eagle and saw that his eyes were closed and his chest was slowly moving up and down.

"Eagle!" Chains caught his friend's face between his fingers and shook it hard. "Look at me, bro."

Eagle's eyes fluttered open, and he stared vacantly at Chains.

"Don't fuckin' die on me. This isn't your time. Stay with me, bro." He kept lightly patting his face.

"How bad is he?" Paco asked.

Chains looked up. "Pretty fucked up. He took two bullets—I think they were both in the chest."

"Doc won't be able to fix this. He needs a hospital." Paco ran his fingers through his hair. "Fuck! We should've killed the bastards the minute they came into the house. Fuck!"

"Don't blame yourself for this. We all knew the risks." Chains glanced back at Eagle and his heart squeezed. "I'll get Crow and we'll take him to the hospital."

"Go on—I'll make sure we clean up this fucking mess around here," Paco said, clasping his hand on Chains's shoulder.

Five minutes later, Crow was burning rubber on the backroads, only slowing down when they reached Alina. The last thing they wanted was some damn badge to pull them over and start asking a ton of questions.

Chains jumped out of the car before Crow had completely stopped it. He rushed into the ER and said, "My friend's been shot."

Immediately the nurses, doctors, and techs sprang into action, and within no time, Eagle was laid out on a stretcher and rushed through the wooden double doors. Chains paced for several minutes before going up to the front desk.

"I need to know what's going on with my brother," he said to the woman behind the counter.

"You're his relative?"

"Yeah."

"What insurance does he have?"

"He's been shot and you're asking me about the fuckin' insurance?"

The curly-haired woman pushed her large-framed glasses up her nose with her index finger and smiled.

"I'm sorry, I didn't mean to sound like I'm not sympathetic because I am. It's just hospital policy to ask."

"No insurance—private pay."

For the next twenty minutes, Chains gave the woman all of Eagle's personal information. The mechanics of it were almost a relief because it kept him from thinking about the real possibility of his friend dying.

"We're all done. I'll check on the status of your brother," the intake woman said.

Chains turned away from the desk and walked over to Crow, who sat hunched in a chair near a muted television set, staring blankly at the screen.

"I checked these fuckers out," Chains said as he sank down next to Crow.

"Don't own this shit, dude. You did what Steel asked and more. We all voted to go forward with this. Bad drug deals happen—you know that," Crow replied in a low voice.

"But … Eagle. Fuck!" Chains pounded the armrest, then leaped up from the chair and started to pace.

"You—*we*—didn't know it was gonna go down like that," Crow said.

"Eagle had a bad feeling 'bout tonight." He blew out a breath, scrubbing his hands over his face. "So did I."

"Me too." Crow stretched out his legs and crossed them at the ankles. "We all did."

"We should've been no shows. Fuck." He glanced over at the double doors. "I wonder what the hell's going on in there."

"I'd say the docs are trying to save our brother's life," Crow replied, his face a mask of glumness.

A blast of cold air rushed into the room, and he turned to look at the front glass doors just as Steel, Sangre, and Scorpio hurried over.

"How's Eagle?" Steel asked, concern etched across his face.

Chains shrugged. "Haven't heard anything yet. He was hurt pretty bad."

"Fuck," Steel muttered. "What the hell happened?"

"A bad deal—the fuckers double-crossed us," Crow mumbled as he continued to stare at the blank television screen.

"How the fuck didn't I predict this?" Steel said.

"It's the fuckers' fault—not the Night Rebels," Scorpio said before flopping onto one of the chairs.

"The damn badges will be here for sure. We got our story straight?"

Sangre asked.

Chains nodded. "I told the doc that Eagle was out riding and someone shot him. I said Crow and I went looking for him when he never came back, and we found him on the side of the road."

"It's kinda weak, but we'll have to go with it." Steel locked gazes with Chains. "How're you doing? You two have been real tight ever since you prospected together."

He averted his eyes to the leaf-patterned carpet. "It fuckin' sucks."

Steel put his arm around Chains and gripped his shoulder. "Life fucking sucks sometimes."

"A lot of the time," Scorpio added.

"We cut outta there damn fast. Were any other brothers hurt?" Crow asked.

"Just minor shit—Doc Bones is patching up Aztec, Brick, and Shotgun. Nothing too serious. Paco said that there were casualties on the other side. They're taking care of all that shit. I thought this would've gone down all right, considering we were dealing with an old man who belongs to a fucking country club." Steel shook his head.

"The old man sent his fuckin' son. I don't know why, but somehow Los Malos got mixed up in this. We're definitely gonna hear from them—some of their members were on the ground and not moving when Crow and I took off," Chains said.

"Why the fuck were those asshole gangsters involved in this deal?" Scorpio said.

Chains shrugged. "Who the fuck knows. I think the asshole's son wanted protection. He didn't seem to trust us from the start. Maybe the family's done business with Los Malos before, although that didn't come up when I did the due diligence stuff."

"And what happened to the motherfucker who did this to Eagle?" Sangre asked.

Chains crossed his arms against his chest. "I took care of him. He won't be doing any more drug deals."

Satisfied murmurs and grunts resounded from the bikers, then they lapsed into an anxious silence as they waited for any word on Eagle's condition.

The minutes turned into hours. The badges had come and gone, and no one was left in the reception area except for the Night Rebels and a redhead with frizzy hair who had replaced the curly-haired intake worker. Finally the wooden doors opened, and a man in his mid-fifties, wearing green scrubs, approached the group.

"Chains?" the man said, a puzzled expression crossing his face.

Chains walked over. "Yo. Are you the doc?"

"Yes. Are you Mr. Mitchell's brother?"

"Yeah. What's going on with him?"

The doctor glanced over at the other men who were fast approaching.

"It's cool," Chains said, gesturing to the guys. "They're here for Eagle, too, and need to hear this."

The doctor slowly nodded. "I'm Dr. Chester, and I was the surgeon for your brother. He's stable right now. He took two bullets, and he's very lucky to still be alive. One of the bullets that I removed was embedded against the sternum—the breast bone—and only caused minor damage. The other one entered his left lung, and that was the one which caused the most problems. He's very lucky that he didn't die from severe bleeding into the lung. I was able to remove the bullet, control the bleeding, and repair it. The biggest risk is infection, so I have him on an IV antibiotic treatment. It was good that you brought him in as quickly as you did." The doctor clasped the clipboard against his chest. "That saved his life."

A mountain of relief washed over Chains, and from the sighs and throat clearings, he knew the other members felt it too.

"How long is he gonna be laid up?" he asked the surgeon.

"I'd like to keep him here for ten days. It's the infection that I'm mostly concerned about at this point. After that, he can go home, but it'll take a couple of months to fully recover."

"When can we see him?" Steel asked.

"He's still in recovery. It'll probably be another hour at least and then he'll be moved to a room. I'm keeping him sedated through the night. It may be better to come back in the morning, but it's your choice. Are there any more questions?" The men shook their heads. "All right, then." Dr. Chester turned around and disappeared behind the wooden doors.

"I'm gonna wait," Chains said, shoving his hands into his leather jacket.

"You tell us if anything comes up, okay?" Steel said. "We're going to head to the adobe and see if we can help out with the cleanup."

"I bet the fuckers never had any of the money," Sangre said.

"They brought half of it—one point two million. Paco got it. The sonsofbitches never had any intention of paying the whole amount," Steel said.

"Who the fuck did they think they were dealing with?" Scorpio asked.

"Los Malos probably fed them some bullshit. Those fuckin' punks didn't expect what they got from us. They even hightailed it and ran away." Chains kicked the bottom of the counter with the toe of his boot.

"Nothing but a bunch of pussies," Crow said, disgust lacing his voice.

"We'll discuss this in church tomorrow. We gotta go now," Steel said.

Scorpio clasped a hand on Chains's shoulder. "Glad Eagle's okay, dude."

Chains lifted his chin and watched his friends walk away. He rubbed the back of his neck as he went over to the vending machine. Taking out a dollar, he inserted it into the slot. A cardboard cup plopped down in a metal vise and black liquid streamed into it. He pushed the button for cream and watched as it dripped down into the coffee. With his cup in hand, he walked over to the chairs and sat down. An older man occupied one of the seats by the large window, his face marked with heavy lines of sadness.

Chains slouched down into the chair and took a sip of coffee: it had a tinny taste but was at least hot. *It's gonna be a long night.*

He stared at the emergency room clock, watching the black second hand sweep around … over and over and over.

Chapter Eighteen

IN THE EARLY morning, Autumn woke with a jolt. Sitting up with her heart pounding wildly, she strained to see in the dark as every nerve inside her tightened. Autumn held her breath and listened for anything that seemed strange, but the only predawn sounds were a distant train moving through the stillness and the chirping of small birds who had begun to stir. Still, her heart beat fast. *Did Bret get in the house?* The chance of that terrified Autumn.

For several minutes, she waited while barely breathing, then slowly began to relax. Cinder jumped up on the bed, and Autumn picked her up and held her close.

"I'm being totally ridiculous," she whispered. Not usually the type of person who got spooked, she found herself on edge ever since Bret's assault the day before.

Glancing at her phone's screen, it read 4:15 a.m., and streaks of anger shot through Autumn. Chains had said he'd come over, but he never showed up. *Not even a damn phone call. Nothing.* At around midnight, she'd figured he wasn't going to show. Chains raised a storm of feelings inside Autumn: anger, frustration, sadness, joy, and confusion. But at this late hour, a new emotion had crept in—worry.

Chains had told her that he had club business that night. Autumn wasn't *really* sure what that meant, but now that she hadn't heard from him, she wondered if something bad had happened. In the past, whenever Bret hadn't followed through on a promise to call her, she'd worry about him being hurt and he was always just fine. His insensitivity and selfishness were the reasons for not following through, but Chains seemed so different from his brother. She couldn't imagine he'd purposely diss her. *But I don't really know him. Maybe he's like Bret. After all, they are brothers.*

Cinder's ears perked up and she stared at the door, her body tense. Autumn stilled. Although the bedroom door was closed, she heard the faint sound of the wood floor creaking on the other side of it. Then the noise of shuffling footsteps along the hallway filled her ears. She clutched the blanket and brought it up under her chin. The footfalls slowed down as they approached her room.

Tingles of fright skated down her spine, and Autumn reached for the phone while her gaze stayed fixed on the door. As the handle twisted and turned, she screamed, and the phone fell to the floor with a *thud*.

Then, the door pushed open, and a figure rushed toward her.

"Autumn, what's wrong?" a deep voice asked as the man neared the bed.

Fear and confusion zigzagged through her, and she pushed back against the headboard, clawing at it.

"It's me, baby. Are you having a bad dream?"

Groping around the nightstand, her fingers found the small lamp and switched it on. Muted golden light cast shadows on the wall and ceiling as her gaze fixed on the advancing figure. *It's Chains.* Relief spread through her entire body.

"You scared the hell out of me!" The blanket dropped down from her hands.

In seconds, he was on the bed, strong arms cocooning her in his warmth.

"I'm sorry, darlin'. I wanted to surprise you," he murmured.

"Well, you did *that*." Autumn tilted her head back and looked up. "How did you get in the house?"

"Yeah … well, we gotta talk about getting you a security system." He brushed his lips across hers. "How're you feeling?"

"Better—the swelling has gone down a lot since yesterday. I iced it every hour after you left." She tightened her arms around his waist. "I was worried about you. At first, I wasn't sure if you blew me off or not."

"I don't do that shit, baby. I should've called, but I got … tied up."

"Did everything go okay?" she asked, noticing that he looked tired and worried.

Giving her a slight smile, he nodded.

"Are you sure? You don't look so good."

"I'm fine." His jaw clenched.

"You can tell me if something's bothering you. Is it Thor?"

He let out a dry chuckle. "Thor's fine, but he's probably pissed that I left him alone again." He shook his head. "Last night, Ruby had to stay in my room because he was going nuts."

Autumn's stomach twisted. "Who's Ruby?"

"One of the club girls. She and Thor get along real well. I'm sure I cramped her style though. There were a lot of members from other clubs at the party last night."

"Party?" She pulled out of his embrace. "Was *that* your club business?"

"Nah. The brothers who stayed behind kept the party going."

"So, club girls live with all of you?"

"Yeah—they get our protection and keep the place clean and do other … jobs."

"Like cooking?"

"Mostly when Lena's off. She's the cook. Crossbones was her old man until he fucked my old lady."

"That must've been awful," she said.

"Fuckin' sucked. It hit Lena real hard. Believe me, we've trashed the fuckers a lot over the years." He chuckled. "Lena's a good woman, but she's still bitter as hell over the betrayal."

"I think you are too."

"Not really—I used to be."

Her breath caught as Chains ran his fingers over her cheeks and along her jaw; her skin tingled at his touch.

"You're so beautiful," he said and moved her tousled hair aside. "Did you miss me?"

"Uh-huh," she mumbled, her body hummed with awareness caused by the heat radiating from him.

"That's good," he whispered as he nuzzled her neck, his beard stubble prickly, his breath warm and soft.

Autumn tilted her head, giving him better access. Chains slowly licked the curve of her ear.

"You smell so good, baby," he murmured against her skin.

She let out a small moan and fell against him.

Chains pulled back and slipped his fingers through her hair to hold her in place; then, he leaned in and melded their mouths together. Autumn's lips parted, and as his tongue slid inside enough for her to taste him, she pressed closer, giving in to the prickle of electricity dancing throughout her body and sparking low in her belly.

Lips, tongues, and teeth tasted and probed deeper, relishing in wet, dark pleasure. Autumn sighed into Chain's mouth, and he let out a low, feral growl as his hands gripped the hem of her purple nightie and slid it high on her thighs while he ground his erection against her—hard and demanding.

"Fuck, Autumn"—his fingers circled their way to her lace panties—"you're already so wet for me," he whispered, touching her through the fabric.

"Oh God … Chains." Jumping from the contact, she arched into him, the tips of her breasts straining against the nightgown's thin material.

Another deep, passionate kiss, then Chains dragged his lips away. His hot panting on Autumn's neck had every one of her nerve endings on alert just before a sharp bite jolted her clit to a full throb. He savagely sucked on the flesh of her neck, and she had no doubt it would leave a disreputable mark, but at that moment, she didn't give a rat's ass.

Then that wicked mouth slid down to her breasts, and when he sucked a pebbled nipple through the fabric, Autumn thought she'd lose it. She gripped the nightshirt and flung it over her head, craving the feel of his lips on her bare skin.

With a satisfied growl, Chains flicked the throbbing nipple with the tip of his tongue before sucking it into his mouth, all the while his fingers pressed harder against her.

Autumn gasped. Breathing him in, she grabbed his hair and pulled on it recklessly.

"That feels good, doesn't it?" His voice was husky and raw.

"Yes, it feels so fucking good." She moaned, opening her legs a bit more.

As his tongue laved her breasts, he pinched her clit, rolling it back and forth, and then one of his fingers moved under her panties and slipped deep inside her.

"Oh, shit," she groaned, bucking against him. Autumn reached out and yanked at the button of his jeans and pulled down the zipper. She heard him suck in a gasp of air as she reached into his pants; his cock was smooth and hard, and she curled her fingers around it, squeezing tightly.

"Fuck, darlin'," he said, his voice hoarse.

"I want you so badly," she whispered.

Chains bent down and kissed her hard and rough, then pulled away. His eyes never left hers as he kicked his boots off and shed his clothes. She stared at the broad expanse of his chest and licked her lips. *He's so damn sexy. Perfect, really.*

When Autumn saw him take out a condom, she said, "I'm on the pill, and I want to feel all of you."

A wicked grin spread over Chains's face. "I'm all in for that, baby."

Then she remembered the *club girls*. "I have to ask if you've been tested though."

Two strong hands gripped her ankles and pulled until she was flat on her back. "Yeah—I'm clean." Chains lowered his gaze to the lace panties. "You're so wet, they're clinging to you." He glanced back up, eyes scorching. Then he climbed back on the bed and hooked a finger under each side of the material, slowly sliding them off her legs.

His lust and desire enveloped her while his words inflamed her.

Chains rocked back on his heels and took in every part of her body. "You make me crazy," he whispered as he reached out and stroked her bare pussy. Leaning forward, he hovered over Autumn, then crashed his mouth down on hers. This time the kisses were deeper, more demanding, more possessive. Autumn gripped his shoulders and clung to him like a drowning woman welcoming a life raft. Being with Chains felt so right, so wicked—so perfect.

As they kissed, his hands glided their way over her breasts, down her belly, and into the wet folds between her thighs. With those deft fingers, he began caressing her with pleasurable, circling strokes. Autumn lifted her hips toward his hand, never wanting him to stop.

"I need to be inside you," he rasped as he pulled away. Chains gripped one leg and placed it over his shoulder, then did the same with the other one. "That's it," he murmured while lightly stroking her sex with the tip of his cock before pushing inside her wet heat.

"Yes," Autumn whispered.

Chains pumped himself into her while groaning her name. He bent over to possess her mouth and then lightly bit her nipples before pounding into her again. Autumn took in the sounds of their coupling and the scent of sex, relishing the feeling of the two of them together. He drove in harder, rougher—his pants and grunts music to her ears. Autumn could feel his desire, the heat from his body, and a connection to him in a way that she'd never had with a man before.

When he pinched Autumn's clit, the building dam of sensations inside her burst, and she came in delicious waves of ecstasy. Chains pounded harder, then stiffened, and a low feral growl erupted from his throat while he buried his face in her breasts.

After what seemed like a long time, Chains rolled off Autumn and drew her near. His heart beat steadily against her ear, and within seconds, she heard his heavy breathing. Reaching over, she switched off the lamp, and the gray light of dawn weakly filtered in through the shutters.

She nestled closer to him, realizing that it was Chains—this rough-around-the-edges outlaw biker—who made her feel safe and desired.

AUTUMN WOKE UP blissfully sore later that morning. She looked over and stared at the empty spot, then the sound of water caught her attention. Just as she pushed up against the headboard, the bathroom door opened and a cloud of steam escaped into the bedroom. Chains stepped out, wearing a towel around his waist as droplets of water glistened off his bare chest and shoulders.

"Morning," he said, stopping in his tracks.

Autumn smiled. "Do you have to leave?"

"Gotta go to church, but I'll be back." A smile twitched on his lips. "In citizens' language that means a meeting at the clubhouse."

"Oh. Can you tell me what the meeting's about?" She stared at him, taking in his muscular chest, lean waist, slim hips, and corded legs.

"No way, darlin'. Club business."

Chains stood by the bed, looking sexy as hell. He ran a hand through his wet hair, the ink around his sculpted bicep danced erotically.

"Like what you see?" He bent down, planting his hands on each of her shoulders.

She inhaled sharply. He smelled clean, like soap and oranges, and a small smile ghosted her lips when she pictured him washing his hair with her citrus shampoo. With her eyes still fixed on his, she slowly nodded.

"I like what I see too." He reached forward and stroked her cheek, his fingers lingering near her mouth.

Slowly blowing out the held breath, Autumn grasped his hand and laced their fingers together. "I'm sure I look awful," she said softly.

"You're always beautiful, baby. Icing your face all night has helped the swelling a lot. The bruises will take some time, though." His jaw hardened as his eyes scanned her face.

"Nothing concealer can't cover." She laughed.

The lyrics from "T.N.T." by AC/DC filled the room, and when Chains jumped back, she admired the way the strong muscles in his back moved, making the skull tattoo on his shoulder ripple as he walked over to the dresser.

He spoke in hushed tones, and after he put the phone back down, he crossed the room and scooped up his clothes.

"I gotta get going," he said, dropping the towel.

Autumn sat unblinking, as she sucked in a breath and held it. His body was impressive, and she'd never stop looking at it, relishing the beauty of it. Her gaze fell to his relaxed dick that hung heavily between his legs, and flutters swirled in her stomach as memories of their sex-fest flashed through her mind.

Chains pulled up his boxers and her eyes cut up to his. Desire smoldered in those brown orbs, and she turned away, a bit embarrassed at being caught ogling him. A hearty laugh deepened the flush creeping up her neck.

"No reason to be shy about admiring the goods, baby." He winked at her, then shrugged on a pair of jeans.

Autumn watched as Chains buckled his belt and then slipped on a leather vest. Patches adorned the front, and plastered on the back of it was the club's logo: three skeletons on motorcycles with flames coming out the back tires. On the top it read *Night Rebels* and the initials *MC* were just under the image; on the bottom were the words *SW Colorado*.

"That's an interesting vest you're wearing. What does the diamond with the *one percent* in the middle mean?" she asked.

"It's our way of saying that we don't live like the rest of you," he answered, winking at her.

She reached down, picked up her nightgown and slipped it over her head, then pushed up from the bed.

"Is it hard to become a member of your club?"

"You gotta prospect first, but that's not open to everyone. A member has to recommend you; then, the club decides if they want you to prospect. Being a prospect is a lowly job, but if a dude can get through it, he's earned the right to wear a full patch." Chains walked over to Autumn and yanked her against him. "You're fuckin' incredible," he said, his hands gliding down her back and cupping her butt.

"You too." She kissed the base of his throat. "How long will you be at … what did you call it?"

"Church." A smile tugged at his lips. "About an hour, then I have to see a friend. I should be back in a few." He pressed his mouth to hers, his tongue delving in deep.

Autumn whimpered and leaned in closer, her arms looping around his neck.

He pinched, then smacked her ass cheeks before pulling away. "Fuck, you drive me wild, woman. I can't keep my hands off you, but if I'm late, Steel will have my head."

"Well, I don't want *that*," she joked, running her hands over his firm butt.

Chains groaned, then stepped away from her. "I should be back around two or so. I'll bring Thor and we can go to Dolores Canyon. Have you been there?"

She shook her head. "I've read about it. There's a lake there, right?"

"Yeah—Arrow Lake. It's not too far from here, and it hasn't been overrun by tourists like Overland Lake."

"Sound great. I can pack a lunch for us and bring some treats for Thor."

Chains walked over and kissed her deeply. "Sounds good, baby," he whispered. "I better get outta here, or we're gonna end up spending the rest of today in bed."

"That wouldn't be a bad thing, would it?" She ran her tongue along his jawline.

"Fuck," he rasped before breaking away. "That'll be our plan for tomorrow." He winked and took out a set of keys from his pocket.

After kissing Chains goodbye, Autumn watched him ride away; then, she closed the door and went into the kitchen to give Cinder some food. As she poured the dry food into the cat's dish, the phone rang.

"Here you go, sweetie." She set the dish down and hurried over to the table to pick it up.

"Hello?"

"Don't hang up on me."

Her stomach roiled upon hearing Bret's voice.

"I'm so sorry about the other night. Please, Autumn, hear me out. I've been sick about it, I really have."

Her instinct was to hang up on him, but she pulled out the kitchen chair and sank down on it. "I'm listening."

"I don't know what got into me. I've been using some new medication for an infection that I've had, and it didn't agree with me. I was acting all kinds of crazy." He let out a dry cough. "Like that night. You've known me for almost two years. I've never been violent toward you, right?"

"That's true," she mumbled.

"So, you know it's out of character for me. I didn't mean to hurt you." There was another cough, then a long pause. "How are you doing? I didn't break anything, did I? Please say I didn't."

"No, but I look like hell. I had to miss a day of work, and I haven't been out of the house since you hit me."

Bret groaned loudly. "I hate even hearing you say that. I've never hit a woman. I don't know what happened."

"Neither do I. You seemed so angry about your brother."

"Yeah, well, he pisses me off. He thinks he's some fucking stud around the ladies. Every girlfriend I had in high school just wanted to date him. I don't know why women like men who are losers."

"The point was, you didn't trust me. I never cheated on you—that's never been my way. You should've known that."

"When it comes to him and women, I always wonder. I just lost it when I saw you with him at Chianti's."

"You were with your ex-girlfriend. Anyway, you broke up with me." Autumn stood up and walked over to the coffeemaker. If she was going to continue talking to Bret, she'd need caffeine for sure.

"Teresa's just a friend. I'm not back with her, and I never cheated on you while we were together—I swear it."

"Thanks for telling me that." She inhaled the scent of the dark roast.

"I don't know, I freaked out about settling down for life, and my mom was really pushing me to get married."

"I was kind of freaked about it too." Opening the cupboard, she took out a mug.

"You were? You seemed so into it," he said.

"It was the hype from your mom and mine. Anyway, you and I were fighting too much for a couple who was about to be married. It just sucks that I paid for a lot of it already, and canceling everything is going to be a real time sucker. I'm grateful Sadie's offered to help me out with that." *Are you going to offer to pay me back for some of the expenses? I bet not.*

"How's the clinic going?"

I called that one. Jerk. "Fine." Grasping the handle, she brought the coffee pot over to the table, then poured the dark liquid into the cup. At the first sip, she closed her eyes, savoring the rich flavor.

"I'm still on a business trip—I've been on this one for the last couple of days. I'll probably be gone for a while."

"Oh." *Why the hell's he telling me that?*

"If you talk to my brother, you can let him know that."

Huh? Strange. "I should be going," she said before taking another sip.

"Autumn, I'd like to take you out to dinner when I get back in town. I think I made a mistake … I miss you."

Didn't see that coming. "You *think*? You don't know?" Autumn chuckled softly. "The truth is, getting married would've been a disaster for both of us—I see that now. We don't really mesh."

"What the fuck does that mean? We've been together for over a year, and have known each other for two, and you've just discovered that we don't fucking *mesh*?" Anger punctuated his words.

"Sometimes people stay together because they've been together for a while. I think that was our case. Face it—you never liked my friends or wanted to go out with them, and I thought your friends acted like they were still living at the fraternity house. It's best that we go our separate ways."

Bret didn't say anything, and if she hadn't heard his rapid breathing, Autumn would've thought he'd hung up. A tense silence crackled over the phone, then he said in a low, terse voice, "You're with Chet, aren't you?"

Autumn finished the coffee, stood up, and walked over to the sink where she rinsed the mug and put it in the dishwasher. Licking her lips, she looked out the window into the backyard. The bare branches of the oak tree swayed slightly, and she saw Tommy—the six-year-old from next door—running around his yard with a small green ball, laughing like a hyena.

"Your silence means you are."

Bret's voice echoed in her ear, reminding Autumn she was still having a conversation with her him.

"My silence means what I do or don't do is none of your business anymore. If you want to know anything about your brother, go ask him. I hope you have a good life." Then, with a single tap on the screen, Bret disappeared. *What an asshole. The decent thing would've been to offer to help me cancel all the damn wedding plans and pay for half of it.*

Bret's call threw her off balance because it wasn't in his nature to do something like that. He *never* apologized while they were together, so she couldn't quite figure out what had prompted him to do so now. Maybe he was worried she'd call the police, or that Chains would come after him.

Autumn snapped her fingers and nodded. *Of course—he's scared Chains will kick his ass. That's why he told me he wasn't in town. I wouldn't be surprised if he were laying low at Teresa's house. How ridiculous to be that afraid of a sibling.* She glanced over at the wedding notebook she'd been keeping, and groaned. Come Monday, she and Sadie would have to start calling the various vendors and canceling the orders. "I'm going to take a real financial hit on this," she muttered under her breath while walking out of the kitchen.

When she reached the second floor, Autumn grabbed a large green towel out of the linen closet and stepped into the master bathroom. A nice hot soak in the tub was just what she needed, replete with scented candles and Enya playing in the background.

She slipped out of her nightshirt, noticing more love bites than ever on her body. The one on her neck would have to be covered before she went to Eli's Delicatessen to buy some things for their lunch. Turning on the faucet, Autumn sprinkled some bath salts that Sadie had given her for her birthday in the summer. While the soaking tub filled, she lit several candles, turned the music on low, and switched off the ringer on the phone.

When the tub was sufficiently full, she sank into the steamy water, slipping beneath the surface to wet her hair. She came up blinking water from her eyes, then settled back and let the warm water swish around her.

Autumn rested her head back and thoughts of Chains floated in her mind. How had he become such an integral part of her life in so short a time? And why the hell didn't she feel one scintilla of guilt about dating Bret's brother so soon after the breakup? Talking with Bret earlier made her happy that he was out of her life. What she needed now was to find out who the hell Ruby was and what the hell those club girls were all about. Suddenly, she found herself plagued by unfamiliar jealousy.

Not wanting to think about Bret, or the strong possibility of Chains crushing her heart, Autumn closed her eyes and let the music take her away.

Chapter Nineteen

AT A LITTLE after two in the afternoon, a barking dog roused Autumn from her nap. A car door slammed just as she pushed up from the couch. The barking drew closer and she shuffled over to the window to see what all the ruckus was about, and her heart did a flip-flop when she saw Chains swaggering up the sidewalk to her house with Thor in tow.

Autumn quickly fluffed her hair, then glanced down at Cinder.

"Be nice to Thor, okay?" Bending down, she scratched Cinder under her chin, then scooped the cat up in her arms and walked to the front door.

She flung it open before Chains rang the bell, and Thor barked excitedly upon seeing her, his white tail wagging a mile a minute. Chains stood there for a moment, his gaze sweeping over her.

"You look real good, Autumn."

The way Chains said her name in his deep voice sent shivers all the way to the pit of her stomach, releasing a slew of butterflies. She bit her inner cheek and shifted in place.

"It's amazing what concealer can do."

He stared intently at her, his gaze disarming in its fervency. "Come here, woman."

Autumn put Cinder down and the cat quickly scampered away, then she stepped on the porch and closed the screen door behind her. Chains gripped her arms and pulled her flush against him, crushing his mouth to hers. It was a messy, wonderful frenzy-of-a-kiss that rocked her to the core. *Incredible.*

Autumn pulled slightly away and smiled. "We're giving my neighbors a good show." She glanced over at Mrs. Hawley who stood on the front porch, staring. The woman was the cul-de-sac's busybody, but Autumn didn't want to give her any more fodder for gossip.

"It's good to give the neighborhood a shake up every once in a while." Chains snapped his fingers and Thor bounded over.

"Cinder's already run away to hide." Autumn opened the screen door and went inside.

Thor dashed around and sniffed everywhere while Autumn searched for her cat. She wanted to reassure Cinder that everything was okay. The cat had never had a dog in her space before, so she wasn't quite sure how her pet would react to a Siberian bursting with energy.

"It'll take some time for them to get used to each other."

Autumn nodded, then bent on one knee and stroked Thor's fur before wrapping her arms around him.

"How're you doing, boy?" When Thor licked her arm, she laughed and then stood up.

"He's crazy about his doc, just like I am," Chains said, his voice thick.

Heading into the kitchen, she glanced over her shoulder at him. "That's good to know.

I'll get our lunch so we can head out."

While Chains packed the SUV, Autumn ran upstairs and went into the walk-in closet in the master bedroom. Sure enough, Cinder was curled up in the corner, big eyes staring intently at the door. Autumn dropped to her knees and petted the soft fur.

"It's okay, honey. There's no danger," she murmured as she continued stroking her cat.

"Are you coming?" Chains's voice boomed from the bottom of the stairs and filtered into the closet.

"I'll be right down," she replied while scratching Cinder under the chin. She planted a quick kiss on top of the cat's head. "I'll be back later," she said before standing. She placed a paper bag in the middle of the bedroom, then headed down the stairs.

Three more bags strategically placed around the first floor had Chains laughing.

"What the hell are you doing?"

Autumn smiled. "It's for Cinder. She loves stumbling across these and cardboard boxes, but I'm fresh out of those. She pounces in and out of them and tears holes to use as tunnels. It's a fun distraction and makes her world feel safe again."

"Never would've thought that, but I don't know much about cats."

"Each pet is different and an owner gets to know what makes her animal tick." She picked up the picnic basket and laced her fingers through his. "I'm really looking forward to this. I work so many hours that I rarely find time to get out of Alina."

"I'm aiming to change that. The next trip out, you'll be on the back of my bike." He lowered his head and kissed her. "You pressed behind me on my Harley makes me hard, woman."

A tingle shivered down her spine at the thought of holding him tight as the wind rushed around. "I can't wait," she whispered, leaning against him.

Thor's barking broke through the sexual haze enveloping her, and she took out the house keys and tugged Chains toward the front door.

Minutes later, they were driving out of Alina. They passed miles of sand and sagebrush before turning onto a small road that took them into a forest of trees and lush vegetation. The contrast in the landscape was breathtaking.

"It's gorgeous," Autumn said and reached her hand across the seat for his.

Chains glanced over at her. "This is one of my go-to places. It's not that far from town, but feels miles away—like I'm the only one left in the world. When life sucks sometimes, this canyon grounds me."

"I bet it's wonderful to ride around the small roads on your motorcycle."

"It is. We're gonna do that for sure. I've been sort of preoccupied lately"—he drew her hand to his lips and nipped it, then gave it a kiss—

"and Thor's been left at the club without me."

"Feeling guilty?" She leaned over and rested her head on his shoulder.

"I guess." Chains brushed a kiss across her forehead.

"I feel like that too with Cinder when I have to work several long days in a row. I've thought about getting another cat so they could keep each other company, but I fear Cinder would be pissed for life about it." She laughed.

"I can see that happening—she's been number one for a long time."

Chains pulled the car off the road, and the three of them bounced over rough terrain for what seemed like miles to Autumn. Then the car stopped and he switched off the ignition.

"You okay?" he asked.

She moved her jaw left and right a few times. "Still working okay."

He tugged Autumn to him and kissed her deeply. "You make me laugh and I like that, woman."

Thor began barking and scratching at the door, and both Autumn and Chains turned around and smiled at the Siberian. Chains jumped out of the car and opened the back door, and Thor dashed out, running into the thicket of trees.

Chains walked around to Autumn's side, helped her out of the car, then grabbed the wicker basket.

"It's much cooler up here than in town. I bet it's a great relief in July and August when it's sweltering in Alina."

"It is."

They walked hand in hand through the wooded forest replete with cottonwoods and ponderosa pines. The wind sighed through the pine needles, carrying a sweet and earthy fragrance. Dried leaves and fallen pine cones crunched under their footsteps, and just ahead, through the shallow veil of trees, Autumn saw the lake. Thor was already at its shore, standing still with his nose up in the air.

"How beautiful," she said as they walked out of the forest. "I can't believe I've never come here before."

Chains stopped and tossed a blanket down on the ground, then placed the wicker basket on top of it. He whistled and Thor rushed over. Chains took out a Ziplock bag from a pocket in his leather jacket and fished out a Milk-Bone. Thor's blue eyes sparkled as he looked intently at his owner.

Warmth spread through Autumn as she watched the two of them interact, and when Chains bent down and hugged Thor close, her heart melted.

Standing up, he said, "Let's take a walk first. It's about a couple of miles or so around."

"That sounds wonderful."

Chains grabbed her hand and tucked it into his, and Thor padded ahead.

Rays of lights danced delicately across the water that mirrored the sky above: cornflower blue with wisps of clouds. Pine trees cast shadows across the shoreline as rippled water gently lapped it. The surrounding area was a kaleidoscope of color: burnt orange, mossy green, flaming red, and harvest gold. A light breeze undulated the surface of the lake and blew Autumn's wispy bangs from her forehead.

The stillness of the area, the warmth of her hand in Chains's, the beautiful surroundings, and Thor's excitement in spending time with them—all made up a perfect day for Autumn. Since she'd arrived in Alina, Autumn had been on what seemed like a hamster wheel: working long hours, usually on call during weekends, and putting most of her energy in building up her business. *Rinse and repeat. Day after day.* And when Bret came into her life, any energy she had left went to him … then the wedding planning for four long months.

She glanced at Chains, who looked pensive as he stared at the water. Since meeting him, her world had turned upside down but in a good way. The short time they'd spent with each other were the best times she'd ever had with any man. Part of her was thrilled by it, but another part was terrified because it seemed like everything was going too fast.

Autumn remembered the story her dad had told her of how her

parents had met at a party while they were college, that when he'd seen her mom across the room, he knew he'd love her forever. Yeah... Autumn had thought it sounded hokey as hell and had even questioned the veracity of it until her mother had told her something very similar about the first time she'd seen Autumn's father. Her mom was a big believer in fate and destiny, but Autumn had always been more practical with that kind of thing than her parents.

But now she wondered if maybe there was something to this whole love-at-first-sight and destiny thing that she'd always dismissed. It would certainly explain why she felt such a strong connection to Chains, and why no man had ever made her *feel* the way he did. And the fate and soulmate aspect gave some insight as to why in the hell she was falling—*correction*, had already fallen in love with him. *And it's been barely a few weeks since I broke up with Bret... Chains's brother.* "Ugh." A groan escaped from her throat.

"You okay?" Chains asked, stopping. He wrapped an arm around her shoulder and drew her close.

"I'm great. I was just clearing my throat. I could get addicted to this place."

He nodded. "It has a way of pulling you in." He stroked her cheek. "Like you do to me."

Autumn nuzzled his neck. "You must know that I'm falling hard for you." She couldn't quite bring herself to admit she was crazy in love with him. Call it pride or self-preservation, but she didn't think she could handle Chains pulling away from her. *That'd be a great one—two brothers dropping me in less than a month.*

"I do, and you must feel that I'm totally mesmerized and captivated by you. No woman has done that to me—not even my ex. So, that's huge, baby."

Mesmerized and captivated are good, right? I mean, he didn't say he loved me, but that's a lot to expect since we've only been together for a short time.

He let out a hearty laugh. "What's going on in that head of yours?"

She turned toward Chains and wrapped her arms tightly around him. "Nothing much except that this is one of the best days I've had."

"It's like that for me whenever we spend time together."

A surge of happiness shot through her, electrifying every cell in her body. Hooking her arms around his neck, Autumn drew his head down and crushed her mouth to his, sucking his tongue, nipping at his bottom lip, and kissing him wildly. With a deep growl, he took control of the kiss, deepening it, and pressing her tighter against him. His hands skimmed down Autumn's back until he cupped her ass, squeezing it while grinding against her. She felt his hard dick and rubbed her body closer, her skin tingling with every feral sound he made.

She broke the kiss, moaning into his mouth.

"What the fuck have you done to me, Autumn?" he rasped before taking her lips again.

She felt the earth below melt away and all time stopped for that moment as she gave in to her senses: his taste—sweet with a hint of tequila, the way he felt—hard and warm, his scent—soap and wind, the sounds he made—grunts and murmurings, and the sight of him—rough and gorgeous.

"I want you so fuckin' bad," he growled.

The sweet laughter of children along with Thor's barks brought her out of the cocoon of sensations and into real time. She pushed back gently and looked over at three children throwing rocks into the lake, and a couple standing near the shoreline, bending over and digging through the sand.

Chains whistled loudly and Thor stopped in his tracks; then, he switched direction and came running toward them.

"You stick with us, buddy," Chains said as he looped an arm around Autumn's waist and began walking.

Before long they'd circled the lake, then Chains shook out the blanket and laid it on the ground again. Autumn sat down, opened the basket, and began to take things out of it.

As they sat eating roast beef sandwiches, a chopped salad with butternut squash, dried cranberries, apples, walnuts, and feta, Chains unscrewed a beer bottle that he'd retrieved from the car and brought it to his lips.

"Is something bothering you?" Autumn asked before taking a small bite of her sandwich.

Shaking his head, he stared at the lake.

"Are you feeling funny about our situation? You know—the whole ex-fiancée thing." She held her breath.

He jerked his head back. "No fuckin' way."

"Then what? I know something's on your mind. You were quiet for most of the walk." Autumn dabbed the corners of her mouth with a napkin, leaned back on her palms, and stretched her legs out on the soft spread Chains had brought.

The muscle in his jaw visibly tightened as he looked over at Thor, who was sleeping at the foot of the throw.

"I'm worried about a buddy of mine. He's in the hospital." Chains glanced over at her, concern settling into the fine lines around his eyes and forehead.

She sat up straight and reached out for his hand to stroke it. "I'm so sorry. What's wrong with him?"

A small pause, then he blew out a long breath. "Someone shot him." He looked away and settled his gaze back on the view in front of them.

Shock reverberated through her and she gripped his hand harder. "That's awful. Did the police catch who did it?"

A slight smile danced across his lips. "The badges are looking into it. Anyway, he's got a raging infection. We thought he'd be back home in a week, and now the doc's saying it could be a lot longer."

"Is that the friend you visited today?"

He nodded. "Yeah."

Sadness spread across his face, and Autumn scooted closer and leaned into him, her hand still holding his. "You should've told me. We could've rescheduled today."

"No, babe, I wanted to be here with you. I needed to get away. Eagle's"—he looked down into her face and stroked her cheek with the back of his fingers—"hooked up to a bunch of tubes and shit. He's out of it right now."

"Is he in ICU?" she asked.

Another pause, this one longer than the first. "Yeah," he whispered.

"Actually, that's the best place for him to be. His doctor's flushing him with antibiotics, and he has a real good chance of pulling through just fine. I know it's hard to see someone you care about suffer, especially when you feel so helpless."

"Yeah—it pisses me the fuck off that I can't help him."

"Is he in your club?"

Chains nodded. "We go back a long time—we're real tight. Fuck," he said, pounding the spot next to him with his fist.

Autumn ran her fingers through his thick hair. "After we're done here, let's go to the hospital. I'll stay with Thor while you spend some time with your friend."

She felt Chains stiffen beside her, and his hand slid to her neck, pulling her head back. His lips were close, his gaze intense, then his mouth claimed hers possessively.

"Autumn," he kept whispering between fervid kisses.

She stroked the side of his face, feeling the faint rough stubble of his beard. Then, his lips trailed along the side of her neck.

"Oh Chains," she whispered. "I want to make it all okay for you."

"You are," he rasped.

She glanced across the lake and saw the couple from earlier sitting on some rocks, watching their children play. "The family's still by the shore. I don't think they're planning on leaving."

Chains pulled away, then looked over and groaned. Autumn smiled and patted her thighs, and he lay down on his back with his head in her lap. As she ran her fingers through his hair, his lids fluttered shut, and she moved her hands over his face, lightly tracing his dark brows, full lips, and strong jawline.

Sitting on the warm blanket, listening to his deep breathing mingle with the small waves that gently lapped against the shore, Autumn had never felt closer to a man than she did to Chains. Crazy? Perhaps. But it felt right, like it was meant to be.

She gazed down at his worry-free face and unadulterated love spread through her. It was one of those moments in time that held the promise of what might be, and Autumn wished she could freeze-frame it, hold it close and never let go.

"I've been waiting my whole life for you," she whispered.

The slanting rays of the late afternoon sun streaked through the trees and bounced off the ripples on the surface of the lake.

Chapter Twenty

Three weeks later

THE YOUNG TEENAGER led Chains and Scorpio to a rundown trailer down a dirt road behind the diner run by "Old Man" Bob. The eatery had been a part of the Alina landscape longer than most people could remember. Old Man Bob's great-grandfather had opened the place up for the weary traveler long before freeways crisscrossed the state. At one time, the place was known for its food and ambience, but over the last three decades, its reputation had fallen by the wayside. Now most of the dishes Bob prepared had grease as the main ingredient, but the diner still had a loyal customer base, which kept it afloat all these years.

"Here it is," the teen said, pointing to a mobile home with faded metal siding.

In front of the trailer was a rusty aluminum picnic table with four folding chairs, and to the left side, an outdoor fire pit and a muddy three-wheeler.

The teenager's eyes darted from Chains to Scorpio, then back to Chains. "Uh … you said you were gonna pay me if I showed you where Benny lives."

"Don't sweat it, kid," Scorpio said.

Chains pulled out a fifty-dollar bill and handed it to the moppy-haired teen. "Make sure you keep your fuckin' mouth shut about where you got the dough."

The boy crumpled it in his hand, then shoved the wadded up bill into his jeans pocket. "Of course." He turned around and walked back down the road.

Benny was a low-level drug dealer—just a cog in the multi-billion-dollar drug industry. He had a full-time minimum wage job that barely paid child support for his two kids and the day-to-day bills. The Night Rebels paid him for information in regard to drug selling, gun smuggling, or whatever else he heard on the streets. As long as Benny didn't fuck with them, they let him deal in dime bags to the locals. Chains and the other brothers understood the dealer's plight: not enough money from honest work to live a somewhat decent life.

Benny had friends in Pueblo who worked in the lower rung of the drug ladder for Los Malos. The Night Rebels offered the dealer a good chunk of money to find out why the fuck Los Malos were in on the drug deal a few weeks before.

Chains opened the screen and knocked on the red-painted door. Strains of punk music filtered out from the trailer, so he pounded harder once more.

"Someone's in there," Scorpio said, jerking his head toward the window.

Chains stepped back and saw the curtains move as if someone was peeking out at them. "Open the fuckin' door!" he yelled as he kicked at it, then stood off to the side just in case someone inside wanted to take a shot at him.

The music stopped, then hinges creaked as the door slowly opened and a dishwater-blonde-haired woman peered out.

"Whaddaya want?" she asked, her voice scratchy and hoarse. She pushed open the screen and stepped onto the small porch.

She wore skinny jeans and a crop top that hung loosely around her boney shoulders. It looked like too much meth and too many nights partying had stripped the flesh off her bones, making her into a breathing skeleton. She stood in the doorway staring at them while picking at scabs on her face.

"Where's Benny?" Chains asked.

"And we're not in the mood for any bullshit," Scorpio added as he walked up to the steps.

"I don't know." She looked over them. "Maybe he's having food. He's always wanting food." A large smile revealed blackened teeth.

Before they could question the woman further, the sound of tires sounded behind them. Chains went for the gun in his waistband, and Scorpio followed suit as they both crouched low and made their way to the picnic table.

"That's him now," the woman said.

The bikers waited until a black Honda Civic parked next to the mobile home. The door opened and Benny slid out.

"Hey, guys," he said.

Chains lifted his chin and Scorpio tipped his head.

"Sorry, I'm late. I had to wait for someone to show up." Benny glanced over at the woman. "Bring out three beers." She nodded, then disappeared inside the trailer.

"You selling shit other than weed?" Chains asked, his gaze fixed on the smalltime dealer.

Benny shook his head vigorously. "No way, dude. I know that shit isn't tolerated in the county." He laughed nervously. "I don't want to get on you guys' bad side."

"Where's your woman getting the meth from?" Chains said.

"Uh … I … uh … make it." Benny waved his arms toward the screen door. "Melinda's been using for a long time. I'd rather she get shit I know is good and pure." He glanced down at the dirt and then back at the porch, avoiding Chains's intense stare.

"And you're not tempted to make a few bucks by selling some baggies?" Chains took a few steps toward him. "Do we look like fuckin' idiots?"

Benny stepped back, his hands raised in front of his chest. "I don't sell the shit in this county. If you heard anything—it's bullshit. I sell in Pinon County and beyond—not in this county." He held Chains's gaze. "I swear on my dead brother's grave, dude. I'm not fuckin' stupid. Why the hell would I bullshit you guys—the Night Rebels?"

"If we find out you're dealing in Alina, we'll come for you," Chains said.

"And it won't be an easy death," Scorpio added.

Benny's small eyes bugged out. "I'm not dealing anything but weed."

"Then you're good." Chains glanced over at Melinda as she walked down the stairs. Benny was in his late twenties, and he was pretty sure Melinda was around the dealer's age but she looked like at least twenty years older due to her crank habit.

"Yeah, I'm good." A smile spread across his face as his shoulders slumped forward.

"Here ya go," Melinda said to Chains as she handed him a bottle of Coors.

"Thanks," he replied as he twisted off the bottle cap. He took a long pull of the beer.

Melinda handed a bottle to Scorpio, then to Benny. "You need anything else, baby?" Benny shook his head, so she turned around and went back inside.

"So what's the word on the streets of Pueblo?" Scorpio asked before bringing the beer to his mouth.

"Los Malos have worked with that dude Eric before." Benny motioned the bikers to sit down at the picnic table.

"In Colorado?" Chains asked.

"No—in Kansas, Oklahoma and, I think, Missouri. The old man didn't want them involved, so when he does a deal, he keeps them out. The old man and his son, Eric, have butted heads on this before. Eric likes the muscle Los Malos gives him because he's fucked over a few buyers in the past."

"Did Los Malos know this was a Night Rebels' deal?" Scorpio said.

"My contact says the word is, they didn't."

"Fuckin' bullshit. I don't believe it for a minute." Chains took another swig of beer.

Benny shrugged. "Maybe they're just sayin' that 'cause they don't want no trouble with you guys. But that's the word—Los Malos didn't know." Benny's gaze went between Chains and Scorpio. "The word is that you iced Eric and a few of the Malos." When he brought the beer bottle to his mouth, the bikers saw the dealer's hand was trembling.

A tense silence fell between the trio. Benny drank the beer in a single gulp and proceeded to let out a long, sustained belch.

Pulling at the label on the amber bottle, he said, "Los Malos was promised a third of the weed."

"Who the fuck did they think they were meeting up with?" Scorpio said.

"Some two-bit drug dealers?" Benny replied.

"In *our* county? Bullshit—they knew. You got anything else?" Chains asked.

"They're playing like bigwigs, but they're scared as shit of you guys and the other biker club you're affiliated with."

"The Insurgents definitely will want to know what the fuck's going on, especially since they were on our turf trying to fuck us over." Scorpio tossed the bottle into a large metal drum near the porch.

"You bikers stick together, huh?" Benny said.

"Damn straight." Chains stood up and threw his bottle into the drum, then nodded at Scorpio.

The well-built biker slipped a hand inside his cut and pulled out three hundred-dollar bills. "Thanks," he said, handing them to Benny.

"If I hear anything else, I'll let you know." The dealer shoved the money into the front pocket of his shirt. "If you need anything, you know where to find me."

Chains grunted, lifted his chin, then turned around and caught up with Scorpio.

"Do you think he told us everything he knows?" Scorpio asked.

Chains nodded. "There's no reason for him not to, but there's no fuckin' way those Malos assholes didn't know we were the buyers."

"I agree. We'll see what Steel wants to do. Since the ATF has been sniffing up our asses, I'm sure he'll wanna lie low for a while. The old man shouldn't have sent his fuckin' son."

"And Gary knew he was dealing with those Malos losers, and they're in Colorado. Bad move," Chains said.

"Maybe he wanted to get rid of the asshole, and he let us do the dirty work." Scorpio stopped in front of the diner. "You wanna get some chow before we head to Durango?"

"Only if I wanna get my damn stomach pumped. We can grab something at Leroy's."

Scorpio chuckled. "I haven't been inside this place in years."

"Well it's a fuckin' dump." Chains glanced down at his phone. "We gotta hustle. Let's just go to a drive-through instead."

"I'm feeling like tacos. You up for that?"

Chains nodded. "Taco Bell's on the way to the highway."

The bikers were going to Durango to pick up Eagle, who had finally gotten cleared from the doctor to go home. The local hospital hadn't been equipped to deal with Eagle's raging infection, so he was transported to the nearest city that had an infectious disease doctor. Eagle had been in ICU for almost two weeks before being transferred to a regular room for three weeks.

"I bet you'll be glad not having to haul your ass to Durango every day," Scorpio said as he slid into Chains's Tahoe.

"It wasn't so bad," he replied as he pulled onto a two-lane road.

Durango was roughly sixty miles northeast of Alina, and depending on traffic, it could take anywhere from an hour or two to get there. After placing their order, Chains steered the car onto the freeway and headed out of Alina.

Two hours later, Eagle rested in the back seat as the bikers made their way to the clubhouse.

"I bet the first thing you do after downing a few shots of Jack is fuck your way through the club girls," Scorpio said as he handed a joint to Eagle and then to Chains.

"Damn straight. My dick's pissed as hell at me." Eagle chuckled.

"Just be happy you still got a cock that can work," Scorpio said.

"You don't know that yet." Chains joked.

"My cock's working just fine. I kept getting a damn hard-on every time this cute nurse bent over me and dabbed my forehead with a cool damp cloth. And that perfume of hers … fuck."

"You getting hard now?" Scorpio let out a hearty laugh.

"Fuck you," Eagle grumbled.

Chains took out a lighter and lit the joint, then inhaled deeply. "The women will be glad to see you—they've missed whatever you've been giving 'em."

Eagle flashed the middle finger, then turned sideways and looked out the window.

"We paid Benny a visit before picking you up," Chains said, glancing in the rearview mirror. "Los Malos claim they didn't know it was a Night Rebels' buy."

"I say that's bullshit," Scorpio said after blowing out a cloud of smoke.

Eagle shook his head. "I don't know. If they knew it was us who was selling the stuff, why the fuck didn't they come with more members? When I first saw all the SUVs heading toward the adobe, I thought we'd be overrun, but then there were only three or four assholes per vehicle. It doesn't make sense."

"We'll see what the other members think about what went down. Steel and Paco are calling church tomorrow."

"Until then, we're gonna party our asses off," Scorpio added.

"Have you been partying?" Eagle asked Chains.

Scorpio smacked Chains on the shoulder. "This dude hasn't fucked a club woman in forever. Ruby's horny as shit, but he's not putting out."

Chains shook Scorpio's hand off him and gripped the steering wheel.

"Did you go and fall for that vet doc?" Eagle asked.

"Yeah," Chains said as his knuckles turned white.

Scorpio jerked back in the seat. "Did you just say you've got a woman? A *citizen*?"

"Yeah," he mumbled.

"I knew you were a goner. When are we gonna meet this lady?" Eagle asked.

Chains shrugged. For the past week, Autumn had been asking to see where he lived and meet his friends, but he'd resisted. He wasn't sure how she'd react to the members and especially to the club girls. She'd been on his mind a lot that day, and he wanted to be with her in the worst way, so he was planning on dropping by her office after he had a drink with Eagle when they got to the clubhouse.

"You can't keep her hidden forever," Eagle said.

"I wanna see what she looks like. Is this the chick Jigger's been talking about?" Scorpio asked.

"It is," Eagle answered.

"Glad to have you as my fuckin' lawyer," Chains grumbled. "I'll bring Autumn by when I do. End of conversation."

Eagle nodded as smoke billowed around him. "I've decided to buy a new bike. I thought about it while I was bored outta my fuckin' mind in the hospital. After going through what I did, a new Harley is the sweet reward."

The rest of the drive home, the conversation centered on everything to do with motorcycles: old models versus new ones, customizing them with artwork and more chrome, adding illegal, altered exhaust systems so the bikes made more noise, and, of course, road stories.

In no time, Chains was back at the bar in the clubhouse, making a toast to Eagle before downing a shot of tequila. The members gathered around their brother, clasping him on the back, pulling him in numerous bear hugs, and bumping fists with him. The club girls buzzed around him, rubbing their barely clothed bodies against him. Lila sat firmly on Eagle's lap while Ruby and Kelly massaged his shoulders. Chains chuckled when Eagle glanced his way: the dude was enjoying this way too much.

As Chains slipped outside, he bumped into Steel, who was hurrying across the parking lot.

"How's Eagle?" the president asked.

"Loving every fuckin' minute of the attention he's getting, especially from the club women."

Steel laughed. "I bet he's been dreaming about this for the past five weeks. You heading out?"

"In a bit." Chains held up the phone. "I gotta make a call."

"Okay. Oh, I've been meaning to talk to you about teaching that online class. It's not going to work, especially now with this Los Malos shit the club's got going on. I just need all the members available all the time. Committing to teaching a class ties you up."

Chains nodded. "I came to that conclusion too. I'm thinking of offering an online video class or something. My wom—" He stopped and kicked at the dirt with the toe of his boot.

"We all know you got a woman." Steel chuckled. "It's been the main gossip at the club for quite a while. Who is she?"

"She's Thor's vet. Autumn's her name. I think she'll fit in with the old ladies real good—especially Breanna. She's so damn smart …" His voice trailed away.

"Can't be that intelligent because she's with you." Steel joked.

Chains flipped his president the bird, then laughed. "I can't say I haven't thought that myself."

"All kidding aside, you're no dumbass. Sometimes it's scary how your mind works. I'm just surprised you went for a citizen."

"Me too, but you know how it is," Chains said.

A grin spread across his face. "Yeah, I know *exactly* what you mean. Breanna just slipped into my life and blew me the fuck away." Steel gripped Chains's upper arm. "Good luck with it. If she's the one, don't let anything"—he jerked his head toward the clubhouse—"or anyone pull you away."

"I don't plan to," he replied.

Steel nodded. "I'll see you at church tomorrow." Then he walked toward the club's entrance.

Chains tapped in Autumn's number as he walked to the Tahoe.

"Hi," she said.

"Hey."

"Did you already pick up Eagle from the hospital?"

"Yeah, and he's doing a great job on getting shit-faced. Whatcha up to?"

"Just going over some tests. It's been kind of quiet here today, at least for me. Thor's doing great—he's stretched out next to the window because of the draft coming through it. Siberians love the cold."

Chains chuckled. "He's gonna love what's blowing in tomorrow. They say the San Juan Mountains are gonna get twenty-four inches dumped on them, which means we're gonna see about eight or ten inches of that."

"Thor will be in heaven. I'm glad you have your friend back with you."

"It's cool." Chains chuckled. "But he'll start getting on my nerves in a few days." He switched on the ignition. "I'm on my way over to see you and pick up Thor. I thought we could go for a ride before the sun goes down."

"You're finally taking me on the back of your Harley-Davidson? I'm speechless."

"That's a first." He teased.

"Oh, you." A giggle rang through the phone. "I'd love to go. I can sneak out early."

"I'll see you soon, baby."

Anxious to see her, Chains stepped on the gas, slowing down only when the phone rang. His mother's name popped up on the screen, and he grumbled under his breath while bringing the cell to his ear.

"How are you, Mom?"

"I'm okay. I need to ask you something. Remember the day you came by to take the box you wanted from the garage?"

"Yeah—I don't need it anymore, so I'll bring it back."

"You can have it, but did you take more than the one?"

"I picked up a few more. You can have them back."

An audible sigh of relief came over the phone. "I've been tearing my hair out wondering where I'd put them. They're full of old photographs and memorabilia of Bret's and Amelia's school years."

"I didn't look through them. I'll return them sometime next week."

"I'm still reeling over Autumn breaking off the engagement."

Chains narrowed his eyes. "Is that what Bret told you?"

"He said she didn't want to go through with it."

"And you believed him, like you always do." Chains slammed on the brakes and the driver behind him honked. He cut his gaze to the rearview mirror.

"Why would he lie about that?" Vexation accented his mother's tone.

"Because he's a liar and always has been. You and Dad just never see it … or don't want to." He pounded his fist on the steering wheel in frustration. "Is he back in town? I've gone to his condo a ton of times, but he's never there or at any of his friends' houses."

"What's going on with the two of you? He told me *you're* dating Autumn. That can't be true."

Chains snorted. Bret already had their mother on his side, making Chains out to be the bad guy and Autumn the heartbreaker. *What a fuckin' asshole.* "Bret's the one who called off the wedding, and before you start denying it, the dipshit contacted me and asked me to do it for him."

"I don't believe that," his mother gasped.

"Of course you don't—Bret's the fuckin' golden boy."

"Chet, watch your language!"

"As far as Autumn goes, yeah, we're together, and I don't give a fuck if you, Dad, or anybody else approves 'cause I'm not asking permission. Bret beat the shit outta her—did he tell you *that one*?"

"He'd never do something like that. Your father's right—you've always been a troublemaker and very jealous of your brother."

"Jealous of a pansy-ass? Nah. Disgusted? Yeah. Disdainful? Fuck yeah. But *never* jealous. So, is the loser at the house seeking protection from you and Dad?"

"Stop talking about your brother like that. What's wrong with you? You abandoned your family to live with hoodlums, and now you're flaunting the fact that you're with that … that horrid woman who broke your brother's heart? Why aren't you normal?"

"If Dad, Bret, and the way you always take Dad's side against me is *normal*, then I'm fuckin' thrilled not to be *normal*. You think what you want. I'm done." He clicked off the phone and didn't pick up when his mom called back.

Anger flashed through him, and Chains took several deep breaths to calm down before he went inside the clinic. Bret had been dodging him ever since he'd abused Autumn. He knew Bret was in town, but he hadn't shown up at his place of work, his condo, none of his friends' houses, or any of his usual haunts. Even upon questioning Teresa at her apartment, she'd claimed that she didn't know where Bret was. Chains figured the asshole was working remotely, and now he was pretty sure he was at their parents' house.

When Autumn had told him a few weeks ago that Bret had called and asked to get back together, Chains had scoured the town looking for him to no avail. A fierce stab of possessiveness had hit him, and it was at that moment he'd realized how much Autumn meant to him.

The phone's ringtone sliced through his thoughts and he picked up his cell and shouted, "What?"

"Don't chew my head off." Autumn's voice was warm and bright like a beam of sunshine.

The anger jabbing his gut dulled, and the corners of his mouth turned up. "Sorry, I didn't look at the name before answering."

"Oh. Who was it meant for?"

"No one, really. What's up?"

"I was wondering how long you were planning to stay in the parking lot." She let out a small laugh.

Chains looked at the front window and saw her peeking out of the Venetian blinds. "I'm coming in."

"Come around back and I'll let you in." A tremor of excitement laced her voice.

Desire replaced anger as he quickly got out of the car. "I'm headed there now." He slipped the phone into the pocket of his leather jacket and hurried across the lot.

When he rounded the corner of the building, he saw Autumn standing just outside the back door. She looked breathtakingly beautiful in a dark green lace top and a pencil skirt, which fit her to perfection, and complemented the dazzling copper highlights the afternoon sun had brought out in her hair. Blood rushed to his groin and his dick twitched.

Autumn's spellbinding eyes danced in merriment as she watched him close the distance between them. As soon as the heady scent of her perfume engulfed Chains, he yanked her to him without thinking, then kissed her deeply.

"I missed you, babe," he whispered.

"We were together last night," she murmured.

"It feels like a fuckin' lifetime." Pulling away, he gripped her hand. "Come on."

Once inside the building, she wiggled out of his grasp, and he followed her into the office. Thor immediately leapt up and rushed over to Chains; he petted the dog, then took out a bully stick from his pocket and gave it to him. The dog dashed over to the corner of the room and happily chewed on the bone.

"He likes that," Autumn said.

"And I like these," Chains whispered as he cupped her tits.

"I'm at work," she said, glancing over his shoulder at the door.

"And why's that a problem?" He nuzzled her neck, then licked and nipped the sensitive spot near her ear, knowing it drove her fucking wild.

"Chains," she whispered, and then pushed away. "Let me lock the door."

He watched her ass move so damn seductively in the tight skirt, and his dick hardened even more. When she came back over, he snagged her around the waist and crushed their mouths together, his tongue charging in as he consumed her. Autumn's large tits brushed his chest with each breath she took; the feel of her nipples hardening fueled his lust even more. He ground against her and a gritty moan ripped through her throat. Chains pulled back, their eyes reflecting one another's desire. Placing her fingers on his crotch, he said huskily, "Feel what you do to me?"

Autumn pressed closer to him as if trying to fuse their heat together. She kissed the base of his throat, then ran her tongue up to his chin.

"Fuck, baby. How do you make me think of you all the time?" he rasped.

"I was going to ask you the same question," she whispered.

He gripped the lace fabric of her top and pulled it over her head and then he stepped back, his gaze taking in her satin bra and the goosebumps carpeting her skin. Chains whistled under his breath as his fingers traced over the fabric.

"Your tits are fuckin' sexy covered in all that soft material." He smiled as Autumn's cheeks reddened. He lowered his head and kissed each breast through the fabric, then dipped his tongue down into her soft cleavage.

She arched her back as her hard nipples strained against the bra. With one fluid movement, he unclasped the front hook and Autumn's heavy tits popped out.

"Fuckin' gorgeous," he said as he played with her nipples, tweaking and then tugging them.

She moaned and squirmed under his touch and he intensified it, loving the sounds she made. Chains flicked Autumn's erect nipples back and forth with the tip of his fingers, and she bucked when he pinched one nipple while capturing the other one between his teeth. Her hands moved down to his throbbing cock and began to unzip his jeans, but Chains batted them away.

"If you touch my dick, I'm gonna blow before I can fuck you, darlin'." Chains then reached behind her, unbuttoned her skirt and pulled it down as she lifted one leg and then the other. He tossed the skirt aside then leaned back on his heels admiring how sexy she looked in nothing but ivory lace panties and high-heeled brown pumps.

"Get over here," he commanded.

She took a few steps then leaned into him. His mouth moved from her shoulders upward, capturing her bottom lip with his teeth before kissing her hungrily.

"Chains," she murmured.

His fingers slid under her panties, parted her swollen lips, and plunged deep inside her wet slit. Autumn gasped then ground against his hand.

"Is it good?" he said hoarsely.

"Yes, so damn good," she panted.

"I fuckin' love how wet you are—it tells me how badly you want me."

She grabbed at the hem of his T-shirt, pushing it up. "I want you real bad."

Chains pulled back and whipped off the shirt, and she leaned forward and licked his tattoos before flicking his nipples with the tip of her tongue. A feral growl rumbled deep in his chest, and he spun her around and with a leg between her, he pushed her forward, bending her over so that her upper body was flat on the desk and her ass was up in the air. He pushed down her panties, ordering her to step out of them, and then he spread her legs wide, exposing her wet pussy and firm ass to him.

He brought his mouth close to her ear and said, "So sexy and ready." Chains unzipped his jeans then pushed them and his boxers down.

She wriggled her butt against his erection and looked over her shoulder and winked, and he about exploded.

Chains leaned over and took her arms and spread them out. "I'm gonna fuck you real hard, darlin'," he whispered before kissing her neck.

"You better," she said, her gaze locked on his.

"You're pretty fuckin' sassy aren't you?" he asked before swatting a firm ass cheek.

Strangled yelps of pleasure escaped through her lips, and her eyes burned with desire. Autumn's behind wiggled again and her thighs tried to clench together, but Chains held them apart. He raised his hand and planted a couple more smacks on that lush ass.

"You like that?" he said as he rubbed her clit, the sweet nub growing rigid with each stroke. He bent down and licked the reddened areas on her butt then gently nipped the soft flesh.

"You're killing me," she moaned softly.

Holding his dick, he pushed the tip of it against her heated wetness then pushed inside, and her pussy grabbed hold of it. Chains pulled out and looked at his cock glistening with her juices. Then he slammed into her, shoving in and out, his fingers digging in her hips.

"You're mine, baby. Don't ever forget it," he grunted while pummeling into her.

"And you better not forget you're mine," she sputtered between pants.

Chains slipped a finger between her drenched folds and feverishly rubbed the side of her sweet spot until tight muscles spasms grabbed his dick as she exploded, her hand covering her mouth to contain her orgasmic sounds.

As her insides clutched around him, Chains couldn't hold back any longer. Throwing his head back, his body stiffened, and he gripped Autumn's hips as he released his hot seed inside her.

"Fuck, Autumn," he growled before pulling her up and wrapping his arms around her. "I've never met a woman like you," he breathed in her ear.

Autumn placed her hands behind her, around his waist. Tilting her head back, he met her gaze. "I'm so happy we found each other," she said softly.

Chains bent down and kissed her deeply then held her close until someone knocked on the door.

"Dr. Stanford?" a woman said.

"Yes, Christina," Autumn replied as she pulled away and started dressing quickly.

Chains pulled up his boxers and jeans then perched on the edge of the desk watching her in amusement.

"Dr. Jenkins wants you in Room Two. He has a cocker spaniel in there and wants your opinion on something."

"Tell him I'll be right there."

Chains drew her to him and she giggled softly, trying to untangle his arms from around her.

"I have to go," she whispered, her gaze darting to the closed door.

He kissed her again then let her go. "How long will you be?"

"Not long. It sounds like Mark wants my input on whatever's going on with the spaniel." She rushed over to an oval mirror on the wall and swiped on her lipstick then unlocked the door. When she was halfway out of the room, she turned to him and said, "That was the best break ever."

He plopped on one of the chairs and watched Thor gnaw at his bone while he thought about her. Chains had thought he'd been in love with his ex-wife, but the way he'd felt about her paled in comparison to the deep and intense feelings he had for Autumn. She rocked his world in so many ways, and there was no way in hell he wanted to live without her. She was the good to his bad, the calm to his anger, and the quiet to the chaos of his world.

Yeah ... Chains, who swore off commitment, was in love. It surprised the hell out of him, but ... he wouldn't have it any other way.

Chapter Twenty-One

SNOW BLANKETED THE sidewalks, lawns, and streets, making them glitter in the cold white light of the full moon. Flakes swirled in an icy wind, clinging to tree branches and bushes. Chains brought the steaming cup of convenience store coffee to his lips and blew on it, his gaze never leaving his parents' house. Since the conversation with his mother, he'd been watching the house for any signs of Bret. From the way his mother *didn't* answer his questions concerning his stupid-ass brother, he knew the pussy was using their place as a refuge.

Chains took a sip of the coffee. Bitter and hot, it burned all the way down his throat. The car's wipers squeaked rhythmically as the snow began to dissipate. Then, the garage door opened and he saw the tail and reverse lights of his dad's SUV light up. He reached for the infra-red binoculars and looked through them.

"Gotcha, asshole," he muttered under his breath as he laid down the binoculars.

Chains waited until his brother turned onto another street before tailing him. With headlights off, he kept a healthy distance between the two cars because there were hardly any vehicles on the side streets as it was. When Bret pulled onto Main Street, the traffic picked up, and from the way the asshole was driving, Chains knew his brother had no clue he was being followed.

The SUV pulled into a space in front of Tequila Willy's—a restaurant and bar that had a small dancefloor. It catered to the young professional group, and Chains shook his head when he saw his brother walk into the place. *Figures.* He searched for a parking place, then called Jigger and Crow to join him. The axe he had to grind was with Bret, not the douchebag's friends, so he wanted the two members to keep the peace while he had a "talk" with his brother.

As Chains waited for his friends to arrive, he kept his eyes glued to the front door of the building. He couldn't believe Bret had dodged him for this long. *What a chickenshit. Did he really think I was just gonna let it slide?* There was no way that was ever going to happen. Outlaws never let anything slide. If it took a week, a month, or years, retribution would be had.

When he saw Crow pass the restaurant, Chains tapped on his horn to let him know where he was parked. Crow nodded and Jigger gave him the thumbs-up as they passed the Tahoe. A few minutes later, the two bikers were inside Chains's car waiting for instructions.

"This'll be quick. I don't want the damn badges involved. Just keep his pansy-ass friends from doing something stupid."

"Do you want us to rough them up?" Crow asked.

"Nah—this has nothing to do with them. If they want to play hero, then do what you gotta do."

"So what's your plan—take him out back and kick his ass?" Crow said.

Chains nodded. "Pretty much."

"How long did your brother think he was gonna be able to avoid you?" Jigger said.

"Fuck if I know. He's always been a whiny-ass pussy. We ready to roll?" Chains switched off the ignition and opened the car door.

The three men crossed the street and entered the establishment. A young woman with short brown hair and false eyelashes threw them a big smile.

"Good evening. How many in your party?" she asked.

"I'm here to see someone," Chains said, brushing past her.

"We're joining another table," Jigger said before following Chains and Crow.

Scanning the area, Chains spotted his brother at a table near the back wall.

"There's the fucker," he said to Crow. "Hang on. I'm gonna check out the back entrance. I'd rather not drag his ass out through the front."

The back door was off the kitchen and down a small hallway from the restrooms. As Chains walked back to where Jigger and Crow stood, a woman called out, "Chet." He turned around and groaned inwardly when he saw Sheila Bixby standing up from a table. *Damn! I don't need her fuckin' things up.*

"This is the last place I thought I'd ever see you!" She laughed, then went in for a hug.

He stiffened and stepped back. "I'm not staying."

Her gaze ran over him. "You look good—real handsome. How's Thor?"

"He's great. Listen, I don't mean to be rude, but I've got people waiting."

Sheila's face slackened. "I didn't mean to keep you. I just wanted to say hi to an old friend, that's all."

"No, it's cool, but I have to go. I'll see you around." He walked away, hoping she'd just sit down and not follow him.

"Who was the chick?" Jigger asked.

"Someone from high school."

"She's a looker," Jigger said, craning his neck to get a better view.

"Did you guys fuck back then?" Crow said.

"Yeah—once." Chains narrowed his eyes. "I'm ready to get this shit over."

Bret was in the middle of a story when Chains came over to him. From the snippets Chains heard, his brother was bragging and lying out the ass. The smile plastered on Teresa's face fell when she looked up and locked gazes with Chains.

"What's wrong?" Bret asked.

She touched her fingers to her lips and mumbled something incomprehensible. Confusion spread across the faces of a couple of Bret's friends, and fear etched across Matt's as he quickly looked down at the table.

Bret pushed back from the table and looked up. "What the fuck are you doing here?" he sneered.

Grabbing him by the front of his shirt, Chains lifted him up out of his chair.

"We need to talk," he said.

"I don't want to talk to you. I'm with my friends"—he glanced at them—"and we're waiting for our food."

"You'll be back. We got some shit to settle."

"Why don't you sit down and join us?" a curly-haired man said.

Crow took a few steps closer to the table and glared at him. "You don't wanna mix in this." He looked around the table. "It's between them—not any of you."

"If you don't want trouble, you'll all get back to your conversation and leave this alone," Jigger said.

The curly-haired man picked up a glass of water and took several gulps. The others fidgeted in their seats, and Teresa looked like she was going to have a nervous breakdown.

Matt leaned back. "We're not involved in this."

Chains nodded. "Make sure it stays that way." Then he dragged a protesting Bret toward the back entrance. A few patrons glanced over but did nothing.

The door opened into the alley and Chains threw Bret down on the snow.

"You fuckin' pussy! You've been dodging me and wasting my time for too damn long."

"I'm telling Mom and Dad, and they're not going to be happy. Dad will make sure you go to jail."

"Be a fuckin' man and stand up!"

"I'm not going to fight you, Chet."

"What, you only beat up women?"

Bret shook his head. "I didn't mean to hurt Autumn. I called and apologized. She forgave me. I didn't do it on purpose."

"How the fuck does that work, asshole? Her face was bruised and swollen for days, and you're telling me you didn't mean to do it? Then, why the fuck did you? Why didn't you stop after the first punch? If you were pissed about me, then you should've punched me, not her."

"I did stop. You know I've never hit a woman before."

"I only know you're a lying sack of shit who hurt Autumn, and she may have forgiven you, but I haven't. Stand the fuck up!"

"I'm not going to. This is crazy."

"I'm done with this shit." Chains bent down and yanked Bret up, then he punched him in the face.

"Shit, Chet! That hurt," Bret said as he tried to run away.

Chains punched him two more times before throwing him on the hard, icy ground. He lifted his leg and was ready to plant his steel-toed boot into his brother's side, but he stopped. Bret lay in a curled up position, his crimson blood staining the fresh white snow.

"Stay away from Autumn."

Bret looked up, his face bloody and swollen. "I think I'm dying."

Chains rolled his eyes as he leaned over and picked up his brother. "You're not gonna die. I didn't even break anything. You got what you gave Autumn. Go inside and clean up."

He took his phone out of his pocket and texted Jigger and Crow to head out, then he watched Bret slip and slide on the ice as his brother walked to the back door.

Before he went inside, Bret looked over his shoulder. "I really am sorry for what I did to Autumn."

"You should be. You treated her like shit—didn't even help pay for canceling the wedding, and then you beat her up? If you weren't my brother, I would've killed you for what you did to her."

Bret nodded, then disappeared inside.

Chains pulled the Tahoe away from the curb just as a police car pulled up in front of Tequila Willy's. In the rearview mirror, he saw Sheriff Wexler step out of the car. The badge would take a report, but that was where it would end. No decent man would blame Chains for what he'd done. That night had been about *an eye for an eye*, and the bad blood they had between them didn't figure into the beating. Bret had hurt Autumn, and Chains had hurt Bret back. It was the flow of life that made things balanced and right, at least in Chains's world.

A few miles away, he pulled the car over and got out, then picked up some snow and washed the blood off his hands. He jumped back into the car and headed over to Autumn's place.

Thor ran out of the house when Chains opened the door and barked up a storm. He opened the garage door and the Siberian dashed out to enjoy the cold weather.

"You're home." Autumn pulled her sweater around tighter as if to keep out the cold.

"What I had to do didn't take as long as I thought." Chains had figured Bret would have at least put up a fight. He wrapped his arms around her and felt her shiver against him. "You better get inside—it's freezing. I'm gonna take Thor for a quick walk, then I'll warm you up." He brushed his lips across hers and stepped back.

Chains watched as Thor ran around the small park near the house, and he realized that the dog needed way more space than what he had at Autumn's home. Chains spent four or five nights a week at her place, and Thor was always with him. The other times, Chains was at the clubhouse with acres of land surrounding it. Siberian huskies were bred to run long distances, and they required a lot of exercise, so the club's setting was perfect for Thor.

A half hour later, Chains was drying the husky off with a large towel Autumn had given him. He refreshed Thor's water bowl, gave him a treat, and went upstairs to take a quick shower.

When he came down, Autumn was dozing on the couch with the fireplace burning brightly and the television on low. He loved looking at her while she slept. There was something about it that made him feel trusted. And lucky.

Chains sank down on the couch and placed her feet on top of his thighs. Cinder, stretched across the top of the sofa, stared at him for a few seconds, then put her head down on her paws. Autumn stirred slightly and then her lids fluttered open.

"Did you just come back?" she asked, stifling a yawn.

"It's been a while." He massaged her feet, the fuzzy material was soft, like a baby's blanket. "I didn't mean to wake you."

"I must've dozed off." She let out a big yawn, then pushed up to a sitting position. "It must've been the wine I had at dinner tonight."

"How was the restaurant? What was the name of it?"

"Thai Mango, and it was delicious. Sadie's obsessed with it the way I am with the Spice Room, so we've been eating a lot of Thai and Indian food lately." She wiggled her toes, then her gaze fell on his swollen knuckles. "What happened?"

He shrugged. "Must've hit them against something." Before Autumn could ask another question, he grabbed her ankles and pulled her toward him.

Laughing, she reached out her arms, and Chains gladly yanked her to him, claiming her mouth in a long, deep kiss.

"Didn't you promise to warm me up?" she whispered against his lips.

"I did," he said as his hands touched her shoulders, sweeping her hair over one of them, as he placed feathery kisses on the side of her neck.

"That feels nice," she murmured.

Chains slowly pushed up the hem of Autumn's nightshirt, his heated gaze fixed on her sheer panties. "I'm gonna warm you up real good, baby."

"You always do." She swiped her tongue across his bottom lip, then placed her hand on his erection. Looking up, he caught her eyes as she slipped it into his sweat pants. He hissed when her soft fingers curled around his dick.

"I want to taste you," she said, pushing back a bit.

Chains jumped up and pulled off his pants, then guided her to the floor where she kneeled between his legs. When Autumn looked up at him with lowered eyelids and slightly parted lips, he thought he was going to lose it. She grabbed the base of his cock and licked up and down his shaft, rolling her tongue around all sides. He leaned back against the cushion, enjoying the burst of sensations rushing through him as she worked his dick.

Autumn kissed and licked the tip, slowly drawing him into her mouth until she took his whole cock down her throat, her lips tightening as she swirled her tongue.

"That feels so fuckin' good, baby," he rasped, his gaze locked on hers.

As she worked her way up and down his hardness, the small whimpers and moans drove him wild. He watched as his cock disappeared between her lips over and over again.

"I don't wanna blow yet, darlin'," he said as he gently pushed her head back.

Autumn leaned back on her knees, then rose to her feet. Without breaking eye contact, she slid her panties down her lean legs and stepped out of them. Then, she leaned over Chains and kissed him as he gripped her hips and guided her onto his lap and his dick.

He swept his tongue across her bottom lip as he trailed a hand up her belly and over the ladder of her ribs to the soft underside of her breast. He covered one of her tits with the palm of his hand and squeezed gently. Autumn arched her back, and he palmed the other breast. Grazing her nipple with his thumb, a guttural moan fell from her lips.

As he flicked, pinched, and pulled at her nipples, she rocked her hips and the warm walls encasing his erection tightened around him like a vise. Chains exhaled a ragged breath before capturing her lips. Autumn hooked her arms around him, and he cupped her ass and lifted her up and down. She bounced and rolled her hips as the coil at the base of his dick grew tighter and tighter.

"That's it, baby. Ride that cock," he growled. "Fuck."

Chains kissed her tits and sucked her nipples, loving how her breasts swayed and jiggled as she fucked him.

"I'm going to come." She moaned, moving faster, more frenzied.

When Chains bucked underneath her, she cried out, spasming all around his dick.

"So good, Chains. So fucking good." She let out a groan.

He held on to Autumn and fucked her until a moment later, when he joined her with a low grunt.

Chains massaged Autumn's thighs as she rested her forehead against his. With his dick still inside her, they stayed like that until both their breathing had returned to normal.

"That was awesome," she said as she moved off him. Grabbing several tissues from the box on the coffee table, she handed them to him before ambling toward the guest bathroom.

Chains wiped himself, then pulled on the sweatpants before tossing the used tissues in the trash and washing his hands. He went back to the couch and emotions crisscrossed through him.

"Do you want anything to drink?" Autumn asked, as she scooped up the nightshirt and shimmied it over her head.

"I'm good. I want to talk to you."

Finger-combing her hair, she glanced over at him. "Nothing serious, I hope." Trepidation filled her voice.

"It's serious, but in a good way, I think." He patted the empty space next to him. "Sit down, darlin'."

Autumn plopped down on the couch and tucked her legs up under herself. "What do you want to talk about?"

Chains pressed his lips together, then exhaled. "The backyard is too small for Thor." He saw her jaw clench and twitch. "I'm just saying ..." his voice trailed off.

"You're dumping me, aren't you?" A slight quiver pierced her voice.

"I'm blowing this all to hell." He shook his head, then chuckled. "What I'm trying to say is that I love you and want to marry you."

Autumn's eyes widened. "Are you serious?"

"I wouldn't be saying it if I wasn't. I know it's too soon, but I feel like we've known each other a long time."

"I was hoping you felt that way. I've been in love with you for a while but was afraid you didn't love me."

"I've been fighting it, but I want to give you my heart and spend our lives together. I want you to be my old lady, darlin'."

Autumn flung herself at him and peppered his face with kisses as she laughed and then cried, all the while saying "Yes" over and over again.

"I'll have your cut made so you can wear it at the club and biker events."

"That sounds great."

"You don't even know what the hell I'm talking about, do you?" He smiled.

"No, but you can explain all that to me later."

He kissed her long and hard, then held her close. "We need to build a house. I saw some land just outta town that's for sale. It's on five acres. That'd be cool for Thor."

"And I can get a horse … maybe two if you're up to riding."

"Never been on a horse, but I'll try it."

"It can be just as much fun as a motorcycle. When we went riding a few days ago, it felt like I was on a horse galloping in a meadow, but much faster. I can't believe this. I'm so happy."

"We're gonna have a good life."

She tilted her head up. "You like kids, right?"

Nodding, he replied, "I do."

"And you want them?"

"Yeah, but we got a bit of time for that." He kissed the side of her head.

"We do, but I'd like to have a couple before I'm thirty-six."

"I can arrange that." He squeezed her tight.

"I love you so much," she said softly.

"Then, it's all perfect."

Chains stared into the fire as he held his woman, the bitter gash inside him from his ex-wife's betrayal finally healed and gone. Autumn was his today and tomorrow, and he wouldn't have it any other way.

Chapter Twenty-Two

Two weeks later

THAT EVENING, AUTUMN stayed late to go over a few lab reports and finish up some paperwork. For the first time since she'd bought the clinic there weren't any animals in the recovery rooms, so she'd sent Rodney and Lauren home for the night.

Darkness crept in and she could see the moon's rays streaming in from a window at the end of the hallway, its long streaks looking like ghostly fingers on the blue-speckled floor. She reached over and turned off the music that had provided a pleasant backdrop to the day's activities. The quiet enveloped her and she was heavy in concentration when the sound of footsteps filtered its way from the reception area. Autumn looked up, expecting to see one of the doctors or employees, but no one was there. Pausing for several seconds, she dismissed the noise to an overactive imagination and looked back at the computer screen to resume her work.

Several minutes later, she heard an unmistakable cough.

"Mark? Is that you?"

Autumn froze and listened: nothing except a tree branch hitting against the building. She meant to call a trimmer to cut back the trees, but she'd been so busy that it had slipped her mind. *Does the scraping of branches against windows and stucco sound like a cough? I'm just spooking myself.*

Shaking her head, Autumn tried to refocus on the lab reports, but she couldn't concentrate anymore as she tried to listen for the slightest sound. *Did someone break into the building?* The clinic carried opioids such as tramadol, a pain medication used by both animals and humans, and hydrocodone, as well as Xanax, a very addictive benzodiazepine. *I can't remember turning on the alarm after Rodney left.* But she must have—it was her habit. Then, she remembered the phone had rung just when the tech had waved goodbye to her.

A shudder of fear crept up her back. *I didn't set the alarm. Dammit! How could I be so forgetful?* She strained her ears, but there wasn't any noise out of the ordinary. Autumn leaned back against the office chair. It was just paranoia. Silly anxiety. The dark night, the suffocating stillness, the wavering moonlight in the corridor had all contributed to her imagination running amuck. A nervous giggle escaped her lips as she looked back at the computer screen. There was only one more report Autumn had to review, and she could finish the paperwork at home. She leaned forward and scanned the results of a feline's blood test.

A creak. Then another. The pressure of footsteps on the hallway floor.

Autumn held her breath for a second and listened, positive that whoever was out there could hear her heart pounding like a jackhammer.

She leapt to her feet and blindly grabbed for a weapon off the desk: an amethyst geode with a miniature mining diorama in pewter. She'd bought it six months before in a souvenir shop in Central City during a weekend trip.

A long, dark shadow flickered on the floor as the footsteps grew louder, closer. Sweat broke out along Autumn's hairline, and she gripped her phone and tapped in Chains's number. *Pick up! Pick the fuck up!*

"Hi, babe." The sound of his voice was reassuring, and a sliver of calmness wove through her.

"Someone's in the building," she whispered. "I'm alone and the footsteps are coming closer."

"I'm on my way. Keep talking to me."

The silhouette of a man stood in the doorway of the office.

"Oh shit! There's someone here."

"Baby, I'm coming."

"Put the phone down." The stranger's voice was cold and menacing.

The man walked into the room, and all the air left her lungs with a low hiss as she stared ahead, too terrified to move.

"Fuck!" Chains yelled.

"I told you to put down the fucking phone. *Now*," the intruder growled.

Autumn placed the phone on the desk without ending the call. At that moment, she couldn't remember if he was staying at her house that night or the club. Since they'd gotten engaged, Chains had been spending most of his time at her home. If he was at her place, he was close, but the clubhouse was a bit of a distance from town.

"What do you want?" she asked, her gaze meeting his penetrating one.

"Sit down," the man said as he settled into one of the chairs in front of her desk.

The stranger looked to be in his late thirties, but there were hints of gray at his temples. His hair was an unruly mop of thick, curly hair. He wore blue jeans and a fitted shirt that showed off his lean and muscular build. His dark eyes were intense and framed by bushy brows. A thin scar down the right side of his face moved when he spoke.

Legs wobbly, Autumn gripped the edge of the desk and sat down.

"Your fiancé owes me money."

"Chains?" She shook her head. "You must be mistaken."

"I don't know who the hell *Chains* is—the guy I'm talking about is Bret Garver. And he owes me a helluva lot of dough."

"I'm not engaged to Bret—we broke up a while ago. I don't know why you'd think I'd pay money Bret owes you. Are you one of the investors in his new business?"

"No—he's got a big gambling debt, and I loaned him the money with interest, of course, and he's been hiding out on me. Bret said he's on the title of this place." The man looked around the office. "You got a nice setup here—it should be worth something."

"You need to leave. I don't know you nor do I know if what you're telling me is true."

The loan shark leaned forward. "This can either be easy or hard—it's your choice, but I'm not leaving until I get some fucking money."

"How much does Bret owe you?"

The intruder's smile was jagged like a broken zipper. He leaned back and thrummed fingers dusted with dark hair on his jeans.

"A hundred thou should do it."

Autumn's eyes widened. "*Dollars*? I don't believe any of this."

The man leaped up and took a gun out of the pocket of his jacket. "I'm tired of this fuckin' bullshit. You better have the money or I'm going to burn this place down." He leaned over and gripped her throat with one massive hand, squeezing tightly.

Autumn choked and gasped for air, her arms swinging wildly until she remembered the geode she'd put down on the desk before sitting down. She reached for it, and with all her strength, she clobbered him over the head.

"Fuck!" he cried. His hand flew away from her throat and went to the blood gushing from his skull. He looked at his red-stained fingers. "You fuckin' cunt!"

Autumn held on to the bloodied geode with both hands. If he was going to kill her, then so be it, but she wasn't going down without a fight.

He raised his weapon, and without thinking, she threw the souvenir at him, knocking the gun from his hand.

"Bitch!" he said, rushing around the desk, but Autumn made a dash for the door.

Knowing he'd probably pick up the gun, her pulse pounded as adrenaline coursed through her veins. When Autumn turned the corner, she heard his footsteps thudding from behind as she rushed to the front door. She yanked at it, but it wouldn't open. *He's going to kill me!* Autumn tried the door again and thought she could feel his breath on the back of her neck.

Looking quickly over her shoulder, Autumn saw one of his legs as he came around the corner.

"No!" she screamed just as the door opened.

"It's me, baby," Chains said as he pulled her away from it.

"He has a gun! He's going to kill me!"

"It's okay—I'm here. No one's gonna hurt you." Chains ran a hand over her hair.

It was at that moment she saw three men in leather jackets holding guns.

"How many are back there?" Chains asked.

"Just the one. He was right behind me." She watched him jerk his head at the three bikers who moved cautiously into the hallway.

"Just relax, darlin', we got it under control."

"I bet he ran out the back door. He'll come back again." She shivered in his arms. "He said that Bret owes him a hundred thousand dollars. He told me Bret borrowed it to pay off his gambling debt. I didn't even know Bret gambled." Memories of Bret asking her for money popped in her mind. *That's why he needed the money—to pay for gambling. He lied to me about everything.*

"Why did he come to you?"

"Bret told him I'd take care of it because I own the building. I don't know what he was thinking—he was probably just desperate to pay this guy off. The man was pretty intimidating."

Autumn heard an anguished cry that split the night. There were a few pops like firecrackers going off and then it was quiet.

"What was that?" she whispered.

Chains swept his lips over her forehead. "I think the loan shark met up with the guys. People do stupid things."

"Do you think he shot at them?"

"Probably. Anyway, he won't be back."

"I know he would've killed me if you hadn't come when you did. I can't believe Bret put me in such a dangerous situation."

"Yeah—I need to talk to him about that. And in the future, if you're gonna stay late at work and no one else is here, let me know and I'll hang out with you."

Autumn snuggled against him. "I love you."

"Me too. I gotta teach you some street smarts, woman."

"I'm already learning." She shuddered.

"That's what'll keep you alive."

Two bikers walked in and glanced at her then turned their attention to Chains.

"You need us to clean shit up?" a man with blond hair and blue eyes asked.

"Clean up?" Autumn said.

"You hit the guy in the head pretty good, baby. You don't want your staff seeing blood in the hallway and your office," Chains replied.

Autumn's face fell. "That's right. What am I going to say to them … to Mark and Marian? This is awful. Should we call the police?"

"No badges," the blond growled.

Chains cupped the sides of her face with his hands. "We'll handle things, darlin'. Don't worry about it." He looked at the bikers. "Do you want me to help out?"

"Nah, we got this. Diablo and Shotgun are out back," said one of the men—this one had dark hair.

"I owe you," Chains said as the men bumped fists then retreated behind the reception area. Are you ready to go home?" he asked Autumn.

"Yes. I'll go get my things."

When she walked into the office, she saw four bikers who immediately stopped what they were doing and waited for her to gather up her files, coat, and purse.

"Thank you," she said before leaving the room.

The men grunted and she quickly walked down the hall, grimacing when she saw the trail of blood on the shiny floor.

"Do you have an extra key?" Chains asked. "The guys will need to lock up. Write down the code to the alarm so they can secure the building when they're done."

"Okay. Are you sure we shouldn't call the cops?"

"Positive."

She handed Chains a piece of paper with the information about the alarm system and a spare key from her ring. In less than two minutes, he was back. He put his arm around her and they walked out into the night.

When they arrived at Autumn's house, she was still spooked from the events of the night. It was like she'd been wound up real tight and hadn't been released.

"You need to calm down," Chains said as he brought over a bottle of wine and set it on the table.

"I'm trying," she said softly. "I've never had anyone pull a gun on me. This whole thing is surreal."

"Let me get you a glass and grab a couple of beers. I'm hungry as hell and pizza sounds real good."

"Okay. Your friends were nice to help out. Are they in your club?"

"Yeah. We have each other's backs, and now that you're my woman, they have yours. What do you want on your pizza?"

"I'm not that hungry, so whatever you want is fine."

Chains placed a glass in front of her then poured a healthy portion of red wine into it before pulling the tab on a can of beer. "I know what you went through is traumatic. We can talk about it if you want."

"Order the pizza first. I'm going to change into something more comfortable. I'll be done in a few." She wanted to take a shower and block everything from her mind.

Thirty minutes later, she heard Chains yell, "Pizza's here," from the bottom of the stairs, and she combed her damp hair then went down to the family room.

"Are you feeling better, baby?" he asked as he opened the pizza box and put a slice on a paper plate then handed it to her.

"A little. It was just so scary. You know how they say your life flashes before your eyes when you think you're going to die? Well, nothing like that happened. The only thing on my mind was getting away from him."

"The instinct of survival. It wasn't your time, darlin'."

She took a bite and chewed, then said, "Do you really believe that?"

"Yeah, I do. I've been in some close situations and I'm still breathing. I had a friend in high school who got shot the week before we graduated. He was in Pueblo visiting family and he got caught in the crossfire of two guys gunning for each other. Three shots were fired, and they all went into him. Died on the spot."

"That's awful."

Chains nodded. "Yeah, it was bad, but it's life. Some people do dangerous as hell things and they die old, some do nothing and they're killed in a car crash or whatever. What happened to you tonight could've been real bad, but you were smart and called me. I'm just happy as fuck you didn't get hurt."

"I feel so grateful."

"And that's a damn good thing. Be grateful for the life you have and live it to the fullest." Chains brought the beer bottle to his mouth.

"Thank you," she whispered.

He leaned over and kissed her. "Now let's discuss our new home." He grabbed another slice of pizza and took a big bite.

For the next hour, they talked about the construction of their new home. Cinder slept in her favorite corner of the couch, close to Autumn, while Thor stretched out on the rug in front of the sofa, next to Chains, and she sat beside the love of her life. The flames dancing in the fireplace cast an orange glow around the room, and after Chains had reassured her that she was safe along with a few glasses of red wine, the incidents from earlier that night seemed like they'd never happened, like it had all been just a bad dream.

"Do you think your parents will ever accept me as part of your family? Your mom has never called me about the breakup, which actually surprises me," Autumn said as she leaned back against the cushion.

Chains quirked his lips. "Bret told my mom bullshit about the breakup which put him in a good light."

She grimaced. "I wondered about that. I like your mom, and I hate that she thinks bad things about me."

"She'll never believe he was the jerk in all of this. It's been a few weeks since I've spoken with my mom, and I haven't talked to my dad since the brunch. As far as I'm concerned, they don't need to know what the hell I do. What about your parents? What do they think about us getting married?"

"They think I'm crazy, but they both told me they've never seen me happier. It turns out, they weren't all that fond of Bret. I kind of picked up on it, but they never said anything to me when I'd ask. They can't wait to meet you, so I thought we could go to Denver for Thanksgiving. Would you be game for that? The holidays are big in my family."

"Yeah, that's cool. I want to meet the people who made such a sexy and special woman." He winked, then picked up the bottle of beer.

"They're going to love you. They may not get the whole biker thing, but they'll definitely relate to the rebel in you. Both my parents were hippies before they realized money is a necessity if you want a decent life. My dad's still a rebel at heart, joining protesters whenever he feels there's been an infringement on our rights. I'd say he's a Constitutionalist for sure. He'd have been right beside George Washington." Warmth spread through her. "He's the best dad. My mom is less radical, but she's a free spirit for sure. I really lucked out with both of them."

"I can't wait to meet them, and I'm with your dad all the way. The fuckin' government is trying to eradicate the Constitution and throw our rights in the damn garbage. It's good that your dad stands against it. We're gonna get along just fine."

"Do you think you'll ever make amends with your family? Your sisters seemed nice."

"I just don't fit in. It used to bother me when I was a kid, but it hasn't for a long time. The only thing we have in common is that we share the same blood. That doesn't mean shit to me. You know who my real family is."

"And they're great. Some are really scary, but I know that they'll always watch over me because I'm with you."

Nodding, Chains put down his beer. "That's the brotherhood."

"I wonder if your parents know about Bret's addiction. I'm still reeling over that."

"Nah—they think he's perfect, especially my old man. If they ever found out, they'd twist it so it'd somehow be my fault." He laughed.

"So you're not going to tell your mom? I think you should. I know you think she doesn't care about you, but deep down she does. She was thrilled you came to the brunch and upset when you left early."

"I guess she's *okay*, she's just not loyal to anyone but my dad. If the old man turned against Bret, she'd be on his side. And that kind of shit, isn't what I want. If I told her about Bret, what would be gained from it? She'd just worry and my old man would talk her out of believing it, and then she'd think I was lying because I wanted to get back at my brother for some dumb reason."

"Well, you know your family better than I do, but I hope for his sake, he gets help. That guy was not joking around. If Bret's not careful, he's going to wind up seriously hurt or killed."

"I'm sure he knows the risks—it's up to him to make the right decision. I can have a talk with him. I want him to know the shit he caused tonight."

"And I better file a quitclaim tomorrow. I want him off the deed to the property."

"Agreed."

"I do think it would be good if you talked to him. Even though he put me in danger, I don't want anything bad to happen to him. He really needs some therapy." She patted his hand. "I wish our house was already done. I can't wait to break ground in the spring. It's going to be beautiful."

"It'll kickass."

"Oh, Breanna called me the other day and asked me to join their old ladies' night out." Autumn giggled. "It sounds so funny calling myself an *old lady*."

He chuckled. "You'll have a good time with them. It's important to build a strong bond with the other old ladies 'cause you'll be spending a lot of time with them. You may not like all of them, but after time, they'll grow on you."

"So far, they all seem pretty nice except for Shannon. I don't think she likes me."

Chains shook his head. "Rooster's her old man, and she and Sam—Tattoo Mike's old lady—had a run of the club for years. They got bumped down when Steel got hitched to Breanna and then our vice president—Paco, you met him, hooked up with Chelsea, pushing those two further down the ladder. Shannon's also pissed because Rooster sometimes has some fun with the club girls."

Autumn looked away. "Do you think that's okay?"

"I think it's *their* business. If you're asking if I'm cool with having fun on the side, the answer is—no fucking way. We're a team, and loyalty and respect mean everything."

Picking up his hand, she kissed it. "I knew that, it's just nice to hear."

"You're it for me, darlin'. I'll be right back."

Autumn stretched her legs out and petted Cinder while she watched the flames flicker.

"Here you go," Chains said as he handed her a wrapped box.

"What is it?" she asked, untying the silver ribbon.

"You'll see."

With her heart beating a mile a minute and her stomach fluttering like crazy, she opened the lid on the blue velvet box. Inside was a sparkling solitaire diamond ring with emerald baguettes on each side of the stone. She picked it up.

"It's gorgeous," she murmured.

Chains took it from her and slipped it on her left ring finger. "I thought you'd like a citizen's symbol of our engagement."

Her lips quirked up. "Was the vest—I mean *cut*—the biker symbol?"

"Yeah—it tells bikers' to back the fuck off, and now this ring will tell citizens the same."

"You're so cute, really." Autumn looped her arms around his neck. "I love you too much."

"There's never too much when it comes to our love, woman."

"We're going to have a wonderful life." She nestled closer to him, then held up her hand, admiring the engagement ring.

"Never doubt it. You just need to understand that the club is a part of me, like your parents are for you. I'd never ask you to choose between them and me, and I don't want you asking me to choose between you and the brotherhood."

"I won't."

"Then, we're good."

"I feel so complete now." Autumn tilted her head back and met his gaze. "You are the man I've been looking for my whole life."

"You rock my world, woman. We were meant to be together."

After two broken engagements and a few dating disasters, Autumn had finally gotten it right. Snuggled against Chains, his arms wrapped protectively around her, she couldn't think of any place she'd rather be than right there with him. She was so excited for the next chapter in their lives, and she couldn't wait to be his wife and for Chains to be her husband.

"I love you," she whispered.

Chains put a finger under her chin and tipped her head backward. His gaze met hers. "And I'll always love you, darlin'." Then he claimed her mouth. He buried his fingers in her hair, tugging her head back a bit more to deepen the kiss. After a long while, he pulled up. "Fuck, baby, once I start kissing you, I just can't stop."

Autumn yanked him back toward her. "Then don't," she said before pressing her lips on his.

And as they kissed and then made love, she lost herself in his touch, his scent—his everything.

Together they made each other whole, and it was simply perfect.

Make sure you sign up for my newsletter so you can keep up with my new releases, special sales, free short stories, and other treats only available to newsletter readers. When you sign up, you will receive a FREE hot and steamy novella. Sign up at: http://eepurl.com/bACCL1.

Find all my books at: amazon.com/author/chiahwilder

I love hearing from my readers. You can email me at chiahwilder@gmail.com.

Visit me on facebook at facebook.com/AuthorChiahWilder
Visit me on twitter at twitter.com/chiah_wilder
Visit me on Instagram at instagram.com/chiah803

Notes from Chiah

As always, I have a team behind me making sure I shine and continue on my writing journey. It is their support, encouragement, and dedication that pushes me further in my writing journey. And then, it is my wonderful readers who have supported me, laughed, cried, and understood how these outlaw men live and love in their dark and gritty world. Without you—the readers—an author's words are just letters on a page. The emotions you take away from the words breathe life into the story.

Thank you to my amazing Personal Assistant Natalie Weston. I don't know what I'd do without you. Seriously, I'd be lost without you. You keep me organized and on track. I so appreciate that! Your patience, calmness, and insights are always appreciated. Thank you for stepping in when I'm holed up tapping away on the computer, oblivious to the world. You make my writing journey that much smoother. Thank you for ALWAYS being there for me! I'm so lucky you're on my team!

Thank you to my editor Lisa Cullinan, for all your insightful edits and making my story a better one. Also much thanks for your insight re: plot and characterization. I definitely took heed, and it made my story flow that much better. I truly appreciate your flexibility in working with this book. Your edits and insights always make my books rock and shine! As always, a HUGE thank you for your patience and flexibility with accepting my book in pieces. I never could have hit the Publish button without you. You're the best!

Thank you to my wonderful beta readers Natalie Weston, Megan Cruder, Sera Lavish, and Barbie McDonald. You rock! Your enthusiasm and suggestions for CHAINS: Night Rebels MC were spot on and helped me to put out a stronger, cleaner novel.

Thank you to the bloggers for your support in reading my book, sharing it, reviewing it, and getting my name out there. I so appreciate all your efforts. You all are so invaluable. I hope you know that. Without you, the indie author would be lost.

Thank you ARC readers you have helped make all my books so much stronger. I appreciate the effort and time you put in to reading, reviewing, and getting the word out about the books. I don't know what I'd do without you. I feel so lucky to have you behind me.

Thank you to my Street Team. Thanks for your input, your support, and your hard work. I appreciate you more than you know. A HUGE hug to all of you!

Thank you to Carrie from Cheeky Covers. You are amazing! I can always count on you. You are the calm to my storm. You totally rock, and I love your artistic vision.

Thank you to Ena and Amanda with Enticing Journeys Promotions who have helped garner attention for and visibility to the Night Rebels MC series. Couldn't do it without you!

Thank you to my awesome formatter, Paul Salvette at Beebee Books. You make my books look stellar. I appreciate how professional you are and how quickly you return my books to me. A huge thank you for doing rush orders and always returning a formatted book of which I am proud. Kudos!

Thank you to the readers who continue to support me and read my books. Without you, none of this would be possible. I appreciate your comments and reviews on my books, and I'm dedicated to giving you the best story that I can. I'm always thrilled when you enjoy a book as much as I have in writing it. You definitely make the hours of typing on the computer and the frustrations that come with the territory of writing books so worth it.

And a special thanks to every reader who has been with me since "STEEL." Your support, loyalty, and dedication to my stories touch me in so many ways. You enable me to tell my stories, and I am forever grateful to you.

You all make it possible for writers to write because without you reading the books, we wouldn't exist. Thank you, thank you! ♥

CHAINS: Night Rebels Motorcycle Club (Book 8)

Dear Readers,

Thank you for reading my book. I hope you enjoyed it as much as I enjoyed writing Chains and Autumn's story. This gritty and rough motorcycle club has a lot more to say, so I hope you will look for the upcoming books in the series. Romance makes life so much more colorful, and a rough, sexy bad boy makes life a whole lot more interesting.

If you enjoyed the book, please consider leaving a review on Amazon. I read all of them and appreciate the time taken out of busy schedules to do that.

I love hearing from my fans, so if you have any comments or questions, please email me at chiahwilder@gmail.com or visit my facebook page.

To receive a **free copy of my novella**, *Summer Heat*, and to hear of **new releases**, **special sales**, **free short stories**, and **ARC opportunities**, please sign up for my **Newsletter** at http://eepurl.com/bACCL1.

Happy Reading,

Chiah

Diesel's Distraction: Insurgents MC
Coming February 2020

Diesel is an **Insurgent**, one of the **largest outlaw MCs** in Colorado. His life is sweet and on his terms. He works hard, parties harder, and hits the backroads on his Harley whenever he wants. The whiskey is always neat, and he's got a string of women fighting to be first in line.

What more could a man want?

Then he sees *her* across the room at the biker bar, leaning over the jukebox, her hips swaying to the music in just the right way. **Curves that won't quit, long legs, and a defiant look in her big blue eyes.** Yeah … she's **pure temptation.**

But she **turns him down** cold, and leaves him fuming. Women don't say no to him.

The problem is he **can't stop thinking about her**, and that's something he's not used to.

Ashley Callahan notices the handsome stranger the minute he walks into the bar. **Their eyes lock** and the **moment is intense** until two women come over and wrap themselves around him.

Just because he's **handsome, rugged, and sexier than any man has the right to be**, Ashley has no interest in being another notch in his belt.

When she leaves the bar, she knows he's not happy but who cares—she'll never see the sexy stranger again.

The following Monday, she starts her new job. When she walks into her boss's office, Mr. Sexy is sitting behind the desk staring at her with those intense eyes and an irritating smirk that keeps growing bigger by the second.

Not only does she have to contend with a handsome, arrogant boss, but she has the feeling someone is watching her.

Diesel senses that Ashley is caught up in something bad, and there's nothing he wants more than to have his spitfire employee in his bed, protecting her.

This is turning out to be quite the ride.

The Insurgents MC series are standalone romance novels. This book describes the life and actions of a gritty outlaw motorcycle club. HEA. No cliffhangers.

Other Books by Chiah Wilder

Insurgent MC Series:

Hawk's Property
Jax's Dilemma
Chas's Fervor
Axe's Fall
Banger's Ride
Jerry's Passion
Throttle's Seduction
Rock's Redemption
An Insurgent's Wedding
Outlaw Xmas
Wheelie's Challenge
Christmas Wish
Animal's Reformation
Insurgents MC Romance Series: Insurgents Motorcycle Club Box Set (Books 1 – 4)
Insurgents MC Romance Series: Insurgents Motorcycle Club Box Set (Books 5 – 8)

Night Rebels MC Series:

STEEL
MUERTO
DIABLO
GOLDIE
PACO
SANGRE
ARMY
Night Rebels MC Romance Series: Night Rebels Motorcycle Club Box Set (Book 1 – 4)

Nomad Biker Romance Series:

Forgiveness
Retribution

Steamy Contemporary Romance:

My Sexy Boss

Find all my books at: amazon.com/author/chiahwilder

I love hearing from my readers. You can email me at chiahwilder@gmail.com.

Sign up for my newsletter to receive a FREE Novella, updates on new books, special sales, free short stories, and ARC opportunities at http://eepurl.com/bACCL1.

Visit me on facebook at facebook.com/AuthorChiahWilder
Visit me on twitter at twitter.com/chiah_wilder
Visit me on Instagram at instagram.com/chiah803

Manufactured by Amazon.ca
Bolton, ON